LUKE JENSEN, BOUNTY HUNTER

LUKE JENSEN, BOUNTY HUNTER

WILLIAM W. JOHNSTONE
WITH J. A. JOHNSTONE

PINNACLE BOOKS
Kensington Publishing Corp.
www.kensingtonbooks.com

PINNACLE BOOKS are published by

Kensington Publishing Corp.
119 West 40th Street
New York, NY 10018

PUBLISHER'S NOTE
Following the death of William W. Johnstone, the Johnstone family is working with a carefully selected writer to organize and complete Mr. Johnstone's outlines and many unfinished manuscripts to create additional novels in all of his series like The Last Gunfighter, Mountain Man, and Eagles, among others. This novel was inspired by Mr. Johnstone's superb storytelling.

ISBN-13: 978-0-7860-2804-7
ISBN-10: 0-7860-2804-1

First printing: September 2012

10 9 8 7 6 5 4 3 2 1

Printed in the United States of America

PROLOGUE

A rifle bullet smacked off the top of the log and sprayed splinters toward Luke Smith's face. He dropped his head quickly so the brim of his battered black hat protected his eyes. A splinter stung his cheek close to his neatly trimmed black mustache.

Luke looked into the sightless, staring eyes of the dead man who lay next to him. "Those amigos of yours are getting closer with their shots, José. Too bad for you that you're not alive to watch them kill me. Reckon you probably would've enjoyed that."

José Cardona didn't say anything. A bullet hole from one of Luke's Remingtons lay in the middle of his forehead, surrounded by powder burns. Most of the back of his head was gone where the slug had exploded out.

More shots rang out from the cabin about a hundred yards away, next to the little creek at the bottom of the slope. The sturdy log structure had been built for defense, with thick walls and numerous loopholes where rifle barrels could be stuck out and fired.

Luke had no idea who had built the cabin. Probably

some old fur trapper or prospector. Those mountains in New Mexico Territory had seen their fair share of both.

Currently, it was being used as a hideout for the Solomon Burke gang. Luke had been on the trail of Burke and his bunch for several weeks. There was a $1,500 bounty on Burke's head and lesser amounts posted on the half-dozen owlhoots who rode with him. If Luke was able to bring in all of them, it would be a mighty nice payoff for him.

Unfortunately, it didn't look like things were going to work out that way. Luke had tracked the gang to the cabin and had been crouched in the timber up on the hill overlooking the creek, trying to figure out his next move, when someone tackled him from behind, knocking him out into the open. They rolled down the hill together, locked in a desperate struggle, even as the man screeched a warning to the others at the top of his lungs.

The big log, which had also rolled about twenty feet down the hill when it toppled sometime in the past, brought the two men to an abrupt halt as they slammed into it. Luke barely had time to recognize the bandito as Cardona from drawings he had seen on wanted posters when he realized the man was about to bring a knife almost as big as a machete down on his head and split his skull wide open.

Without having to think about what he was doing, Luke palmed out one of his Remingtons, eared back the hammer as he jammed the muzzle against Cardona's forehead, and pulled the trigger.

The point-blank shot blew Cardona away from him, and the dead outlaw flopped onto the ground behind the log. Luke had rolled over and started to get up when a bullet had whipped past his ear. Instinct made him drop belly down behind the log. A second later, more rifles opened up from the cabin and a volley of high-powered slugs smashed into the fallen tree. If it hadn't been there to give him cover, Luke would have been shot to pieces.

As it was, he was pinned down on the slope. The trees above him were too far away. If he stood up and made a dash for them, Burke and the others in the cabin would riddle him with rifle fire. Trying to crawl up there would make him an even easier target. The grass was too short to conceal him.

He was stuck with a dead man for company, and it was only a matter of time until some of those varmints slipped out of the cabin and circled around to catch him in a crossfire. Luke's craggy face was grim, in spite of the ghost of a smile lurking around his mouth.

In plenty of tight spots during the years he'd spent as a bounty hunter, he had always pulled through somehow. But he had known his luck was bound to run out someday.

After all, he had already cheated certain death once. A man didn't get too many breaks like that.

From time to time, he rose up long enough to throw a couple shots at the cabin, but not really expecting to do any damage—too long range for a handgun. His nature wouldn't let him die without a fight, though. He could put up a better one, if his Winchester wasn't still in the saddle boot strapped to his horse, a good hundred feet upslope. Might as well have been a hundred miles.

"Blast it, José, I must be getting old, to let a clumsy

galoot like you sneak up on me," Luke said, keeping his eyes on the cabin.

Cardona had been a big, burly man, built along the lines of a black bear. Like all the other men in Solomon Burke's gang, he'd had a reputation for ruthlessness and cruelty. He had killed seven men that Luke knew of during various bank and train robberies, and was probably responsible for more deaths in addition to those. But he wouldn't be killing anybody else.

Luke took some small comfort from that. He tracked down outlaws mostly for the bounties posted on them, and he wasn't going to lie about it to himself or anybody else. It pleased him to know, because of him, men such as Cardona were no longer around to spread suffering and death across the frontier.

More bullets pounded into the log. One tore all the way through it and struck a rock lying on the slope, causing the bullet to whine off in a ricochet and bringing a thoughtful frown to Luke's face. He realized the log had been lying there long enough to be half-rotten in places. He holstered the Remington he was still holding and drew a heavy-bladed knife from its sheath on his left hip. Attacking the log with the blade, he hacked and dug at the soft wood.

It didn't take him long to break through and see what he'd been hoping to see. The log was partially hollow. Luke began enlarging the opening he had made and soon realized the hollow part ran all the way to one end of the log. He could see sunlight shining through it.

It took fifteen minutes of hard work to carve out a big enough hole for him to fit his head and shoulders through. By the time he was finished, sweat was dripping down his face.

He sheathed his knife and looked over at Cardona. "*Adiós, José.* If I see you again, I reckon it'll probably be in hell."

Luke wormed his way through the opening into the hollow log. Down below in the cabin, the outlaws hadn't been able to see what he was doing. He could only hope none of them had snuck around to where they could observe him. If they had, he was as good as dead.

He began shifting his weight back and forth as much as he could in those close confines. He felt insects crawling on him. His nerves twanged, taut as bowstrings. The log began to rock back and forth slightly. Bunching his muscles, he threw himself hard against the wood surrounding him. Over the pounding of his heart, he heard a faint grating sound as the log shifted.

Suddenly, it was rolling.

He let out a startled yell, even though rolling the log down the hill was exactly what he'd been trying to do. Up and down switched places rapidly.

With nothing between the log and the cabin to stop it, the crazy, bouncing, spinning, dizzying ride lasted only a few seconds.

The log crashed into the side of the cabin with a loud cracking sound just as he had counted on. Luke bulled his way out of the broken trunk, pulling both Remingtons from their cross-draw holsters as he did so.

He was on his feet when one of the outlaws appeared in the doorway, unwisely rushing out to see what had happened.

Luke shot him in the chest with the left-hand Remington. The slug drove the owlhoot back, making him fall. His body tangled with the feet of the man behind him. Luke blasted that hombre with the right-hand gun, then pressed himself against the cabin wall and waited. The men inside couldn't bring their guns to bear on him from those loopholes, and the log walls were too thick to shoot through. If anybody tried to rush out through the door, he was in position to gun them down. And, if the door was the only way out, he had them bottled up.

Of course, he couldn't go anywhere, either. But a stalemate was better than being stuck behind that log and his enemies having all the advantage.

As the echoes of the shots rolled away through the mountain valleys, a charged silence settled over the area. Luke thought he heard harsh breathing coming from inside the cabin.

After a few tense minutes, a man called out. "Who are you, mister?"

"Name's Luke Smith." He wasn't giving anything away by replying. They already knew where he was.

"I've heard of you. You're a bounty hunter!"

"Am I talking to Solomon Burke?"

"That's right."

"Who are the two boys I killed in there?"

Burke didn't answer for a moment. "How do you know they're dead?" he finally asked.

"Wasn't time for anything fancy. They're dead, all right."

Again Burke hesitated before saying, "Phil Gaylord and Oscar Montrose."

"José Cardona's dead up on the hillside. I blew his brains out. That's nearly half your bunch gone over the divide, Burke. Why don't you throw your guns out and surrender before I have to kill the rest of you?"

That brought a hoot of derisive laughter from inside.

"Mighty big talk, Smith. You step away from that wall and you'll be full of lead in a hurry. How in blazes are you gonna kill anybody else?"

"I've got my ways." Luke looked along the wall next to him. One of the loopholes, empty now, was within reach.

"We've got food, water, and plenty of ammunition. What do you have?"

"Got a cigar."

"Well, go ahead and smoke it, then," Burke told him. "It'll be the last one you ever do."

Luke kept his left-hand gun trained on the doorway. He pouched the right-hand iron and reached under his coat, bringing out a thin, black cigar. He bit off the end, spit it out, and clamped the cylinder of tobacco between his teeth. Fishing a lucifer from his pocket, he snapped it to life with his thumbnail. He held the flame to the end of the cigar and puffed until it was burning good. "Smell that?"

"Whoo-eee!" Burke mocked. "Smells like you set a wet dog on fire."

"It tastes good, though," Luke said. "I've got something else."

"What might that be?" Burke asked.

Luke took another cylinder from under his coat. Longer and thicker than the cigar, it was wrapped tightly in dark red paper. A short length of fuse dangled from one end. Luke puffed on the cigar until the end was glowing bright red, then held the fuse to it.

"This," he said around the cigar as the fuse began to sputter and spit sparks. He leaned over and shoved the cylinder through the empty loophole. It clattered on the puncheon floor inside the cabin.

One of the other men howled a curse and yelled, "Look out! That's dynamite!"

Luke drew his second gun and swung away from the wall as he extended the revolvers and squared himself up. As the outlaws tumbled through the door, trying to get away before the dynamite exploded, he started firing.

They shot back, of course, even as Luke's lead tore through them and knocked them off their feet. He felt the impact as a bullet struck him, then another. But he stayed upright and the Remingtons in his hands continued to roar.

Solomon Burke, a fox-faced, red-haired man, went down with his guts shot to pieces. Dour, sallow Lane Hutton stumbled and fell as blood from his bullet-torn throat cascaded down the front of his shirt. Young Billy Wells died with half his jaw shot away. Paco Hernandez stayed on his feet the longest and got a final shot off even as he collapsed with blood welling from two holes in his chest.

That last bullet rocked Luke. He swayed and spit out the cigar, but didn't fall. His vision was foggy, because he'd been shot three times or because clouds of powder smoke were swirling around him, he couldn't tell. The

Remingtons seemed to weigh a thousand pounds apiece, but he didn't let them droop until he was certain all the outlaws were dead.

Then he couldn't hold the guns up anymore. They slipped from his blood-slick fingers and thudded to the ground at his feet.

I might not live to collect the bounty on these men, but at least they won't hurt anybody else, he thought as he stumbled through the cabin door. The single room inside was dim and shadowy.

The cylinder he had shoved through the loophole lay on the floor near a table. The fuse had burned out harmlessly. The blasting cap on the end was just clay and the "dynamite" was nothing more than a piece of wood with red paper wrapped around it. Luke had used it a number of times before. Outlaws tended to panic when they thought they were about to be blown to kingdom come.

Ignoring the fake dynamite, he stumbled across the room. Sitting on the table was the thing he had hoped to find inside.

It took him a couple tries before he was able to snag the neck of the whiskey bottle and lift it to his mouth. Some of the liquor spilled over his chin and throat, but he got enough of the fiery stuff down his throat to brace himself.

He leaned on the rough-hewn table and tried to take stock of his injuries. He'd been hit low on his left side. There was a lot of blood. A bullet had torn a furrow along his left forearm, too, and blood ran down and dripped from his fingers. The bullet hole high on his chest was starting to make his right arm and shoulder go numb.

He needed to stop the bleeding before he did anything else. With little time before his hands quit working, he pulled the bandanna from around his neck and used his teeth to start a rip in it. He tore it in half and managed to pour some whiskey on the pieces. He pulled up his shirt, felt around until he found the hole in his side, and shoved one wadded-up piece of the whiskey-soaked bandanna into the hole.

But that was just where the bullet had gone in. Wincing in pain, he located the exit wound and pushed the other piece of bandanna into it.

That left the hole in his chest. All the gun thunder had deafened him for a few moments, but his hearing was starting to come back. He listened intently as he breathed, but didn't hear any whistling or sucking sounds. The slug hadn't pierced his lung, he decided. That was good.

The bullet hadn't come out, either. It was still in there somewhere. Not good, he thought. Fumbling, he pulled his knife from its sheath and used the blade to cut a piece from his shirttail. Lucky he didn't slice off a finger or two in the process. He upended the bottle and poured whiskey right over the wound, then bit back a scream as he crammed the piece of cloth into the hole.

That was all he could do. His muscles refused to work the way he wanted them to. He had to lie down. He took an unsteady step toward one of the bunks built against the side walls. The world suddenly spun crazily around him. The floor seemed to tilt under his feet. His balance deserted him, and he crashed down on the puncheons, sending fresh jolts of pain stabbing through him.

He felt consciousness slipping away from him and knew if he passed out, he probably wouldn't wake up again. He tried to hold on, but a black tide swept over him.

That black surge didn't just wash him away from his primitive surroundings. To his already fevered mind, it seemed to lift him and carry him back, back, a bit of human flotsam swept along by a raging torrent, to an earlier time and a different place. The darkness surrounding him was shot through with red flashes, like artillery shells bursting in the night.

BOOK ONE

CHAPTER 1

The bombardment sounded like the worst thunderstorm in the history of the world, but unlike a thunderstorm, it went on and on and on. For long days, that devil Ulysses S. Grant and his Yankee army had squatted outside Richmond, pounding away at the capital city of the Confederacy with their big guns. Half the buildings in town had been reduced to rubble, and untold numbers of Richmond's citizens were dead, killed in the endless barrages.

And still the guns continued to roar.

Rangy, rawboned Luke Jensen felt the floor shake under his feet as shells fell not far from the building where he stood. It had been one of Richmond's genteel mansions, not far from the capital itself, but recently it had been taken over by the government. One particular part of the government, in fact: the Confederate treasury.

Luke was one of eight men summoned tonight for reasons unknown to them. They were waiting in what had been the parlor before the comfortable, overstuffed furniture was shoved aside and replaced by desks and tables.

In the light of a couple smoky lamps, he glanced around at the other men. Some of them he knew, and some he didn't. The faces of all bore the same weary, haggard look, the expression of men who had been at war for too long and suffered too many defeats despite their best efforts.

Luke knew that look all too well. He saw it in the mirror every time he got a chance to shave, which wasn't very often these days.

For nearly four long years, he had worn Confederate gray—ever since the day he had walked away from the hardscrabble farm tucked into the Ozark Mountains of southwestern Missouri and enlisted. Behind him he'd left his father Emmett and his little brother Kirby, along with his mother and sister.

It had been hard for Luke to leave his family, but he felt it was the right thing to do. Fighting for the Confederacy didn't mean a man held with slavery, although he figured that was what all those ignorant Yankees believed. Luke didn't believe at all in the notion of one man owning another.

At the same time he didn't think it was right for a bunch of Northern politicians in By-God Washington City to be telling Southern folks what they could and couldn't do, especially when it came to secession. The states had joined together voluntarily, back when they'd won their freedom from England. If some of them wanted to say "thanks, but so long" and go their own way, it seemed to Luke they had every right to do so.

Even so, if they'd just kept on wrangling about it in the halls of Congress, Luke, like a lot of other Southerners, would have pretty much ignored it and gone on about his business. But Abraham Lincoln had to go and send the army marching into Virginia, and the battle along the creek called Bull Run was the last straw as far as Luke was concerned. He'd been raised to avoid trouble if he could, but when a Jensen saw something wrong going on, he couldn't just sit back and do nothing.

So he'd been a soldier for four years, fighting against the Northern aggressors, slogging along as an infantryman for a while before his natural talents for tracking, shooting, and fighting got noticed and he was made a scout and a sharpshooter.

He knew three of the men waiting in the parlor with him were the same sort. Remy Duquesne, Dale Cardwell, and Edgar Millgard were good men, and if he was being sent on some sort of mission with them, Luke was fine with that.

The other four had introduced themselves as Keith Stratton, Wiley Potter, Josh Richards, and Ted Casey. Luke hadn't formed an opinion about them based only on their names. He didn't blame them for being close-mouthed, though. He was the same way himself.

Remy fired up a cigar and said in his soft Cajun accent, "Anybody got an idea why they brought us here tonight?"

"Not a clue," Wiley Potter said.

"The treasury department has its office here now," Dale Cardwell pointed out. He smiled. "Maybe they're finally going to pay us all those back wages we haven't seen in months."

That comment drew grim chuckles from several of the men.

Remy said, "I wouldn't count on that, my frien'."

Luke didn't think it was very likely, either. The Confederacy was in bad shape. Financially, militarily, morale-wise . . . everything was cratering, and there didn't seem to be anything anybody could do to stop it. They would fight to the end, of course—there was no question about that—but that end seemed to be getting more and more inevitable.

The front door opened, and footsteps sounded in the foyer. Several gray-clad troopers appeared in the arched entrance to the former parlor. They carried rifles with bayonets fixed to the barrels.

A pair of officers followed the soldiers into the room. Luke and the other men snapped to attention. He recognized one of the officers as a high-ranking general. The other man was the colonel who commanded the regiment in which Luke, Remy, Dale, and Edgar served.

The two men in civilian clothes who came into the room behind the general and the colonel were the real surprise. Luke caught his breath as he recognized the President of the Confederacy, Jefferson Davis, and the Secretary of the Treasury, George Trenholm.

"At ease," the general said.

Luke and the others relaxed, but not much. It was hard to be at ease with the president in the room.

Jefferson Davis gave them a sad, tired smile and said, "Thank you for coming here tonight, gentlemen," as if they'd had a choice in the matter. "I know you'd probably rather be with your comrades in arms, facing the enemy."

Stratton and Potter grimaced slightly and exchanged a quick glance, as if that was the last thing they wanted to be doing.

"I've summoned you because I have a special job for you," Davis went on. "Secretary Trenholm will tell you about it."

Luke had wondered if they were going to be given a special assignment, but he hadn't expected it would come from the president himself. It had to be something of extreme importance. He waited eagerly to hear what the treasury secretary was going to say.

"As you know, Richmond is under siege by the Yankees," the man began rather pompously as he clasped his hands behind his back.

Luke preferred Confederate politicians to Yankees, but they all had a tendency to be windbags, as far as he was concerned.

"Although I hate to say it, it appears that our efforts to defend the city ultimately will prove to be unsuccessful," the secretary continued.

"Are you saying that Richmond's going to fall, sir?" Potter asked.

Trenholm nodded. "I'm afraid so."

"But that doesn't necessarily mean the Confederacy is about to fall as well," Davis put in. "Our glorious nation will persevere. The Yankees may overrun Richmond, but we will establish a new capital elsewhere." He smiled at the treasury secretary. "I'm sorry, I didn't mean to interrupt."

"That's quite all right, Mr. President. No one in this room has more right to speak than you." Trenholm cleared his throat and went on. "Of course, no government can continue to function without funds, so to that end, acting on the orders of President Davis, I have assembled a shipment of gold bullion that is to be spirited out of the city and taken to Georgia to await the arrival of our government. This is most of what we have left in our coffers, gentlemen. I'm not exaggerating when I say the very survival of the Confederacy itself depends on the secure transport of this gold."

Luke wasn't surprised by what he had just heard. For the past few days, rumors had been going around the city that the treasury was going to be cleaned out and the money taken elsewhere so the Yankees wouldn't get their grubby paws on it.

The secretary nodded toward Luke's commanding officer. "Colonel Lancaster will be in charge of the gold's safety."

"You're taking the whole regiment to Georgia, sir?" Dale asked.

The colonel shook his head. "Not at all, Corporal. That would only draw the Yankees' attention to what we're doing." Lancaster paused. "We're entrusting the safety of the bullion—and the future of the Confederacy—to a smaller detail. Eight men, to be exact." He looked around the room. "The eight of you who are gathered here."

CHAPTER 2

Luke had figured that out even before Lancaster said it. The idea seemed obvious. Getting the gold out of Richmond would require speed and stealth, and no one was better at moving fast and quiet than he and his fellow scouts.

It seemed like a mighty big risk, though, turning over a fortune in gold to only eight men. Of course, as long as they were loyal to the Confederacy, it didn't really matter.

"I'll be going along as well," Colonel Lancaster pointed out. "I've been relieved of my command of the regiment and given this task."

"I know you'd rather be with the men you've led in such sterling fashion, Colonel," Jefferson Davis said. "However, we all must make sacrifices for our noble cause."

"Of course, Mr. President," Lancaster said stiffly.

Davis turned back to Luke and the other scouts. "No one is going to order you enlisted men to accept this assignment. If there are any of you who don't want to go along, speak up now, and it won't be held against you. You'll be allowed to return to your units. All we ask is that you say nothing about this. Secrecy is the watchword until the bullion is safely on its way to Georgia."

Luke looked at his friends. Remy shrugged and told Davis, "Mr. President, I don't think any of us are gonna say no to this job."

"That's right," Edgar said. "If this is something that will help the Confederacy, you can count on us, sir."

"I knew that." Davis smiled. "I knew you valiant lads wouldn't let me down, but I felt it was only right to ask. Thank you for justifying my faith in you."

"You can thank us when we get that gold where it's goin', Mr. President," Stratton said.

Luke had been quiet so far, but he asked, "When are we leaving?"

"Tonight," Colonel Lancaster said.

"That soon?" Potter was surprised.

"Do you have a problem with that, Sergeant? Something you need to do here in Richmond before you leave?"

Potter grunted and shook his head. "Permission to speak freely, sir?"

"Go ahead," Lancaster told him.

"Richmond's turned into a hellhole ever since the Yankees showed up on our doorstep, and as far as I'm concerned, the sooner we get out of here, the better."

As if to punctuate his comment, another shell fell somewhere nearby, and the blast shook the house enough that little bits of plaster sifted down from the ceiling.

The general said to Davis, "You should get back to somewhere safer, sir. The colonel and I can handle this."

"Very well, General." Davis turned to the treasury secretary. "Come on, George."

The troopers escorted the two politicians from the room. Once they were gone, Colonel Lancaster said, "The gold is being stored in a warehouse not far from here. It's packed in crates in a couple wagons and covered with canvas so they'll look like supplies."

"No offense, Colonel," Luke said, "but are you sure that's a good idea? With the city cut off like it is, people are starting to get pretty hungry. They're liable to come after food quicker than they would gold."

"How else would you suggest we transport it, Jensen?" the colonel snapped.

Luke shrugged. "I don't know, sir," he admitted. "As scarce as everything is these days, folks are going to be interested no matter what it looks like."

"That's why it's up to us to get the wagons out of the city quickly, and with as little fuss as possible. We have civilian clothes at the warehouse for all of you, as well. Hopefully that'll keep you from drawing too much attention."

Luke didn't know about that, but the idea of getting some fresh duds appealed to him. His gray uniform was worn and ragged and covered with stains from too many nights spent sleeping in the mud. The black bill of his forage cap was crooked and broken. His shoes were more hole than shoe leather.

His only possessions still in good shape were his

Fayetteville rifle and his Griswold and Gunnison revolver, both of which he kept in excellent condition. His life often depended on them.

The general shook hands with all eight of the scouts and wished them luck, then Colonel Lancaster said gruffly, "Let's go. We'll dispense with military formality since we're supposed to be civilians, but don't forget who's in charge here."

Luke didn't think Lancaster was likely to let that happen.

"I don't know about you boys," Ted Casey said with a wide grin, "but I feel like a whole new man in this getup!"

The civilian clothes they had donned when they reached the warehouse weren't new—some of them even had patches here and there—but they were clean and in much better shape than the uniforms the eight men had been wearing.

Colonel Lancaster, as befitted his rank, was dressed in the only real suit, including a flat-crowned planter's hat. Other than his ramrod-stiff backbone, in those clothes and with his florid face and thick side-whiskers, he might have been mistaken for a plantation owner.

The other men were dressed more like overseers on that hypothetical plantation, in boots, whipcord trousers, linsey-woolsey shirts, and leather vests. They wore an assortment of headgear ranging from broad-brimmed hats to tweed caps.

Luke had snagged one of the hats he thought made

him look like a plainsman. Such men rode through the Ozarks from time to time, on their way to or from the vast western frontier, and Luke had always admired them.

His revolver was tucked in the waistband of the trousers. Most enlisted men didn't carry handguns, but since scouts often had to do some close-quarters fighting, they had been issued revolvers along with their rifles. Luke considered himself pretty handy with either weapon, and with a knife, too, for that matter.

He didn't think about it very often, but he had killed quite a few men during his time in the army. It was war, of course. That was what soldiers did. He had killed more than his share up close, though, sneaking up on Yankee pickets and slitting their throats or driving his knife into their backs so the blade penetrated the heart. He had felt the hot gush of enemy blood on his hand, heard the death rattle, and borne the weight of a suddenly limp body that had to be lowered to the ground quietly. He had seen the terrible damage gunshots did to human flesh, especially at close range.

Those memories didn't haunt his sleep, but they were part of him and always would be.

Wiley Potter, Keith Stratton, Ted Casey, and Josh Richards clustered together near one of the wagons. Luke saw them casting furtive glances at the canvas-covered cargo in the back of the vehicle.

"Like dogs lickin' their chops over a big ol' soup bone, eh?" Remy said quietly as he came up beside Luke.

"You can't blame them. I sent some mighty hard looks at those wagons myself. I've never been this close to so much gold." Luke snorted. "Hell, back home I might go as long as a year without seeing as much as a double eagle."

"I suppose I'm more accustomed to it, seeing as I spent a lot of time in the gambling halls in New Orleans. The money always flowed freely there."

"Maybe so," Luke said. "Where I come from, money flows more like quicksand."

Dale asked Lancaster, "Are we going to be riding on the wagons, Colonel?"

"We'll have a driver and a guard on each wagon," Lancaster explained. "The other four of you, plus myself, will be on horseback and serve as outriders."

"Horses sound good," Casey said. "I always hankered to ride something better than an old mule. They turned me down for the cavalry because that was all I had."

"You'll take turns at the jobs, at least starting out. I don't care who does what, though. You can settle that among yourselves."

Dale commented, "I wouldn't mind handling one of the teams. I used to drive a freight wagon before the war."

"So did I," Edgar offered. "I reckon I'll take the other driver's job starting out."

None of the other men volunteered to ride on the wagons as guards. Luke and Remy looked at each other. Luke shrugged, and Remy said, "We'll take the wagons, too, Colonel."

Lancaster nodded. "Fine." He looked to Potter, Stratton, Casey, and Richards. "You men will find your horses in the alley behind the warehouse. Bring them around front and mount up. You can fetch my mount as well." He motioned to the uniformed soldiers who had been waiting in the warehouse, guarding the gold shipment. "Open the doors."

The troopers swung the big double doors back while Luke and his friends climbed onto the wagons. Luke settled down on the seat of the first wagon beside Dale. "Sure you can handle this?"

"Oh, yeah. To tell you the truth, I've never been that comfortable in a saddle."

"I was riding almost before I could walk, at least according to my pa," Luke told him.

The mention of Emmett Jensen put a pensive look on Luke's face. Luke had joined up first, back in '61, but he had suspected his pa wouldn't be able to stay out of the fight for long. Sure enough, Emmett had enlisted, too.

Proving that the world really was a small place, the two of them had run into each other at Chancellorsville, even though they were in different regiments. Hundreds of thousands of troops rampaging around those Virginia woods, and yet father and son had practically bumped heads.

That wasn't the last time, either. Anytime their units were anywhere near each other, one of them would seek out the other so they could visit in the lull between battles. Neither of them got much news from home, but Emmett was confident his youngest son Kirby was keeping things going on the farm.

"Kirby may be just a boy," Emmett had said during one visit, "but he's got something special inside him. I don't think I've ever seen a boy willing to work harder or more determined to do the right thing."

"He'll have the farm waiting for us when we come back," Luke had said.

"Shoot, he may not even need our help!" Emmett had replied with a grin.

It had been a while since Luke had seen his pa. He hoped Emmett was all right. Both were soldiers, so who knew what might happen. It was a dangerous line of work.

When the wagons rolled out of the warehouse into the darkness, Colonel Lancaster and the other four outriders were waiting on horseback.

"I'll lead the way," Lancaster declared. "I want a rider on each side of the wagons. Keep an eye out behind you as well. We don't want anybody sneaking up on us."

"Did the colonel tell any of us exactly where we're going?" Luke asked Dale as the party set out over the rough, cobblestoned streets.

"Not that I know of," Dale replied.

"I might say something to him about that the first time we stop. He's bound to have a map or something, but if anything happened to him, we wouldn't know where we were supposed to take this—Luke stopped himself before he said the word *gold*—"cargo."

"Yeah, that's true," Dale agreed. "All we know is that we're headed for Georgia, but Georgia's a pretty big place."

It was pretty far away, too, Luke thought, and almost anything could happen between here and there. He felt the unaccustomed burden of responsibility weighing on his shoulders. He wasn't used to taking care of anybody but himself or maybe two or three of his comrades. He'd never had anything like the fate of the Confederacy riding on his back before.

The city was dark except for the few fires started by exploding artillery shells. The Yankee bombardment continued. It went on almost around the clock. Luke didn't see how the city could hold out much longer.

A shell screamed overhead and landed maybe half a mile behind them, blowing up with a huge explosion. Dale looked back over his shoulder at the pillar of flame rising into the black sky. "What do you think it'd be like if one of those things landed right on top of us?"

"We'll never know," Luke said.

"Because it won't happen?"

"Because if it does, we'll be blown to smithereens before we know what happened."

"You really know how to make a fella feel encouraged, Luke—" Dale stopped short and hauled back on the reins. Colonel Lancaster had come to an abrupt halt in front of the wagon team. Garish, flickering light spilled over the cobblestones as a large number of men, many of them carrying torches, surged around a corner up ahead.

"That looks like trouble," Dale muttered.

Luke was thinking the same thing. He knew mobs made of desperate civilians and deserters had taken to roaming the streets of Richmond. The army was trying to keep things under control, but it was getting more difficult with every passing day as the Yankee siege continued. Already there had been several riots.

And it looked like the two wagons were in the path of

another one, as one of the men in the forefront of the mob yelled, "There are some wagons! There might be food in them!"

It was an easy conclusion to jump to. A starving man saw food everywhere.

The man waved his torch forward, and with a full-throated cry sounding like the howl of a wounded animal, the mob surged toward the wagons and riders.

CHAPTER 3

Luke saw Colonel Lancaster look around as if searching for a way out. In the narrow street it would be difficult and time-consuming to turn the wagons around, and there were no alleys nearby down which they could escape.

Fleeing wasn't going to do any good. As close as the mob was, the starving men would be able to overtake the wagons without much trouble.

"Get ready to fight if you have to, Dale," Luke said as he pulled the Griswold and Gunnison revolver from his waistband. He stood up and almost called Lancaster "Colonel," catching himself just in time. He took a breath and shouted, "Mr. Lancaster, get out of the way!"

The army and the Confederate government wanted the bullion shipment kept secret, along with the fact that those with the wagons were soldiers. But the secret would be out if the mob swarmed over the wagons. Although the last thing he wanted was to hurt any of his fellow Southerners, Luke would do whatever was necessary to protect the gold. He hadn't seen any firearms in the crowd, only torches and makeshift clubs. Figuring it was a small risk, he raised the revolver.

As Lancaster yanked his horse to the side, out of the line of fire, Luke thumbed back the hammer and squeezed the trigger. The Griswold and Gunnison was a .36 caliber weapon modeled after the Colt Navy and not noted for its accuracy. But the range was short, and he sent the pistol ball slamming into the cobblestones just a few feet in front of the mob's leaders.

They stopped in a hurry.

The other members of the escort lifted rifles or pulled out pistols.

Luke knew hunger could make a man risk a great deal, up to and including his life. He cocked the revolver again and raised the barrel until he was aiming right between the eyes of the man who'd urged the mob into action. He didn't know if the man was one of the leaders or just someone who'd been moved to shout, but he wanted to be certain the man was aware of the danger he was facing.

"You fellas stay right where you are!" Luke warned them. "We'll shoot if we have to, make no mistake about that!"

"You can't kill all of us!" somebody yelled.

Somebody in the back of the crowd, Luke noted. "No, but we can do for half of you. Maybe more than that."

That estimate was good only if every member of the escort emptied his guns and scored a hit with every shot, which was highly unlikely, but the members of the mob probably wouldn't bother to do that ciphering.

"And you'll be the first one to die, mister," Luke went

on, addressing the man he'd aimed at. "Is it worth dying for something you can't even eat?"

The man looked scared, but he asked, "What is it? What's in those wagons?"

"Manufacturing equipment," Luke said. He didn't know where that answer came from, but it struck him as a good one. "We're trying to get it out of town while we still can."

"What sort of equipment?"

Luke bit back a curse. The varmint was awfully curious for somebody who had a gun pointed at him. "Leather goods. Tool and die presses."

He wasn't sure that answer even made sense. He didn't know anything about manufacturing, but recalled hearing that phrase once from a fellow who owned a saddle shop.

He figured the stubborn man would want to take a look at the contents of the crate, but before that could happen, somebody else called out, "You don't have any food?"

"Just our own provisions for the trip," Luke answered, putting some sympathy in his voice. "And we're going to be on mighty short rations just like everybody else."

"We might as well let 'em go," another man grumbled. "Can't eat a bunch of damn machinery."

"They've got horses," yet another man said.

"I'll be damned if I'm far enough gone that I'll eat horse meat! Let 'em pass!"

After that bit of discourse, the crowd seemed to be of two minds. Some agreed they ought to let the travelers go, while others were so angered by the fate that had befallen them they wanted to hurt somebody, anybody, for any excuse. It was a delicate balance, and Luke knew it could tip at any second to the side of violence.

He glanced at his companions. They looked tense and ready to fight, but were scared, too. Only fools would not be scared in the face of an angry mob. Luke hoped none of them panicked and got trigger-happy. All it would take was one shot to set off an orgy of killing.

Finally, the man in the lead stepped aside and swung the blazing brand. "All right, go on and get out of here." He raised his voice to the others in the mob. "Get out of the way! Let them pass!"

The men crowded to the sides of the street. As the wagons and riders passed between them it was uncomfortably like running a gauntlet. As the lead wagon rolled by the man with the torch, Luke told him, "You made a wise decision, friend. Good luck to you."

"You're the lucky ones," the man said with bitterness in his voice. "You're getting out of Richmond. Maybe the Yankees will catch you and kill you, but even if they do, it'll be quick. The ones left behind here will be a long time dying."

As he reloaded the expended chamber, Luke had a feeling the man's grim prediction was correct.

The gold escorts didn't encounter any more trouble as they made their way to the city's edge, but Luke knew they were far from being out of danger yet. The Yankees patrolled heavily around Richmond to keep the city's inhabitants bottled up while the artillery bombardment continued.

Colonel Lancaster dropped back alongside the lead wagon and said to Luke, "I appreciate your help with that mob back there, Jensen, but don't forget that I'm in command here. The way you took charge bordered on insubordination."

Well, then, you should've come up with some way to get us out of that mess, Luke thought, *instead of sitting there looking scared and confused.* He kept that opinion to himself, of course. "That's not the way I meant it, Colonel. I was just trying anything to keep those fellas from swarming over us."

"I understand," Lancaster said with a nod. "Just remember in the future that you look to me for your orders."

"Yes, sir."

The colonel rode ahead again, and Dale said quietly, "If we'd waited for him to figure out what to do, we'd all be dead now."

"More than likely," Luke agreed. "The colonel's a good commander out in the field, but I'm not sure he's really cut out for a job like this."

"That's why I'm glad you're with us, Luke. You can think on your feet about as well as anybody I ever saw."

Luke took that compliment in silence. He had never thought of himself as any sort of strategist or tactician. He was just a fellow who wanted to stay alive and was willing to do almost anything to accomplish that goal.

Their route took them north out of the city, which was opposite from where they wanted to go, but Luke understood why. The heaviest concentration of Yankee forces was south of Richmond. The scouts had to take the wagons north, then circle far to the west, well behind Union lines, and make a fast dash southward. It was the long way around, but a direct route just wasn't possible.

Lancaster called a halt. "I want to be out of the city by dawn. The farther away we can get, the better."

"How will we dodge those Yankee patrols?" Stratton asked.

"We'll have to do some good scouting." The colonel nodded toward Luke. "That's why I want one of you men to give Jensen the horse you're riding. I want a mount for Duquesne, too."

"We've done plenty of scoutin', Colonel," Richards protested. "You can send a couple of us."

Lancaster shook his head. "Jensen and Duquesne have served under my command. I know what they can do. You other men were recommended to me, but I haven't seen you in action yet. Now, dismount, a couple of you."

There was some angry muttering, but Richards and Casey swung down from their saddles.

"Keep your eyes open, Dale," Luke said to his friend.

"You bet I will," Dale promised.

Taking his rifle with him, Luke hopped down from the wagon seat. Richards handed him his reins and climbed up to take his place.

Once Luke and Remy were mounted, Lancaster told them, "Follow this road we're on and see if the way is clear up ahead to the bridge about a mile from here. If it is, one of you come back and tell us, and we'll come ahead."

"What if the Yankees have blown up the bridge, Colonel?" Luke asked.

"Then we'll have to find another way," Lancaster replied as if that were the most obvious thing in the world, and Luke supposed it was.

Crossing the river was probably going to be the most difficult part of getting out of Richmond, Luke thought. If the Yankees really wanted to keep the citizens and the Confederate government trapped in the city, the first thing they should have done was destroy all the bridges.

But that would make it more difficult for them to get in and out of the city from the north once Richmond had fallen, so maybe one or two bridges were still standing. In normal times, the small road the Confederates were on was little used and might be overlooked, along with its bridge spanning the river.

Those were anything but normal times, however.

Luke and Remy moved forward, leaving the buildings on the edge of town behind. Trees crowded in on the road from both sides as they rode northward. Although the sky behind them was bright with the orange glow of fires and the flashes of exploding shells from the Yankee barrage, the darkness grew thicker the farther they went. Luke eyed the trees warily. A Yankee cavalry patrol could be hidden in there, and he wouldn't see them until they opened fire.

But he might be able to hear them. He kept his ears open, listening for hoofbeats, the jingle of bit chains, or coughs, and he watched his horse's ears. If the animal smelled other horses, it would prick its ears in the direction of the scent.

Nothing. Only the slow thud of hoofbeats from his and Remy's mounts.

"We're fortunate," the Cajun whispered. "I don't think anybody's out there right now."

"Yeah," Luke breathed, "but I wouldn't count us lucky until we see whether the bridge is there."

The road was fairly straight, with only a few curves in it. They had just ridden around one when a large structure loomed in front of them about two hundred yards away. Luke recognized it as the covered bridge that crossed the James River.

"That's it," Remy said. "It's still there."

Luke grinned in the darkness. "Yeah." His eyes searched the shadows around the bridge, looking for any sign of movement. "Seems to be deserted, too. But we'd better take a closer look before one of us goes back and tells the colonel the path is clear."

"Absolutely." Remy heeled his horse into a slightly faster gait. "Let's go."

Luke started to call out to his friend and tell him to slow down, but Remy was right, they didn't really have any time to waste. As Colonel Lancaster had said, the farther away from Richmond they were by morning, the better. Luke rode after Remy.

They were about fifty feet away from the bridge when a sheet of orange muzzle flame split the night.

CHAPTER 4

Luke's only warning was a sudden toss of his horse's head a split second before the shots rang out, giving him just enough time to duck.

It was a good thing he did. As it passed over his head, he heard the sinister hum of a minié ball.

He pulled the revolver from his waistband—he had five rounds ready—and cocked the gun as he brought it up, turning the cylinder from the empty chamber on which the hammer had rested.

As several men on horseback burst out of the trees just short of the bridge, Luke thumbed off a couple rounds. Even though he couldn't see their uniforms, he knew they had to be Yankee cavalrymen.

More shots blasted as muzzle flames continued to tear orange gashes in the darkness. He pulled hard on the reins to whirl his horse around and flee, but saw something that made him stop short.

A match had flared into life on the bridge. He could think of only one reason why somebody would be striking a lucifer out there.

To light the fuse attached to a keg of blasting powder.

The Yankees hadn't destroyed the bridge yet, but only because they were just getting around to it.

"Cover me, Remy!" Luke yelled, and he did something the Yankees wouldn't have expected in a million years. If he'd had time to think about it, likely he wouldn't have done it.

He charged straight at them.

Luke leaned forward over his horse's neck as he sent the animal lunging toward the cavalrymen. The revolver in his hand roared twice more. He saw one of the troopers topple loosely from the saddle. A glance over his shoulder told Luke his friend had taken cover in the trees at the side of the road and opened up with his revolver. Remy was firing, too.

The Yankees were confused. Instead of fleeing, as they had expected, the two Confederates were putting up a fight. The patrol's charge had broken up, and the horses were milling around in the road.

Luke's horse thundered between a couple Yankees. One of the cavalrymen drew a saber. Silvery moonlight winked off the blade as it started to slash toward Luke. He still had one round in the revolver. Tipping up the barrel, he triggered the gun.

The .36 caliber slug caught the saber-wielding cavalryman in the throat. A fountain of blood, black in the moonlight, sprayed from him as he went backward out of his saddle. Luke flashed past, unharmed.

With no time to reload the revolver, he jammed it back in his waistband. Up ahead, sparks flew in the darkness as the lit fuse burned toward a small keg filled with blasting powder. It would be enough to destroy the bridge. Even if the explosion didn't blow the bridge in two, the fire it was bound to start would finish the job.

The fuse lighter stood in the middle of the bridge, vaguely illuminated by the sputtering glow. Confused by the unexpected fight of the Confederates, he took too long to decide whether to flee or stay. Luke was already on the bridge, his horse's hooves ringing on the planks and echoing from the arched cover.

The Yankee lifted a rifle and fired. The ball whipped past Luke's head.

Luke kicked his feet free of the stirrups and left the saddle in a diving tackle that sent him crashing into the enemy soldier. The collision's impact drove the man backward off his feet.

Luke landed hard, too, knocking the breath out of him. He gasped for air as he scrambled to his knees. The powder keg was about ten feet from him, sitting against the wall on the left-hand side of the bridge. The fuse had only a few inches left to burn.

The Yankee wasn't interested in fighting anymore. He just wanted to get the hell out of there before the powder went off and he was blown to bits. Leaping to his feet, he raced for the north end of the bridge.

Luke threw himself at the keg, snatched it up, and plucked the fuse from it as he rolled over. As he came up again, he flung the keg after the fleeing Yankee.

It landed beside the man and bounced past him. He screamed in sheer terror and stumbled, falling and hitting the ground right at the end of the bridge. He rolled over a couple times and came to a stop with the keg resting on its side a few feet away from him.

Luke heard the swift rataplan of hoofbeats and looked back to see the cavalry patrol had regrouped. They charged toward him. Their revolvers roared as they opened fire.

Luke lunged toward the closest decorative opening in the cover of the bridge as bullets sizzled through the air right behind his back. Down at the far end of the bridge, the Yankee who'd lit the fuse screeched, "Stop shooting! Hold your—"

It was all he got out before one of the wild slugs aimed at Luke struck the powder keg. Luke saw the fierce burst of flames from the explosion out of the corner of his eye as he dived through the opening in the bridge cover.

There wouldn't be enough left of that luckless Yankee to bury.

Luke had problems of his own. He was plunging through empty air toward the black surface of the James River.

He barely had time to drag a breath into his lungs before he struck the chilly water and went under. The river closed over him. He kept sinking for a moment before he was able to right himself.

He wasn't the best swimmer in the world, but he stroked his arms and kicked his feet, fighting his way back to the surface until his head broke out of the water.

While he tried to stay afloat, gun thunder pealed and echoed along the bridge. The Yankees weren't shooting at him, Luke realized. A separate fight was going on under the arched cover. Muzzle flashes were visible through the openings in the walls.

Since nobody seemed to be trying to kill him at the moment, he struggled toward the northern bank, which was closer. By the time he got there, the shooting had stopped and a couple horsemen emerged from under the cover near the site of the blast.

Luke didn't know how he was going to put up a fight. His revolver wasn't loaded, and getting dunked in the river probably had ruined his caps and powder. He still had his knife, but he wasn't in any shape for hand-to-hand combat against overwhelming odds.

The Yankees could just sit there and shoot him while he tried to climb out of the river.

"Luke! Luke, is that you?"

The familiar voice sent a surge of relief through him. "Remy! Down here!"

The Cajun laughed. "Come out of there, you old water rat!"

With river water streaming from his clothes, Luke clambered onto the bank and collapsed. Remy dismounted and went down to help him.

"What happened?" Luke asked as he made it to his feet with Remy's assistance.

"Lancaster and the others heard the shooting and came to see what was going on. You and I had already done enough damage to the Yankees that they were able to wipe out the rest of the patrol."

"Anybody hurt?"

"No, we were lucky. How about you?"

"I reckon I'm all right. Just wet and tired. My ammunition's probably ruined, too."

"Don't worry about that. We'll be able to scavenge plenty of powder and shot from those dead Yankees, not to mention their guns."

"And their horses," Luke suggested. "It won't hurt for us to have some extra mounts."

"Most of the horses have bolted, but we might be able to catch a few."

By the time Luke and Remy reached the road, the wagons had crossed the bridge. They had to steer around the gaping hole in the ground where the keg of blasting powder had gone off, but there was room enough at the side of the road for them to manage that.

Colonel Lancaster said, "From what Corporal Duquesne tells me, if we'd come along a little later this bridge would already be gone. The same would be true if not for your swift action, Jensen. Good job."

"Thank you, sir. And thank you for coming along and taking a hand in the fight."

"When we heard the shots, I should have ordered the drivers to turn the wagons around. We should have gone back and looked for another way out of the city. It really wasn't wise of me to risk our cargo just to see what was happening to the two of you." The colonel shrugged. "But everything seems to have worked out all right. Just don't expect me to keep on pulling your fat out of the fire, Jensen."

"No, sir, I won't." Luke managed to keep the irritation

he felt out of his voice. He'd just been following orders when all hell broke loose.

"We'd better move quickly now," Lancaster went on. "There are probably more Yankee patrols in the area. They would have been expecting to hear an explosion, but when their men don't come back, they'll start to wonder what happened. We don't want to be here when they come to find out."

Luke knew that was true. He started looking for his horse and found the animal grazing peacefully on the grass at the side of the road.

He couldn't do anything about his wet clothes except wait for them to dry. That would be miserable, but he could put up with it. He found his hat on the bridge where it had fallen off when he tackled the Yankee.

The Confederates hastily helped themselves to guns and ammunition from their fallen foes. They were trying to catch some of the Yankee cavalry horses when Lancaster said, "No, leave them here."

"It never hurts to have extra mounts, Colonel," Stratton suggested, unknowingly echoing what Luke had said earlier to Remy.

"Those horses have U.S. army brands on them," Lancaster pointed out. "If we're captured, it's unlikely we'll be able to talk ourselves out of a firing squad, but it would be even more difficult if we were in possession of Yankee cavalry mounts."

"The colonel's got a point there," Luke said. "It might be better if we just make do without them."

Nobody put up an argument. A short time later, the

group was on the move, following the road into the rugged, wooded countryside of northern Virginia.

Riding on the wagon with Dale again Luke looked over at Wiley Potter, who rode alongside the vehicle. "Thanks for coming to help me back there."

"Well, sure, Jensen," Potter said. "What else could we do? We're all on the same side, ain't we?"

CHAPTER 5

After the fight at the bridge, the scouts didn't run into any more trouble. A couple times they heard hoofbeats coming along the road and quickly found places where they could pull the wagons off into the trees. Yankee cavalrymen galloped past without even slowing down, never realizing how close the Confederates were.

The riders could only be Yankees. Nobody else would be out and about at night. The people who lived in the area were huddled in their houses and cabins, hoping and praying they wouldn't be slaughtered before morning by the northern invaders.

Luke thought about his ma and Kirby and Janey back on the farm. There had been fighting in Missouri, although not as much as in the east, and widespread bloody raids by guerrilla forces on both sides. He hoped none of the violence had come near the Jensen family farm.

By morning the Confederates were several miles north of Richmond. As the sun came up, Potter and Casey found a cave-like opening under a rugged bluff topped with trees, and Dale and Edgar drove the wagons into it at Colonel Lancaster's command. There was room for the horses under the bluff, too.

"We'll stay here today," the colonel said. "Traveling in daylight is too risky while we're still this close to Richmond. When we swing west and then south we'll be less likely to run into the Yankees, so we can stay on the road more and make better time then."

Based on what he had seen so far, Luke had doubts of Lancaster's ability to be in charge of the mission, but he agreed with the colonel's decision. They were all tired and needed some rest, and it would be better for them to lie low for a while.

They made an unappetizing breakfast of hardtack and salt jowl. No coffee. Luke wasn't sure how long it had been since he'd had real coffee, but it hadn't been anytime recently, that was for sure. They took turns sleeping while two men stood guard at all times.

When it was Luke's turn to watch, he was paired with Ted Casey. They hunkered in some brush near the wagons, and the first thing Casey did was reach for a tobacco pouch and papers in his shirt pocket.

Like stopped him with a hand on his arm. "You can't roll a quirly."

"Why not?" Casey asked with a frown.

"Because the smell of tobacco smoke can travel a pretty good distance. The road's only about a quarter mile away. You don't want some smart Yankee coming along, smelling your smoke, and getting curious enough to come over here and take a look around."

Casey let out a disgusted snort, but he shrugged and

put away the pouch. "If they was smart, they wouldn't be Yankees."

"They probably think the same thing about us Confederates," Luke pointed out.

"Don't start talkin' about how they just think they're doin' the right thing and how we shouldn't hate 'em because of that."

"They're *not* doing the right thing," Luke said with conviction. "They invaded our homes. Of course we have to fight them. But the ones I really hate are the politicians from both sides who kept prodding and poking at each other until they felt like they had to start a war over something that could have been settled without one."

"What are you talkin' about?" Casey asked.

"Did you know that more than twenty years ago, some congressmen from the South were already talking about ending slavery? Their plan was to get rid of it in stages, so the southern economy wouldn't be ruined in the process. If the northern politicians had just gone along with that idea, by now a lot of the slaves would be free, maybe even all of them, and there wouldn't have been any need for this war. But the Northerners turned it down flat. They'd already started making speeches about how all the slaves had to be freed at once, or they wouldn't go along with it."

Casey gave him a dubious squint. "I never heard nothin' about anything like that. You're makin' it up."

Luke shook his head. "Nope. I read about it in an old newspaper I came across once."

"You know how to read, eh?"

"My ma saw to that. And once I learned, I had a liking for it."

That was true. As a boy and a young man, he had read every book and newspaper he could get his hands on. Unfortunately, in the part of the country where he'd grown up, reading material wasn't all that common.

But some of the settlements had schools, and whenever he could, Luke would ride over to one of them, sneak in, and "borrow" whatever books he could find. He always took them back once he'd finished reading them, so he didn't consider it stealing. He was just doing whatever he had to in order to feed his thirst for knowledge.

One of the few good things about the war was that churches across the South had donated Bibles for the troops, so Luke got the chance to read the Good Book from cover to cover, more than once.

Sometimes he came across other books, usually in abandoned houses. He'd nearly always had some sort of volume of prose or poetry tucked away in his gear, and he read them until they fell apart from exposure to the elements.

He didn't have a book with him at the moment, but maybe once they got to Georgia he could scrounge up a few. He had read some plays by an Englishman named Shakespeare, and he had a hankering to read more.

"I don't understand it," Casey said. "I thought those Yankees were so all-fired anxious to have the slaves freed, and now you're tellin' me they turned down a chance to have that happen and went to war instead."

"The politicians in Washington raised a big stink about slavery because they didn't want folks up north thinking too much about the way we were starting to develop more industry here in the South. All those rich men who own factories up there didn't like that. They didn't like the contracts our businessmen were starting to make with businesses in England and other places in Europe, either."

Luke grunted disdainfully, then went on. "The way they saw it, we weren't supposed to do anything except grow the crops. They'd do everything else the country needed and rake in all the money. They stirred up a bunch of well-meaning people who had real doubts about slavery and got them to fight a war over it. But if you want the truth, all you have to do is look around. You don't see any factories still standing in the South, do you?"

Casey frowned as if thinking about the question hurt his head. "It's all about states' rights. That's what we're fightin' for."

At this point, all we're really fighting for is survival, Luke thought. But he said, "It's true the North tried to trample on the rights of our sovereign states, but consider this . . . the Southern businessmen building those factories and making those contracts with the British wanted the money from those things as much as the Northern industrialists didn't want them to have it."

"So what you're sayin' is the politicians and the fellas with a lot of money on both sides have got us fightin' each other because they want to keep rakin' it in?"

Luke shrugged. "Draw your own conclusions, Casey. All I'm saying is the whole situation is a lot more complicated than what most folks think. One side yells about slavery and the other side yells about states' rights, but like nearly everything else in life, most of it always comes back to money."

Casey nodded slowly, as if the implications of what Luke had said were sinking into his brain. After a moment, he said, "You know what we need to do?"

"What's that?"

"We need to get our own hands on some of that money the varmints are fightin' over."

Luke laughed softly. "Men like you and me don't get rich, Casey. It's just not in the cards. And I don't really care. If this war was over tomorrow, I'd go back home and be mighty happy to do it. My family's farm isn't much, but if we have faith and work hard enough, it'll take care of us."

"There's better ways to get rich. Easier ways." And with that, Casey turned his head to stare hard at the wagons.

Luke stiffened as he saw where the man was looking. A harsh note came into his voice. "You can forget about that. That gold belongs to the Confederacy. Thinking otherwise is the same thing as committing treason."

Casey shook his head and said hastily, "You've got me all wrong, Jensen. I'm not thinkin' anything except I'll be glad when our turn at guard duty is over so I can get me some more sleep." He yawned, but Luke wasn't sure if it was genuine. "It was a hard night, and I'm still tired."

"It was a hard night," Luke agreed, thinking about the encounter with the mob in Richmond and then the fight with the Yankee patrol at the bridge.

Casey grinned as he poked a fist against Luke's upper arm.

"Your problem is you got too many thoughts in that head of yours. A man's brain ain't built to work that hard, Jensen. Me, all I think about is whiskey and women and killin' Yankees, and that's plenty."

"I figure it'll be a while before we get any whiskey or women," Luke said, "but it wouldn't surprise me if you get your fill of killing Yankees before this is all over."

CHAPTER 6

After talking to Casey, Luke felt the need for some solitude. He took his rifle, climbed to the top of the bluff hanging over the wagons, and stretched out among the trees so he could gaze around the countryside.

Other than numerous columns of smoke rising in the distance marking the location of Richmond, he couldn't see any signs of the war from where he lay. Here and there, the vegetation was starting to turn green with the approach of spring. A few birds winged through the blue sky.

It would have been a tranquil, beautiful scene if not for the never-ending rumble of artillery, which could be heard even so far from the capital city. The sound of the bombardment was a constant reminder of the ugliness lurking beneath the apparently peaceful surface.

He and his companions were putting that behind them, at least for the moment, Luke reminded himself. He was sure the war would catch up to them again, probably sooner rather than later, but he was going to enjoy the solitude while he could.

Weariness stole over him, begging him to close his eyes. He fought it off, knowing if he gave in to the temptation, he would fall asleep. The possibility of the Yankees sneaking up on the escort on his watch was unacceptable.

To help keep himself awake, he looked down at the brush where Ted Casey still hunkered. He caught a glimpse of the scout through the branches, but only because he knew where the man was. Luke thought it was very unlikely anybody else would spot Casey.

He recalled the way Casey had looked at the wagons while they were talking about getting rich. The memory brought a frown to Luke's face.

As soon as President Davis had explained the details of the mission the night before, Luke had worried about entrusting the safety of so much gold to such a small group of men.

It made sense from a tactical standpoint. Nine men and two wagons could move a lot faster and attract a lot less attention than a company of soldiers.

But if some of those men turned out not to be trustworthy, it could lead to trouble. Luke knew he could trust Remy, Dale, and Edgar, and Colonel Lancaster was completely devoted to the Confederacy. The other four men were unknown quantities. In the long run, how would they react to the temptation of all that bullion?

Of course, they could be wondering the exact same thing about him and his friends, Luke reminded himself. Potter, Stratton, Richards, and Casey certainly hadn't held back when it came to fighting the Yankees at the bridge. They had pitched right in, risking their lives for the cause . . . and also to save him and Remy.

Thinking about the cause made Luke ponder the future. It was pretty obvious the Confederate government couldn't survive without the funds represented by that gold. Even if they made it safely to Georgia with the wagons, and the government set up a new capital there, would it mean anything except the Confederacy would cling to existence by its fingernails for another few weeks?

General William Tecumseh Sherman had already stormed through Georgia, leaving much of it in ruins. Atlanta—what was left of it after the Yankees had burned the city—was in Union hands. Once Richmond fell, as seemed inevitable, Grant could just turn around and march south, and the remnants of the Confederacy would be caught between two overwhelming forces.

The glorious cause, Luke thought bitterly. But despite his own cynicism, he knew he would fight to the end. Jensens didn't give up, even in the face of certain defeat. Sometimes events had a way of taking unexpected turns.

Even so, Luke didn't hold out much hope the mission would really change anything.

He lay on top of the bluff until it was time to wake up Dale for a turn on guard duty. He climbed down, went into the cave-like overhang, and reached under the lead wagon to where Dale had wrapped up in a blanket.

A shaken shoulder brought Dale out of his slumber. "Trouble?" he asked in a groggy voice.

"Nope," Luke told him. "Everything's quiet. But it's your turn to stand guard."

Dale yawned and stretched.

"One thing," Luke went on quietly after glancing around to see that no one was going to overhear. "Keep an eye on Casey, Stratton, Potter, and Richards."

"Why?" Dale asked with a frown.

"I just think it would be a good idea, until we're sure how much we can count on them."

Understanding dawned in Dale's eyes. "All right, Luke. But so far they haven't given us any reason not to trust them."

"Maybe not," Luke said, not wanting to get into the details of his conversation with Casey just yet, "but we want things to stay that way."

Before the sun went down that evening, Edgar Millgard built a small fire under the bluff. The overhang would disperse the smoke enough that it wouldn't be noticed. He cooked more of the salt pork, and they had biscuits with the meat instead of hardtack. "Don't get used to eatin' so fancy," he warned the men with a grin. "We don't have much flour."

They washed the food down with brackish water from their canteens. Josh Richards sighed. "I sure could use a real drink right about now."

"No liquor," Lancaster snapped. "We can't afford to let our guard down, even for a minute."

"Don't worry, Colonel," Richards drawled. "I was

just wishin'. We don't have any redeye, anyway." He glanced over at Stratton and winked fast.

Luke barely noticed it, but it made him wonder. A little later, while they were saddling the horses, he pretended not to see Stratton until he bumped into the man.

When Stratton turned with a scowl and said, "Hey, be careful," he was close enough that Luke caught a faint whiff of whiskey on his breath.

"Sorry, Stratton, that was my fault. I wasn't watching what I was doing."

Stratton shrugged. "Well, no harm done. So don't worry about it."

Luke was going to worry about it, though. He was going to worry that either Stratton or Richards—or one of the other two, he supposed—had managed to sneak a bottle or a flask into their gear.

Drinking itself didn't bother Luke. From time to time he liked to have a beer or a shot of corn liquor. But he'd never had the thirst for the stuff some men did, and he agreed with Colonel Lancaster. They didn't need anything to distract them from their mission. They had been given the job of taking the bullion to Georgia, and as soldiers, it was their duty to carry out those orders.

It was just one more reason to keep an eye on the four men, he told himself.

Before they left the camp, Luke went over to Lancaster. "I've been thinking about something, Colonel."

"What's that, Jensen?"

"You seem to be the only one of us who knows exactly where we're going."

Lancaster frowned. "What's your point? I'm the only officer with this detail. The rest of you are just enlisted men. I'm the only one who needs to know."

Luke ignored the man's annoying arrogance. "Begging your pardon, sir, but if anything were to happen to you, we wouldn't know where to deliver the gold. I was thinking that if you had a map or something—"

"So you'd know exactly where to avoid if you tried to abscond with these wagons?" Lancaster broke in.

Luke couldn't stop himself from responding angrily. "Colonel, I never said such a thing. I never even thought it!"

"Well, I can't take any chances. President Davis himself picked me for this mission, and I don't intend to let him, or the Confederacy, down. So you just concern yourself with your own responsibilities, Corporal, and let me worry about everything else."

There was nothing Luke could do except grit his teeth for a second. "Yes, sir, Colonel." He turned and went back to the wagons.

Remy was helping Dale hitch up the team to the lead wagon. He inclined his head toward Lancaster and asked, "What was that about, *mon ami*?"

"Remember we talked about how the colonel is the only one who knows where we're going?" Luke asked.

"Sure."

"Well, I said something to him about it . . . and he wasn't inclined to share the information . . . which he told me in no uncertain terms."

Dale chuckled. "I never minded serving under the colonel in the field. Thought he did a pretty good job, in fact. But put him out here in command of a small group like this and he's sort of a jackass, ain't he?"

"So far," Luke agreed.

"You think he can manage to get all the way to Georgia without getting himself killed?"

"It's not him I'm worried about," Luke said. "I'd just as soon get the rest of us there without us getting killed."

CHAPTER 7

They traveled through the night without encountering any trouble, and after resting the next day Colonel Lancaster announced they would turn and head west for a night before starting south again. "We'll be well clear of Richmond, so we shouldn't run into any trouble."

"We'll be behind Yankee lines," Potter said.

"Yes, but all their attention is focused on Richmond now. As long as we avoid their supply trains and relief columns, we should be fine. I'm relying on you men for that."

Several more days passed without incident. They traveled by day, since they were off the main roads and needed light to see where they were going. Also, they were moving through country where none of them had been before, so they didn't know the terrain. Sometimes they found their way blocked by a ravine or a ridge the wagons couldn't handle, and were forced to backtrack until they found another route.

They were making progress southward, and that was encouraging to Luke. He didn't know how long it would take them to reach Georgia—a couple weeks, more than likely, he thought—but at least they were heading in the right direction finally. He just hoped the Confederacy hadn't collapsed by the time they got there.

In a way, that would be simpler, he mused as he rode ahead of the wagons, scouting with Remy. If the damned war was over, they could just surrender and be done with it. Admitting defeat to the Yankees would be a bitter pill to swallow, but at least they would all be alive.

Of course, in that case the Union would seize the gold. Off it would go to Washington. That bothered Luke, too, but the final fate of the gold was really none of his business.

He suspected Potter, Stratton, Richards, and Casey were all sneaking drinks now and then, but none of them got drunk so he didn't say anything about it. Lancaster seemed oblivious to what was going on, but that was nothing unusual. The colonel was oblivious about a lot of things.

Several times they had to take to the woods and find hiding places when Yankees were in the vicinity. Once they watched from the concealment of trees while a lone supply wagon rolled slowly past, accompanied by a handful of tired-looking blue-clad troopers. In whispers, Stratton and Potter urged Lancaster to let them attack the wagon.

"There's bound to be provisions in there we could use," Potter said.

"And we can kill all them blue bellies before they know what's goin' on," Stratton added.

Lancaster shook his head stubbornly. "We can't

risk the shots drawing attention. We'll stay here until they're gone."

Stratton and Potter didn't argue, but Luke saw them looking at the colonel with a mixture of scorn and hatred. He didn't have a very high opinion of Lancaster himself, but those two looked like they wanted to murder him.

The bad feelings he had about the mission grew stronger as they continued heading south. More than a week had passed since they left Richmond when they paused to rest the horses one afternoon and suddenly heard something they hadn't heard in quite a while.

Female voices.

Casey's head came up like a bloodhound catching a scent. "Hear that, fellas? There's womenfolks somewhere close by!"

Luke heard it, all right. Several women, by the sound of it, and they were laughing. The voices were coming from the other side of a thick stand of trees.

"We'd better check that out, Colonel," Stratton said to Lancaster.

"Yeah, there's no tellin' but what they might be spyin' on us," Richards said.

It didn't sound to Luke like the women were spying on them. He thought it would be better to move on as quickly as possible.

But Lancaster nodded. "All right. Three of you go find out who they are and what they're doing here. Jensen, Casey, and Potter, you go."

Luke would have rather gone with a couple of his friends, but he nodded and got his rifle from the wagon.

He and Casey and Potter slipped into the woods, moving quickly but quietly.

The stand of trees wasn't very thick. A couple minutes later, the three men came to a creek. A covered wagon was parked on the other side of the stream. A woman perched on the seat with a shotgun across her knees.

"Holy Moses," Casey breathed.

He was looking at six women standing knee-deep in the creek, stripped down to their underthings. They were taking advantage of the creek and the warm afternoon to bathe. The flimsy garments were soaked and clung to their bodies.

"You know what kind of women those are?" Potter asked in a whisper.

Luke knew. It was pretty obvious. They ranged in age from late teens to early thirties, he judged, although soiled doves led such hard lives they often looked older than they really were. Such women always followed the armies. Union, Confederate, it didn't matter. Luke figured such women could have been found with the Greeks outside the walls of Troy. "Must be Yankees around here. Otherwise those women wouldn't be here."

"I don't care about that," Casey said. "I just want to go say howdy to them."

Potter grunted. "I want to do a hell of a lot more than say howdy."

Luke understood. He was as human as the next man, and the sight of all that wet, bare, female flesh made him react just like Potter and Casey. But they had other things to worry about. "We'd better leave them alone.

We'd just be asking for trouble if we start bothering with them."

"You're not in charge here, Jensen," Potter snapped.

"No, but the colonel wouldn't want—"

"The hell with the colonel! Come on, Ted."

Before Luke could stop him, Potter straightened, stepped out of the trees, and called, "Howdy there, ladies."

The women in the creek shrieked and giggled in surprise, but the older woman on the wagon seat instantly swung up her shotgun and pointed it across the stream. "Howdy yourself, you damn Rebel. You come a step closer and I'll blast you to hell!"

Potter held up his hands. "Whoa, there, ma'am. I don't mean any harm. I just came along and saw all these beautiful young fillies, and I had to say hello." As Casey stepped out of the trees, Potter went on. "My friend here feels the same way."

"That's right," Casey said with a broad grin on his face.

Still under cover, Luke saw what was about to happen. "Casey, no!" He started forward, but was too late.

Casey's hand came up with a gun in it. The revolver roared, and across the creek, the woman on the wagon rocked backward as the bullet drove into her. One barrel of the shotgun boomed as her finger jerked on the trigger, but the weapon was angled upward and the load of buckshot went harmlessly into the air.

The woman swayed forward, dropped the shotgun, and pitched off the wagon seat, landing on the creek bank in a limp sprawl. Luke could tell by looking that she was dead.

The screams that came from the whores in the creek weren't playful any longer. The girls were terrified.

Potter drew his gun and said in a loud voice, "Shut up! Nobody's gonna hurt you!" He glared at Casey. "Why the hell did you shoot the old woman?"

"I don't like people pointin' guns at me," Casey said. "Anyway, you heard her call me a Rebel. She was a Yankee madam, nothin' to be worried about."

Even though Luke had seen far, far more than his share of violence over the past four years, the callous way Casey had murdered the woman sickened him. He was about to draw his own gun and coldcock the varmint from behind when footsteps rushed through the trees toward them. He looked over his shoulder and saw Remy and the other men coming to see what the commotion was about.

"Hold your fire!" Lancaster called, even though no one was shooting. "Damn it, what's going on here?"

As they emerged from the trees, the man all gaped at the women in the creek, who were now huddled together in frightened silence. Even Lancaster stared at them.

Casey holstered his revolver and said coolly, "That old biddy over yonder by the wagon tried to blast us with a shotgun, Colonel. I stopped her."

"I heard those shots," Lancaster said, "and so did any Yankees within a mile of here! Come on. We have to get moving while we still have the chance."

"No offense, Colonel," Casey said, "but I'm not goin' anywhere until I've had a chance to get to know one of those gals a mite better. That one with the yaller hair, I'm thinkin'."

Luke saw how things were shaping up. Stratton and Richards had drifted toward Casey and Potter. Remy, Dale, and Edgar had moved up alongside Luke. Lancaster was in the middle.

The colonel realized it wasn't a very good place to be and stepped back quickly. "I've given you men an order. By God, I expect you to carry it out!"

They were standing on the knife-edge of bad trouble, Luke sensed. He had felt such impending violence in the air many times, and seldom did it end well.

However, something intervened. From the corner of his eye, he saw one of the soiled doves break away from the others. The blonde Casey had mentioned, in fact. She scrambled out of the creek onto the bank and snatched up the shotgun the older woman had dropped.

With their attention focused on each other, none of the other men saw it happening until it was too late. Potter finally noticed the blonde and twisted toward her, his hand clawing for the gun at his waist.

Luke's revolver came out with blinding speed. He leveled the barrel at Potter and drew back the hammer. The sinister metallic sound made Potter freeze.

"Don't do it," Luke warned.

Across the creek, the blonde screamed, "Get out of here, damn you! One barrel of this scattergun's still loaded! I'll cut you all down! I ought to do it anyway, for killin' Maddy!"

Potter's gun was in his hand, already cocked, but it was still pointed at the ground. He looked at Luke through eyes slitted narrow with hate. "You're takin' the side of a bunch of damned whores over your friends?"

"I don't recall you and me being friends, Potter," Luke said. "We just have the same job to do, that's all."

"And that job's in danger the longer we stay here," Lancaster said. "We have to go. Now."

For a second Luke thought Potter was going to lift his gun and pull the trigger, anyway. If he did, the creek bank would erupt in gunfire. They might all die, especially if the blonde cut loose at the men with that shotgun. She very well might do just that, considering the other whores had scrambled out of the creek and taken shelter behind their wagon.

Potter laughed and shook his head. "I'll never figure you out, Jensen." He lowered the hammer of his revolver and stuck the gun back in his waistband. "But I reckon you and the colonel are right. There might be a Yankee patrol gallopin' toward us right now, so we better light a shuck."

"But, Wiley—" Casey began.

"I said we're goin'."

Casey cast a regretful glance at the blonde. Clearly, he might have dared that shotgun to get at her. But too much else was against him at the moment. He nodded. "Yeah, come on, fellas." He pointed a finger across the creek at the blonde and added, "I'll see you again one of these days, darlin'."

"You better hope I don't see you first," she said as her mouth twisted in a snarl.

Luke didn't put his gun away until the men had gone back to the wagons. He saw Potter glancing at him several times as they got ready to move. It was hard to read the man's expression, but Luke knew he had made an enemy.

The outriders mounted up, and the drivers and guards climbed onto the wagons. With no Yankees in sight, they moved out smartly, still heading south.

Remy brought his horse alongside the wagon where Luke and Dale were riding. "The next time those girls see Yankee soldiers, they're gonna tell them about us."

"I expect you're right," Luke said.

"And that blond belle, she be a smart one, Luke. She heard Casey and Potter call the colonel by his rank, and she heard him givin' us orders. She'll figure out that, civilian clothes or not, we're soldiers. Confederate soldiers."

Luke nodded. He knew Remy was right.

And because of what had happened at that creek, he knew their mission had just gotten harder.

CHAPTER 8

The rest of that day, everyone in the group kept looking behind them fairly often, checking their back trail. The same thought was in their minds: one time, they'd look back and see Yankee cavalry chasing them.

It didn't happen, though. By the time they camped that night, they hadn't encountered anyone else.

The next day passed without incident as well, and Luke began to hope if the whores had told somebody about what had happened, the Yankees were too busy to worry about some strange-acting Confederate soldiers dressed in civilian clothing.

They were somewhere in eastern Tennessee, Luke figured, maybe in the Smoky Mountains, and the terrain grew more rugged. The wagons followed narrow, twisting trails running between steep, heavily wooded slopes. Luke watched those mountainsides intently, knowing the dark valleys were perfect for an ambush.

The travelers avoided settlements, but every now and then they passed isolated cabins with small garden patches nearby. The people living there barely subsisted on what little food they could grow, along with any small game they could trap. Obviously, it wasn't much. The people who came out of those rickety cabins to watch them pass were gaunt and hollow-eyed. They looked like it had been months since their bellies were even half full.

The children were the worst, Luke thought. His heart went out to them as they stared up at the wagons and riders with dull, defeated eyes. He wanted to give them something to eat, but he and his companions were already on short rations. His own belly spent a lot of time growling in hunger. The soldiers couldn't do any hunting because of the attention the shots might attract.

They were approaching one such cabin when an old man with a long white beard limped onto the trail to stop them.

Lancaster called, "Get out of the way, old-timer," but the man didn't budge. Dale hauled back on the reins to bring the lead team to a halt before they ran over the old man. Lancaster cast an irritated look over his shoulder, and Luke knew it was because Dale had stopped the wagon without waiting for the colonel's order.

"What do you want, old man?" Lancaster asked.

The man raked gnarled fingers through his long white beard before answering. "I don't know who ye are or where ye be goin', but I want you to take my grandson wi' ye." He turned his head and nodded toward the shack, where a skinny boy about twelve years old stood on the leaning porch. He was barefoot and wore only a pair of ragged overalls.

"I'm sorry, we can't do that," Lancaster said.

"If he stays here, he'll starve, sure as shootin'," the old man insisted. "The only chance he's got to live is goin' somewheres else, somewheres they have more food."

A harsh laugh came from Potter. "Then he's out of luck, old-timer, because it's like this all over the South. The Yankees have burned and looted and torn down until there's nothing left. The boy might as well stay here and starve instead of starvin' somewhere else."

The old man lifted a trembling hand. "Ye can't mean that. There's got to be someplace better. There's got to be a place where folks still have some hope."

"If there is, we haven't seen it," Lancaster said. "I'm sorry, sir, but we have to be moving on. Now, if you'll get out of our way . . ."

In desperation, the old man reached for the halter on the colonel's horse. "Please . . . you got supplies . . ."

"Not enough to share," Lancaster snapped. "Not even enough to last us until we get where we're going." He pulled his horse to the side, out of the old man's reach. "Get out of—"

He didn't say any more. At that moment, a shot boomed and the old man's head jerked as a sizable chunk of it was blown away by a rifle ball. Blood sprayed in the air, turning his white hair pink.

The shot came from just behind them and to the right, Luke judged. While he was turning on the wagon seat to locate the threat, the thought crossed his mind that the shot had been aimed at Lancaster. When the colonel moved his horse suddenly, it sealed the old man's fate.

More shots roared. Tongues of flame spurted in the

trees almost at the edge of the trail. Luke whipped his rifle to his shoulder and fired at one of the muzzle flashes. A man in a dirty blue uniform and black forage cap staggered out from behind a tree, clutching his chest where Luke's bullet had gone. The Yankee soldier collapsed.

The rifle was good for only one shot, and Luke didn't have time to reload. He dropped it at his feet and yanked the revolver from his waistband as he used his other hand to shove Dale off the seat. He followed, diving after his friend.

The bushwhackers seemed to be on the right side of the road. As the Confederates returned the fire, they hurriedly took cover behind the wagons. The saddle mounts bolted down the trail, but that was a problem to worry about later, Luke thought . . . if any of them survived.

Crouching behind the lead wagon, he tried to make his shots count, waiting for a glimpse of blue before he pulled the trigger. Fortunately, the Yankees cooperated. There was no telling where those Union troops were from, but they didn't seem to have much experience at the sort of hill fighting the Southerners did. Nobody grew up in the Ozarks without learning about the dangers of bushwhackers.

Three more men fell to Luke's shots, and the heavy fire from his companions was taking a toll, too. The wagons with their cargo of bullion provided good cover. No bullets could penetrate those crates full of gold bars.

Luke glanced at the other men. They were all on their feet. He couldn't tell if any were wounded, but they were all still in the fight, something that couldn't be said for the Yankees.

The officer in charge of the ambush realized the same thing. He shouted over the sound of gunfire, "We'll overrun them! Charge!"

That was just about the worst thing those Yankees could have done. As they burst out of the woods, yelling and shooting, they were met by a hail of bullets from the wagons.

The first rank went down as lead tore into them, then the second, and the charge disintegrated into a chaotic milling around, turning the soldiers into sitting ducks. A few tried to flee back into the trees, but they were gunned down.

An eerie silence fell as clouds of powder smoke drifted over the trail and around the wagons. Luke risked a look. It appeared all the Yankees were on the ground. A few were writhing around and groaning in pain, but most of them lay in the limp sprawl that signified death.

If there had been enough of them, maybe they could have overrun the wagons and finished off the Confederates with their bayonets. But the attack had fallen short

"Check those men," Lancaster ordered.

Stratton tucked away his pistol and drew a knife. He looked over at Richards and grinned. "Josh and me will take care of it, Colonel."

Richards grinned, too, and pulled out his own knife.

Luke knew they intended to cut the throats of the Yankees who were only wounded. He didn't like the idea of killing defenseless men, but this was war, after all.

A sob made him turn around. The boy who'd been on

the porch had come onto the trail, falling to his knees beside the body of his grandfather. He was leaning forward over the corpse, crying.

Luke reloaded his pistol and his rifle, then walked over to the boy and rested a hand on his shoulder. "Come on, son. That won't do any good. Your gramps is gone. I'm sorry."

"The . . . the Yankees came marchin' up a while ago," the youngster managed to say. "They told Grampa that . . . that there would be some wagons comin' along . . . They said they'd been chasin' you for days . . . and wanted him to stop y'all somehow. Grampa didn't want to do it . . . but they said they'd kill us both and burn down our place if he didn't . . . He had to do it, mister. He had to."

"I reckon he did." Luke had already figured out something like that must have happened. "There's no shame in a man doing whatever he has to in order to protect his family. You remember that, son."

"But then they . . . they shot him anyway!"

"I think that was an accident. They were trying to shoot one of us."

"He's dead, though, either way."

There was no denying that. Luke didn't even try to. He couldn't do anything for the boy except squeeze his shoulder again and leave him there to mourn his grandfather.

When he went back over to the wagons, he asked Remy, "Anybody hurt in our bunch?"

"Edgar got nicked on the arm, but Dale's patching it up. The colonel's hat's got a hole in it, so he came mighty close to shakin' hands with the devil. But that's all."

"We were lucky."

Remy nodded. "Very lucky. Maybe the fates, they are smilin' on us for a change."

Luke thought they had been pretty fortunate the whole trip, but he didn't point that out.

Colonel Lancaster said, "I don't know if there are any more Yankees in this area, but if there are, they're bound to have heard this battle. We need to get moving again quickly. Somebody move that old man's body out of the way."

"We could bury him, Colonel," Luke suggested.

Lancaster shook his head. "There's no time for that. Let's go. We'll all ride on the wagons until we catch up to our horses."

Luke thought it was likely the saddle mounts had stopped to graze somewhere along the trail. Once they were away from the sound of shots and the smell of powder smoke, they would have calmed down fairly quickly.

The boy had gone back to the shack and disappeared inside. Luke and Remy picked up the old man's body and carried it carefully off the trail. They had just returned to the wagons and climbed on when the youngster emerged from the cabin carrying an old squirrel rifle.

"You and your damned war!" he cried shrilly. "I hate all of you!" He started to lift the rifle.

Potter's revolver streaked out and blasted. The slug smashed into the boy's frail chest and lifted him off his feet as it drove him backward. Dust puffed up around him as he landed on the ground.

There hadn't been time for the other men to do anything. Lancaster turned to Potter and said in a horrified tone, "You shot that boy!"

"He was about to point a rifle at me," Potter said coolly as he reloaded the expended chamber. "Damned if I was gonna sit here and let him shoot me."

Luke hopped down from the wagon and walked over to pick up the rifle the boy had dropped. The youngster lay a couple feet away, staring sightlessly at the sky. Luke tried not to look at those open, empty eyes.

He checked the rifle and said in disgust, "I don't think this old relic would have even fired! You killed him for nothing, Potter."

Potter's shoulders rose and fell. "I didn't have any way of knowin' that, now did I?"

That was true, Luke supposed. He threw the squirrel rifle aside. The boy and his grandfather lay dead on one side of the road, more than a dozen Yankees on the other. Once again Luke and his companions were surrounded by senseless death.

After all the things he had seen . . . all the things he had *done* . . . he wondered if by the time the war was finally over, he would have any soul left at all.

CHAPTER 9

The gold escort continued south, hoping the Yankees who'd ambushed them were the only ones on their trail. Luke thought it likely the women they'd encountered beside that creek had sent the soldiers after them.

Each day without an ambush or confrontation the Confederates became more aware the Yankees had other things to deal with, like the collapse of the Confederacy. The atmosphere of gloom and despair hung over the landscape like actual clouds. The air smelled of smoke, rotting flesh, and defeat.

It seemed to Luke like a month had passed since they left Richmond, but he knew it hadn't quite been two weeks. "We're getting close to Georgia now," he commented to Dale one day. "Have to be."

"I think you're right," Dale said. "What are you gonna do once we get where we're goin', Luke?"

"I guess that'll be up to the colonel. Maybe he has orders for what we're supposed to do next. If not, I guess I'll stay wherever the new capital is and try to do what I can to help." Luke shook his head. "No point in trying to go back to Richmond, even if we could get there."

"I got a feelin' you're right about that."

The trail entered a long, straight stretch between two mostly bald knobs. Luke frowned at the hills, thinking it would be another good spot for an ambush.

But when the trouble came, it popped up right in front of them through sheer bad luck. A Union cavalry patrol came trotting around a bend in the trail just beyond the knobs.

The Yankees regarded anybody who wasn't wearing the blue as an enemy. Sunlight winked on steel as the officer in charge of the patrol whipped his saber from its scabbard and shouted, "Charge!"

Just like that, the Confederates were in another fight, and there wasn't any good cover on either side of the road.

All they could do was shoot it out.

Luke brought his rifle to his shoulder, drew a bead on the officer leading the charge, and pressed the trigger. The rifle roared and bucked against his shoulder. Through the powder smoke stinging his eyes, he saw the Yankee topple off the galloping horse.

Their commanding officer's death didn't slow down the other cavalrymen. They kept moving forward, blazing away with pistols as they raced toward the wagons and the outriders.

Colonel Lancaster tried to wheel his horse around and gallop back to the cover of the wagons, but he jerked in the saddle as at least one bullet found him.

A crimson stain bloomed on the colonel's shirt as he galloped past the lead wagon.

Dale grunted in pain beside Luke, but he didn't have time to glance over and see how badly his friend was hurt. He had his revolver leveled at the charging Yankees. As he squeezed off his last two rounds, another cavalryman fell, taking his mount down with him. Another horse ran into the fallen animal and upended as well. The trail suddenly became a welter of flailing hooves and swirling dust.

The back of the charge was broken. Only three Yankees remained mounted. They whirled their horses and fled. A few final shots from the Confederates followed to speed them on their way.

Luke turned to Dale and found his friend clutching a bloody left shoulder. "How bad is it?"

"Don't know, but it hurts like hell," Dale replied through clenched teeth. "I'll be all right. See about Remy and Edgar."

Luke twisted on the seat to look back at the other wagon. Remy was reloading and seemed to be all right. He glanced up and gave Luke a brief nod to signify as much. Edgar waved to indicate he was unharmed, too.

Lancaster had galloped past both wagons before coming to a stop. Luke had a feeling the horse had been running blindly, that the colonel was no longer in control. He glanced back to where the horse had stopped. Lancaster was still mounted, sitting hunched over in the saddle.

Casey trotted his horse back to check on the officer. He put a hand on Lancaster's shoulder and leaned over to take a closer look at him. Then he turned and called to the others, "Hey, the colonel's shot to pieces!"

"Get him down from his horse," Luke said, "but be careful with him."

Casey frowned as if he didn't like the idea of Luke giving him orders, but he dismounted and reached up to take hold of Lancaster. Stratton got to them in time to swing down from his saddle and give Casey a hand.

They lowered Lancaster onto his back in the grass at the side of the trail. All the men gathered around him, even the wounded Dale Cardwell.

Lancaster was still alive. His eyes were open, and his mouth moved like he was trying to say something. He couldn't get the words out, though. Nothing came from his mouth except trickles of blood at each corner.

The colonel's shirt was so bloody it was hard to tell for sure, but it looked like the man had been hit at least three times. Clearly, the wounds were bad ones.

Luke figured Lancaster had only minutes to live, if that long. He dropped to a knee beside him. "Colonel, can you hear me? Colonel!"

Lancaster managed to make a sound, but it was just a choked, incoherent moan. From the look in his eyes, he wasn't aware of anything except the pain that filled him.

"Colonel, listen to me!" Luke urged. "We need to know where we're going. Colonel, do you have a map? Can you tell me—"

"He can't tell you nothin', Jensen," Potter said. "He's next thing to dead, can't you see that? We're on our own now."

"Don't say that just yet," Luke snapped. "We can't give up—"

A grotesque rattle came from Lancaster's throat. When Luke looked at the colonel again, he saw that Lancaster's eyes were starting to glaze over.

"Well, he's sure enough dead now," Potter drawled, "and like I said, we're on our own. Question is, what are we gonna do?"

"Go check those Yankees and make sure they're all dead," Luke said as he reached over to close Lancaster's eyes. "Remy, patch up Dale's shoulder."

"*Oui*."

"Then we'll get moving," Luke went on. "We can't afford to wait around. Three of those troopers got away. They'll go tell other Yankees what happened. We need to get off the trail and find a place to hole up for a while."

He glanced up. No one except Remy, who was tearing pieces off his shirt to bind up the wound in Dale's shoulder, had moved to do what he said. "Blast it, get moving."

"Hold on just a minute, Jensen," Potter said. "I don't recall anybody puttin' you in charge."

"Somebody's got to take over," Luke said. "Or would you rather stand around and argue about it until a whole company of Yankee cavalry shows up?"

Potter thought it over for a couple seconds, then shrugged.

"All right, we'll do what you say . . . for now. But this ain't settled."

Luke didn't expect it to be, but for the moment he

would take what he could get. He said to Edgar, "Let's put the colonel's body in one of the wagons."

"Why not leave him where he lays?" Stratton suggested.

"Because I want to search him later and see if he's got any written orders or a map on him."

That answer satisfied the others, and they went about their business. All the fallen Yankees were dead except for a couple, and Casey didn't waste any time slitting their throats. Luke and Edgar carried Lancaster's body over to the second wagon and placed it alongside the crates containing the gold bullion. By that time, the crude job Remy had done of bandaging Dale's wound had stopped the bleeding.

"Somebody tie the colonel's horse behind the second wagon," Luke said. "We'll take it with us."

That done, they followed the trail for another half mile until Luke spotted a narrow path leading off into a thick stretch of woods. He was driving the lead wagon since Dale couldn't handle the team with a wounded arm and drove between the trees, calling back to Remy, "Once we're all off the trail, get a branch and wipe away our tracks as far back as you can."

Remy waved a hand in acknowledgment of the order.

The path was little more than a game trail. Trees and brush crowded in on the wagons from both sides. Branches clawed at the men. Several times the wagons' sideboards scraped against tree trunks, and Luke worried they would get stuck. Finally, they broke out into a small clearing. It was big enough to turn the wagons around and go back out the way they had come in, but it would be a challenge.

When Remy rode in a few minutes later, he said, "Not only did I wipe away our tracks, but I pulled some brush in front of the opening as well. If any Yankees ride by, they may not even notice a gap big enough for the wagons."

Luke nodded his approval. "That was good thinking. Let's get the colonel out of the wagon so I can check his pockets."

"Robbin' the dead?" Potter asked mockingly.

"Checking for a map or orders, like I said before."

"You go right ahead. I ain't fond of handlin' dead men."

Neither was Luke, but he made himself do it. He searched all Lancaster's pockets but didn't find anything except a couple bloodstained letters from the colonel's wife. He didn't read them, tucking them back into Lancaster's pocket. He didn't have any right to intrude on the colonel's private life.

Since that search came up empty, Luke opened Lancaster's saddlebags next. He was luckier there, finding a leather dispatch case with a folded map inside. As the others gathered around, he spread the map on the ground and studied it. After a second, his finger poked a spot that had been circled. "Copperhead Mountain, That must be where we're going. There's probably a settlement nearby where the government's going to set up." He straightened as he folded the map. "That's where we're going, anyway."

Wiley Potter's voice was flat and hard as he said, "I'm not so sure you're right about that, Jensen."

CHAPTER 10

Luke stiffened. Somehow, he wasn't surprised by what Potter said or the thinly veiled threat in the words. "What are you talking about?"

"All you've got is a map," Potter said. "You don't know that this Copperhead Mountain place is where we're supposed to go."

"It's the only thing in the colonel's belongings that has a destination marked. I think we all know that's what it means."

"Maybe," Stratton said. "But we don't have to go there, now do we?"

"Lancaster's dead," Richards added. "The mission's over."

Luke shook his head. "What makes you think that? Just because we've lost our commanding officer, doesn't mean we don't still have our orders."

"Orders from who? Jeff Davis?" Potter laughed. "The president of a country that may not even exist by now? Hell, Richmond could have fallen the day after we left, for all we know!"

Edgar said, "Even if Richmond fell, the war's still going on. General Lee hasn't surrendered. The way those Yankees keep attacking us proves that."

"Edgar's right," Remy said. "Our responsibility still lies with the Confederacy."

Casey finally put into words what was uppermost in all their minds. He pointed at the wagons and exclaimed, "But there's all that gold just sittin' there!"

It had happened even faster than Luke thought it would. The temptation of that fortune in gold bullion had been there all along, of course. Lancaster's presence and the men's habit of taking orders had held it in check.

But Lancaster was gone, and all Potter, Stratton, Richards, and Casey could think of was how they could be rich men. All they had to do was forget about delivering the gold to Copperhead Mountain, take the wagons, and strike out on their own. If they headed west, they might be able to leave the war behind them. There had been battles between Union and Confederate forces out on the frontier, but not many.

Luke glanced right and left. Remy, Dale, and Edgar stood with him, as he had known they would. They faced the other four men across a short distance. No guns were drawn—yet—but everyone was tense and ready for trouble.

It might not be possible to reason with the others. That much gold had a way of making a man's brain not work as well as it usually did. But Luke was going to try. "Look, you know we're not going to let you take those wagons. That gold belongs to the Confederacy. If we do anything with it except deliver it where we're supposed to, we'll be thieves . . . and traitors."

Potter let out a contemptuous snort. "How can you betray a country that don't exist anymore?" he demanded.

"You don't know that."

"Hell, Jensen, you've got eyes! There's no way Richmond was able to hold out. The streets are probably full of Yankees by now. And if Lee *hasn't* surrendered yet, he's got Grant chasin' him across Virginia. It's only a matter of time until what's left of the army is cornered. Lee's not gonna fight to the death, and you know it. He'll surrender."

Luke suspected Potter was right about that. General Robert E. Lee cared too much about his soldiers to let them be slaughtered to the last man in a futile cause.

But that still didn't change anything. They had their orders.

"Forget it, Potter. From the looks of that map, we're not far from Copperhead Mountain. We can be there in another couple days. And that's where we're going with that gold."

"That's your final word?" Potter asked. Next to him, Casey nervously licked his lips, anxious to grab for his gun. So were Richards and Stratton.

From what Luke had seen of those men, they were probably faster on the draw than Dale and Edgar. He and Remy might be able to match them, but that wasn't good enough. If it came down to a fight, he and his friends would probably die.

Some of the others would die, too, but more than

likely one or two of them would survive. Those survivors would be very rich men.

The ones who didn't make it would be dead, and that worry lurked in Wiley Potter's eyes. Potter didn't want to risk his own life to make somebody else rich.

That realization was confirmed a second later when Potter burst out, "Ah, the hell with it!"

"Wait a minute, Wiley," Stratton protested. "What do you mean?"

"I mean I don't feel like dyin' over this," Potter declared.

Casey looked stricken. "The Confederacy don't need that gold," he said with a whining note in his voice. "It oughta be ours!"

"A man can always get rich if he's smart enough," Potter responded. "But not if he's dead!"

Luke didn't relax and let his guard down. He didn't trust Potter, not for a second. It could be some sort of trick. "You'll go on to Copperhead Mountain with us?"

"I didn't say that," Potter replied. "Look, we've fought Yankees over and over again on the way down here. They're probably lookin' for us right now. Our luck's bound to run out sooner or later. I've had enough of this war, Jensen. I'm riding away. The rest of you do whatever you damned well please."

"In other words, you're deserting," Luke said in a hard voice.

Potter surprised him by laughing. "You think I care what you call it? You can't betray a country that doesn't exist, and you can't desert from an army that's probably surrendered by now. All I know is I'm done with it."

"Me, too," Stratton said.

"And me," Richards added.

Casey still looked like he wanted to shoot somebody, but he gave a grudging nod. "Yeah, I'll go along with the others. I reckon bein' alive is the best thing."

"So, Jensen," Potter said. "Is it settled . . . or is it going to be a fight?"

Luke glanced at his companions. Remy shrugged a little. Edgar gave him a tiny nod. Dale just looked like he was in pain from that wounded shoulder.

"Go ahead and get out of here, if that's what you want to do." Luke didn't bother trying to keep the scorn out of his voice.

"We're taking the horses."

"Go ahead. We've got the colonel's horse. Remy can ride it. I'll handle one wagon and Edgar the other."

Potter smirked. "Sounds like you've got it all figured out. You'll be a real hero when you get to Copperhead Mountain with that gold. That is, until the Yankees take it away from you and you see what a waste it all was."

"I'll know that I followed orders, anyway."

"Yeah, that'll buy you a lot." Potter jerked his head at his allies. "Come on. I want to put some distance behind us before any more blue bellies can catch up to us."

"Wiley, are you sure about this?" Stratton asked.

"I'm sure. We'll have other big chances later on. Stick with me, boys, and we'll all be rich sooner or later."

The others still didn't look happy about it, but they followed Potter's lead and mounted up. Potter took a small bag of supplies from one of the wagons and held it up to Luke, raising his eyebrows. Luke nodded for him to take it.

The four men didn't follow the path back toward the road. They struck out across country, soon vanishing in the thick woods.

"Deserters," Edgar said in disgust. "Lousy deserters."

"Maybe worse than that," Remy said. "You don't trust them, do you, Luke?"

"Not one bit. We'll keep our eyes open in case they double back and make a try for the gold."

"So now we have to worry about the Yankees *and* those four," Dale said. "Things don't get any easier, do they?"

Luke shook his head. "Hardly ever."

They buried Colonel Lancaster's body in the woods and stayed hidden in the little clearing all night. Several times Luke heard a lot of hoofbeats in the distance and thought it was likely the Yankees were hunting for them. None of the searchers came close to the wagons, though. Luke wondered if that was because they really hadn't gone very far from the site of the battle with the cavalrymen. The Yankees might have expected them to head on south as quickly as possible.

Nor was there any sign of Potter, Richards, Stratton, and Casey. Luke hoped the four men really had lit a shuck for the frontier. It would certainly make things easier.

By morning, Dale had developed a fever and lay stretched out under one of the wagons.

Luke looked at him, then at the others. "If we move him, we take a chance on him getting worse."

"We could stay here another day," Remy suggested.

"Give the Yankees that much more time to get tired of lookin' for us."

That sounded like a pretty good idea to Luke. They continued lying low and took turns wiping Dale's face with a wet cloth to keep him cool as he tossed and muttered. It was all they could do for him.

The fever broke the next night. Dale was still weak, but a lot more coherent the morning after that. As he sipped a little broth Edgar had made from the salt pork, he said, "We gotta get movin' again. That gold needs to get to the new capital."

Luke had his doubts whether that new capital even existed, but on the chance that it did, they had to continue their mission. He nodded. "We'll hitch up the teams."

Dale was able to sit up and ride on the seat of the lead wagon next to Luke. Edgar handled the other wagon while Remy rode ahead to scout their route. He came back to report that the trail was clear.

"Lots of tracks, though, and they're pretty recent," Remy said. "There are still plenty of Yankees in these parts. Might be better if we started travelin' at night again."

"That won't be easy since we don't know exactly how to get where we're going," Luke said. "We've got the colonel's map, though. Maybe we can figure it out."

Late that afternoon, they had to leave the road hurriedly to avoid a cavalry patrol. Luke and Edgar managed to pull the wagons behind a hill before the blue-clad troopers rode past, but it was close.

"You're right," Luke told Remy. "We'll travel at night the rest of the way, starting tonight. We'll stay here and let the horses rest for a few hours, then try to put a few more miles behind us."

They made a cold supper from rations that had dwindled to almost nothing. For days, they had gotten by on about half the food they really needed. Luke's belly felt empty all the time. The trek wouldn't last much longer, he told himself, and then things would be better.

Remy did a little more scouting while it was still light and returned to tell the others, "There's a river about a mile from here. It's shallow, and there's a good ford. We shouldn't have any trouble gettin' across."

"And we can fill up our water barrels and canteens while we're at it," Edgar said.

That sounded like a good plan to Luke. When they had rested for a while and it was good and dark, they started the wagons rolling south again.

The moon hadn't risen yet when they reached the river, but Luke saw stars reflected in its placid surface. Remy rode out in front of the wagons so the others could see how deep the water was. Luke figured it was only about a foot.

"The bottom's good and solid," Remy said. "The only problem is that the bank on the other side is a little steep. It'll be a hard haul for the teams gettin' all that weight up to the top. But I reckon they can do it."

"All right, let's go." Luke slapped the reins against the backs of his team. The big draft horses leaned into their harness. Water splashed around the wheels as the wagon began fording the river.

Luke made the crossing without any problem and started up the grade on the far side as Edgar's wagon rolled out of the water behind him. Remy sat his horse to one side.

Suddenly, what felt like a sledgehammer slammed into Luke, low down on his back. He cried out in agony as the impact drove him forward. Dropping the reins, he slumped over and almost pitched off the seat to land under the hooves of the team. At the last moment he twisted his body and fell to the side, landing with stunning force beside the front wheel.

He had never felt such pain in his life. It swelled and burst into a fiery explosion that seemed as big and hot as the sun. As Luke lay there gasping for breath, he heard shots, heard men cry out. Remy cursed and gasped. Edgar roared in defiance, a bellow that was cut short by a flurry of gunfire.

They had been ambushed. The question was whether the bushwhackers were Yankees . . . or those damned deserting curs, Potter, Stratton, Richards, and Casey.

He got his answer a moment later when hoofbeats sounded close beside his head. Instinctively, he tried to jerk away from them, but his body wouldn't work anymore. All he could do was lie there and twitch.

"I don't hear you giving any orders now, Jensen," a man's harsh voice said.

Wiley Potter. Luke recognized the voice, even though he couldn't respond to it.

He thought his gun was still tucked in his waistband and tried to edge his hand toward it. A gun roared, and mud from the riverbank splattered in his face as the bullet tore into the ground beside his head.

"You're beat, Jensen," Potter said. "You might as well

admit it. The other three are dead, and you soon will be. And that gold's goin' with us, just like it was supposed to all along. You stupid idiot, did you really think we were just gonna ride away and leave it?"

Luke was hurting too much to force his thoughts into any coherent order. He shifted a little, and an even more terrible wave of agony made him scream.

"Your back's busted," Potter went on. "That was a hell of a shot I made, if I do say so myself. You're gonna be a long time dyin', Jensen, and I'm going to sit right here on my horse and enjoy every minute of it. So you go ahead and scream. It's music to my ears."

"Wiley, we can't stay here too long." That was Stratton. "We need to take these wagons and get movin'. Why don't you just put a bullet in his head and be done with it?"

Casey laughed. "What fun would that be? I'm with you, Wiley. I want to listen to Jensen scream while he's dyin'."

Luke's mind cleared abruptly. He understood what they'd been saying and forced himself to cut short the agonized cries coming from his tortured throat. He wasn't going to give them the satisfaction.

But his resolve was short-lived, as the pain made him cry out again. Several of the deserters laughed, obviously enjoying Luke's torment.

They weren't going to have much longer to indulge their sadistic glee. A darkness that had nothing to do with night was closing in around Luke, washing over his mind like a black tide. *This is what dying feels like,* he thought in a final moment of clarity.

"He's dead," he heard Wiley Potter say.

That was all. After that, the darkness was complete.

BOOK TWO

CHAPTER 11

When Luke Jensen was ten years old, he fell out of a tree and broke his left arm. It hurt like blazes, and he couldn't hold back the tears as his pa set the bone and splinted the arm.

"No need to cry," Emmett Jensen had said. "That don't make the arm feel any better, does it?"

"Hell yes, it does!" Luke had yelled.

Emmett had laughed too hard to get on to him for cussing. Luke's ma took care of that later, fussing at him until he wished he'd broken his ears instead of his arm.

Luckily, Emmett had set enough broken bones that he knew what he was doing, so his oldest son's arm healed cleanly and Luke didn't suffer any loss of strength or movement in it. He never forgot how bad it hurt when it happened, though.

A couple years later, while getting some wood from the pile next to the back door of the Jensen cabin, he was stung on the right hand by the biggest scorpion he'd ever seen. It felt like somebody had shoved a dull knife through his palm.

The hand swelled up and got almost as red as a beet, and for a while the family worried that he would lose it. Emmett was prepared to cut the hand off if it meant saving Luke's life, but first, he rode up into the hills and brought back an old granny woman who scoured the countryside for plants, made a foul-smelling poultice out of them, and bound it onto Luke's hand.

Within a day the swelling started to go down and the redness went away. By the time a week had passed, the hand was back to normal and Luke couldn't even see the place where the scorpion had stung him.

He remembered what that had felt like, too, and took particular satisfaction in stomping every one of the ugly little varmints he saw after that.

The pain radiating from his back made breaking his arm seem like stubbing his toe. That scorpion sting was nothing more than a mosquito bite. Without a doubt, the current pain was the worst agony Luke had ever experienced in his life.

He wasn't sure how long he lay there, awash in suffering, before he realized the pain meant he wasn't dead.

His pulse hammered an insane rhythm inside his skull. He tried to force his eyes open, but couldn't do it. There wasn't enough strength in him even for a tiny task like that. All he could do was lie there and drag ragged breaths into his body.

After another unknowable length of time, he became aware of light striking his eyelids. He tried again to lift them, and succeeded.

Sunlight lay in a dappled pattern around him. Lying on his stomach on damp ground, his head was turned to the right, his left cheek pressed against the dirt. After a moment, he figured out the sun was shining down on him through some tree branches. Trying to make his brain work provided a welcome distraction from the pain.

He tried to remember how he'd gotten there. At first, everything up until that moment was a blank slate in his mind, but slowly the details began to fill in. He remembered the gold, the journey from Richmond, the friends who had been with him . . .

Then the ambush and Wiley Potter's sneering voice telling him the others were dead and he was dying. In fact, he recalled Potter saying, "He's dead."

Potter had been wrong about that. Luke was too weak to move, but he sure wasn't dead. Not yet, anyway.

Since Potter had been wrong about him, maybe the bushwhacker had been wrong about the others, too. Luke yelled, "Remy! Dale! Edgar! Can any of you hear me?"

It was only when he heard the faint croaking sounds that he realized he wasn't yelling at all. He'd only thought that he was. *He* was the one making those incoherent noises. Finally, after what seemed like another hour, he struggled to get out the name, "R-Remy . . ."

He heard some birds in the distance, the wind stirring the branches in the trees, the tiny lapping sound of the river flowing nearby, but that was all.

He had to get up and look for them. He might still be able to save them.

The gold was gone. Luke knew that. Potter and the other deserters would have taken the wagons with them when they left him for dead, so Luke didn't waste time worrying about that. His only concerns were saving his own life and helping his friends if he could.

He needed to get up and see how badly he was hurt, but one thing at a time, he told himself. First he wanted to look around. He moved his hands enough to dig his fingers into the dirt and brace himself. Then, with a grunt of effort, he lifted his head.

A yell burst from him as even that much movement set off a fresh explosion of pain. He wanted to drop his head, close his eyes, and retreat back into the welcoming darkness.

Instead, he forced his head from side to side in small, jerking motions.

He couldn't hold back a sob as he saw Dale lying on the ground a few yards away. The young man's face was unmarked and his eyes were open, but flies were crawling around on them. He was dead, no doubt about it. His clothes were black with blood where he'd been shot.

Remy and Edgar had fallen in the other direction. Edgar's face was a hideous ruin where several shots had struck him, but Luke recognized his friend's burly build. Remy was disfigured as well, with most of his jaw shot away. The flies were feasting on their spilled blood, as well.

Luke groaned and let his head fall. There was nothing he could do for his friends, after all. Nothing he could do except save himself and maybe go after Potter and the others once the pain in his back got better.

He didn't know how long he lay there, stretched out on the riverbank. The earth turned and the sun moved in the sky, and he was no longer in the shade. When the heat began to bother him, he tried to heave himself up to his hands and knees so he could crawl where it was cooler.

The muscles in his arms and shoulders bunched, and the upper part of his body lifted slightly, but that was all. Luke pushed on his hands again to move upward, but was unable to move high enough. He tried to press against the ground with his knees . . . and realized he couldn't *feel* his knees. He couldn't feel any part of his legs.

Horror washed over him. His body seemed to end at his lower back, where the bullet had struck him and the pain was so bad. Below that, however, nothing hurt. His legs might as well not have been there, and for one sickening moment, he believed they weren't. He thought Potter had sawed them off before leaving.

Slowly, Luke moved his right hand next to his hip. Breathing heavily against the pain, he twisted his neck and looked along his body. He couldn't see very well, but caught enough of a glimpse to know his right leg was still there.

He slumped down. The effort had made his heart pound crazily and left him breathless. As he gasped for air, he remembered a farmer back in Missouri named Claude Monroe, who'd been kicked in the back by a rambunctious mule. The accident busted something in Monroe's back, and after that he was never able to walk again. He had lived for a couple years, lying in bed or sometimes lifted into a chair, before he'd taken an old flintlock pistol, carefully loaded and primed it, and blown a hole right through his head.

He wouldn't have to do that, Luke thought as a hysterical laugh worked its way up his parched throat. No, he would die right where he was . . . on the riverbank . . . more than likely. He knew from the terrible thirst gripping him that he'd lost quite a bit of blood, and he might be losing more all the time without being aware of it. The easiest thing in the world would be to just give in to the pain that enveloped him, and wait for death. So easy . . .

There was no dramatic moment, no stirring speech he made to pull himself back from the brink of despair. It was just that after a while he got so thirsty he thought he might as well try to get a drink from the river. He moved his left arm next to his left hip and cautiously looked under his arm to see if his left leg was still there. It was. He pushed and clawed at the ground in an effort to turn himself around.

When he got far enough around, the steep slope worked against him, and before he knew what was happening, he was rolling down toward the water, his useless legs flopping loosely.

So, I'm going to fall in the river and drown in a foot of water. As that thought flashed across Luke's mind he reached out, caught hold of a root growing from one of the trees on the bank, and stopped himself at the edge of the river.

He hung on to the root with one hand while he reached out with the other and cupped it in the stream. When he brought that hand to his mouth, the water he sucked out of his cupped palm was the sweetest he'd ever tasted.

Thirst made him ignore the pain in his back. His movements grew frenzied as he drank. He missed sometimes and splashed water over his face. It felt good.

Then his stomach lurched, and he spewed up all the water he had managed to guzzle down. The spasm made him cry out.

The sickness faded after a few minutes. Luke lay there a little longer and started drinking again, slower.

He kept it down.

When his thirst wasn't so desperate, he twisted around and looked up at the top of the riverbank again. In his condition, the slope seemed impossible for him to climb. He would be better off just staying close to the water, so he could get another drink later.

Making that decision was all he could manage. Closing his eyes, he rested his head against the ground, content to lie there and wait for . . . something.

What he got wasn't good. A short time later, it started to rain.

Luke hadn't noticed the sun going behind the clouds, hadn't been aware the day was growing dark and ominous with the approach of a storm. He had no idea what was happening until thunder suddenly boomed so loud it shook the earth underneath him.

Or was that artillery fire? He had felt the earth move plenty of times in Richmond as the Yankees pounded the city with their big guns.

No, definitely thunder, he thought as several large raindrops pelted the back of his head. In a matter of seconds, a torrent was sluicing down around him.

Luke lifted his head, tilted it back as much as he could, and shouted at the heavens, "Go ahead! Rain on me, damn you! After everything that's already happened to me, how much worse can this be?"

He wasn't sure if he actually bellowed out the words or just thought them, the way he'd thought he was calling his friends' names earlier. But either way, the sentiment was real.

Unfortunately, a few minutes later he realized his situation *could* get worse.

When he looked along the banks, he saw how they were washed out in places. That was why the root he'd grabbed was sticking out of the ground. It meant the river had a tendency to rise when it rained. If the marks on the bank were right, the water could come up higher than the place where he was sprawled.

But how long will it take to do that, he asked himself? *And how much will it have to rain before I'll be in danger?*

He couldn't answer those questions, but it was a downpour, no doubt about that. A real toad-strangler, they'd call it back home. All along the banks, miniature waterfalls were already forming as rain landed higher up and ran down to the river, raising its level drop by drop.

And there were millions of drops.

Luke started laughing again. By all rights, he should have been dead already. How many more times could he manage to dodge the reaper? When was his luck going to run out?

Soon, he thought. Soon.

The water would climb up his body until the current plucked him away from the bank and spun him out into the stream and sucked him under. Tomorrow his lifeless body would wash up somewhere downriver. He could see that grotesque image in his mind, plain as day.

But he wasn't going to give in to that fate without a fight. His father had made it clear to him at an early age that Jensens didn't have any back up in them. Don't go lookin' for trouble, Emmett had told him, but don't ever go runnin' away from it, either. And if the devil finds you, spit in his face.

Luke reached up the bank, dug his hand into the mud, and pulled.

The ground was wet and slick, but he clawed at it stubbornly, grabbed another root, dug in with his elbows, and shoved. He got his body turned so he was facing up the bank again instead of lying sideways on it.

Even if he'd been able to use his legs, it would have been difficult to crawl up that muddy slope. With only his arms to pull himself along, it was sheer torture. The burning pain in his arms and shoulders dominated the misery in his back.

Slowly, inch by agonizing inch, he pulled himself up the riverbank.

After what seemed like hours, when he was too exhausted to go on, he turned his head, looking under his arm, and realized he was only a couple feet higher than when he'd started out. He looked back along his body as best he could.

His feet were already in the water. The river had risen about a foot, and the current was running fast, which meant more and more water was coming down from upstream.

Gritting his teeth, Luke tried to haul himself higher.

He made another few inches, maybe half a foot, and his strength deserted him again.

Maybe what he ought to do was try to roll over onto his back, he thought. Then the rain, which was still coming down with blinding force, might drown him before the river rose high enough to do the job.

The problem was, he was too weak to roll over.

Luke laughed. "You got me," he rasped. "I'm done for. Fought all I can fight. I'm sorry, Pa. Wish I could see you again. You and Ma and Janey and Kirby . . . but this is where it ends for me."

His head fell forward. Mud covered his face, clogged his nose, choked him. He coughed and fought free of it, his instincts refusing to let him die. The rain washed some of the muck from his eyes.

And he was able to see the slender fingers reaching down and wrapping around the wrist of his outstretched right hand. Thunder boomed again and lightning flashed.

Luke Jensen blinked in amazement as he rose up as best he could, carefully turned his head, and saw the face of the angel who had reached down from heaven to lift him from earth.

It was funny. He'd always figured when he died, he'd be headed in the other direction.

CHAPTER 12

"Damn it!" the angel yelled.

Confused, Luke blinked rainwater out of his eyes. He'd never gone to prayer meeting all that much, but he didn't remember any preachers he'd ever heard saying anything about angels cussing.

"Come on, mister!" the beautiful vision urged. "You weigh too much for me to lift you by myself. You gotta help me some!"

Understanding sunk slowly into Luke's brain. Despite the pretty face, it was no angel above him but rather a flesh-and-blood girl. She wasn't wearing heavenly robes and didn't have wings, either. She was dressed in tattered overalls, a woolen shirt, and a battered old black hat with rainwater streaming from the brim.

She tugged on his wrist. "Mister, can you hear me? The river's comin' up. If we don't get you off this bank, you're gonna drown."

After fighting on his own for what seemed like an eternity, the sheer fact that someone else was trying to save him filled Luke with gratitude and relief. That feeling was short-lived, though, because he realized she was right. "Can you . . . get help?" he croaked.

"No time!" she said. "This ol' river comes up mighty quick when it rains like this. Goldang it, I told Grampaw I heard somebody yellin' last night!"

"You better . . . fetch him. Has he got . . . a horse or . . . a mule?"

"Yeah, but like I told you, there ain't enough time for that." She dug the heels of her bare feet into the bank and got hold of his wrist with both hands. As she hauled hard on his arm, she said through clenched teeth, "Can't you push . . . with your damned legs?"

Luke couldn't, and he didn't have a chance to explain it. Just then her feet slipped in the mud and she sat down hard as her legs went out from under her. With a startled cry she started sliding down the bank toward him.

She didn't go very far. His head butted her in the stomach and stopped her. Her thighs rested on his shoulders. She put her hands on the ground and pushed herself away from him.

"Dadblast it!" she cried. "Don't you go gettin' any ideas, mister!"

"The only idea I have . . . is not drowning," Luke said. "Let's . . . try again."

The girl scrambled up and took hold of his wrist again. Luke used his other hand to grasp one of the tree roots and pulled. The combined effort was enough to break him free of the sticky mud. He slid upward almost a foot.

"Hang on," Luke told her. "Let me . . . get hold of . . . another root."

She waited until he had a good grip, and then both of them grunted with the strain as they lifted his mostly dead weight. He wound up higher on the bank.

"Here we go," the girl urged. "We're gettin' it now."

They had made some progress, that was true, but Luke didn't know how much longer his strength would last. He was already drawing on reserves he hadn't known he possessed.

The rain was falling harder, turning the riverbank into a swamp. Knowing there was a risk he would slide back down and lose all the ground he had gained, he reached up to grasp another root and pull himself higher with the girl's help.

But the roots were about to run out, he saw with a sinking heart. The top of the bank was only about six feet above him, but it might as well have been six miles. The rest of the slope was nothing but slick mud.

"You've got to hang on here," the girl told him. "I'll go find a branch or something I can reach down to you!"

"You can't hold my weight," Luke said.

"I'll figure out a way. It's our only chance!"

Luke nodded his agreement and got a good grip on the last root. "Okay."

With obvious reluctance even though it was her idea, she let go of his wrist and clambered up the bank, slipping and sliding. When she disappeared over the top, he felt a sharp pang of loss. There was a chance he would never see her again, and for some reason that bothered him as much as the possibility that he was about to die.

He hung on to the root for dear life as the rain

continued to pound down on him. The river was making a rumbling sound, and he wondered if the water was already plucking at his legs. He still couldn't feel anything below the waist.

The jagged end of a gnarled tree branch nearly poked him in the face. He looked up and saw the girl lying on top of the bank, extending the branch down toward him. All he could see of her was her head, arms, and shoulders.

"Grab it!" she called. "Pull yourself up!"

Luke let go of the root with one hand and grabbed the branch. "I don't want to pull you over!"

"You won't! I've got it! Now climb, damn it!"

Luke shifted his other hand to the branch. Its rough surface provided a pretty good grip. He looked up at the girl again, and she gave him an encouraging nod.

He didn't see how it was going to work, since she probably didn't weigh even a hundred pounds soaking wet, the way she was at the moment. But he tightened his hands and hauled hard on the branch, and to his surprise, his body followed. Reaching hand over hand, he continued pulling himself up.

When he glanced at the girl, he saw pain etched on her face. Supporting his weight was obviously painful. Not wanting to hurt her any longer, he summoned all his strength and energy and continued climbing up the branch.

When he was finally close enough, she reached out and grabbed his shirt, pulling hard. He added his efforts and surged up and rolled over the top of the bank. He came to a stop on his back and had to push himself onto his side to keep the rainwater from filling his nose and mouth.

"C-careful," she said. "After all that, we d-don't want you to drown now."

Luke blinked water out of his eyes and looked over at her. She still wore the soaked wool shirt, but she had taken off the overalls. The suspenders were tied around the trunk of a tree while one of the legs was tied around her ankle. That was why she'd been hurting, he realized. The strain of his weight had gone through her whole body, passing through her hands on the branch to her shoulders, along her body, and through her ankle.

When he turned his head, he saw the surface of the river racing along about three feet below the edge of the bank. He almost hadn't made it.

This girl, whoever she was, had saved his life.

"Th-thank you," he gasped out.

"Don't thank me yet," she said. "The river could still get out of its banks."

Her hands were scraped raw from the rough bark, he saw as she sat up. Rain washed away the blood seeping from the wounds.

"I'll fetch Grampaw and the wagon," the girl went on. "He's pretty strong for an old fella. We oughta be able to lift you into the wagon." She paused. "Your legs don't work at all, do they?"

Luke shook his head. "No, I can't even feel them. I was . . . shot in the back."

"Last night?"

He nodded wearily.

"Then that was you I heard hollerin'. I wanted to come see, but Grampaw wouldn't let me. He said to let the damn Yanks and the damn fool Rebs shoot each other, that it weren't nothin' to us either way."

Luke didn't know exactly what she meant, but it wasn't the time to discuss it.

The girl untied the overalls from her leg and scrambled to her feet. "You could have the decency to close your eyes, seein' as how I ain't got no pants on and I saved your life and all."

Incredibly, Luke felt himself smiling. "Yes, ma'am." He squeezed his eyes shut. "Could I ask you one more favor?"

"What's that?"

"Tell me your name."

She hesitated, then said, "Emily. Emily Sue Peabody."

"You sound like a good Georgia girl, Emily Sue Peabody."

"I am. Where are you from?"

"Missouri. My family has a farm up in the Ozarks."

"Then you must be a soldier, in spite of what you're wearin'. Otherwise you wouldn't be so far away from home."

"I was a soldier," Luke said. "But not any more."

That was true. The gold was gone, his friends were dead, and he had spent the past day on the razor's edge of death. It wouldn't surprise him one bit if he closed his eyes and opened them again to find himself in Hell.

"What's your name?" Emily asked.

"Luke Jensen."

"Well, I'd say that I'm pleased to meet you, Mr. Jensen, but right now that'd be a plumb lie. Now don't you move . . . Come to think of it, I guess you won't, will you?"

"Not likely."

"I'll be back quick as I can with the wagon. I'd take it kindly if you don't die in the meantime."

"I'll . . . try not to," Luke said as a new wave of exhaustion washed over him. His eyes closed. He heard the swift splashes as Emily hurried away over the wet ground.

Maybe it was his imagination, but he thought it wasn't raining quite as hard. Even if the downpour stopped, it wouldn't mean the danger was over. All the water that had fallen upstream still had to go somewhere. The whole area might flood. If it did, he would be helpless.

I'm pretty much helpless either way, he reminded himself. All he could do was lie there and wait for Emily to come back.

"Emily Sue Peabody," he murmured. It was a pretty name for a pretty girl.

Thinking about her made the pain not quite so bad.

CHAPTER 13

The sound of wagon wheels creaking brought Luke out of his stupor. Rain still fell, but it was definitely not pouring down as hard.

The wheels stopped, and he heard a thud as somebody jumped down from the wagon. Footsteps ran over to him.

"You ain't dead, are you, Mr. Jensen?" Emily asked.

He opened his eyes and lifted his head. "I'm . . . still here," he croaked.

Emily bent down to look at him. "Good." Then she turned her head to call, "He's still alive, Grampaw!"

"I'm glad to hear it," replied a voice cracked with age. "I'd hate to think you dragged me out in this rain for nothin'! My rheumatiz don't like this damp weather at all."

Luke looked past Emily and saw a man with long white hair and a drooping white mustache coming toward them. The years had bent him some, but he was still fairly tall and his shoulders were broad with strength.

He reminded Luke of a thick-trunked old oak tree draped with moss.

"Let's roll him onto his back so I can get hold of him under his arms and drag him," the old man suggested.

"We can pick him up and carry him," Emily said. "I'll help you."

"No, the other way will be easier," her grandfather insisted.

"He said he'd been shot in the back. Draggin' him like that's liable to hurt him even worse."

The old man frowned. "You might be right about that," he admitted. "All right, get on that side of him. I can take most of the weight, but you'll have to support some of it."

"I've got it." Emily moved to loop both arms around Luke's right arm in a secure grip.

Her grandfather took Luke's left arm in the same fashion. "All right, you ready? Lift!"

With grunts of effort, they straightened, hauling Luke upright for the first time since the night before. Emily's feet slipped a little in the mud as the strain of his weight hit her, but she managed to keep her balance and didn't lose her grip on him.

"This'd sure be easier if you could walk, mister," the burly old-timer said, "but since you can't . . ."

Half dragging, half carrying him, they started toward the wagon, which Luke saw had a team of four raw-boned mules hitched to it. They looked like pretty sorry specimens and the wagon wasn't much better. Every step the old man and Emily took sent pain jolting through him, but he gritted his teeth and didn't cry out.

He recalled how he had screamed after Potter shot him, and the memory filled him with shame. He wasn't going to let himself act like that in front of Emily Sue Peabody and her grandfather.

That wasn't the only shame he felt. The knowledge that he had driven right into that ambush, had lost the Confederacy's gold, and gotten his friends killed had started to gnaw at him. He had known good and well there was a chance Wiley Potter and the others would double back and make a try for the bullion. For a couple days he had watched very closely for any signs of an ambush.

But he guessed he'd let his guard down, especially while he was concentrating on getting the wagon up the steep slope of the riverbank. All it had taken was that moment of carelessness, and he had lost everything.

Well, not everything, he corrected himself. He was still alive, even if just barely. Remy, Dale, and Edgar couldn't say that much. The guilt Luke felt because of that ate at his insides all the more.

When they reached the wagon, the old man said, "Mister, you grab on to the sideboard and help hold yourself up whilst Emily puts the tailgate down. Hop to it, girl."

Luke grasped the side of the wagon as tightly as he could. When Emily had the tailgate lowered, they helped him around to it and lowered him facedown over the gate. Luke's weight kept him there while they lifted the lower half of his body and shoved him into the wagon bed.

That hurt like hell, too.

"I can see where the bullet tore his shirt," the old-timer commented. "Looks like the rain washed out most of the blood. Maybe it did the same for the wound. If it didn't, he'll likely die of blood poisonin' in a day or two."

"Grampaw!" Emily said.

"Just tellin' you the truth of it," her grandfather said. "I'll wager the fella's already thought of that his own self."

"I . . . have," Luke gasped from where he lay with the side of his face pressed against the rough boards of the wagon bed. "I appreciate you . . . trying to save my life anyway."

"It was the girl's idea," the old man said. "I got no use for either side in this war. Haven't ever since it took my boy and my two grandsons."

That explained the bitter undertone in the old-timer's voice, Luke thought, as well as Emily's comment that her grandfather didn't want to get involved in the Yankees and the Confederates shooting each other. He thought he had already lost enough to the fighting, and he was probably right about that.

Luke didn't consider himself a Confederate anymore, not after the way he'd let down the cause by losing that gold. But it didn't really matter since, as Emily's grandfather had mentioned, he expected to die from his wound in the next few days.

He would worry about guilt when and if he survived.

"Might be a good idea if you was to climb up there with him and hold him as still as you can," the old man told Emily. "It's gonna be a rough ride, and bumpin' around's just gonna hurt him worse."

"You're right." She climbed into the wagon bed and sat down next to Luke. Her grandfather got on the seat and took up the reins, yelling at the mules and slapping them with the lines until they lurched forward into a walk.

The jarring motion sent fresh bursts of agony through Luke's body, just as the old-timer had predicted. His breath hissed between clenched teeth, but again he managed not to yell. Emily lay down beside him and put her arm around his shoulders, hanging on tightly to brace him against the wagon's rocking and bouncing.

He couldn't help being aware of the warmth of her torso pressed to his. If he responded to it, he didn't know it, but somehow it comforted him anyway. Gradually the pain eased a bit.

He didn't know how far it was to their destination or how long it took to get there, but finally the wagon came to a halt.

"We're here," Emily said. "This is our farm."

Luke felt the wagon shift as the old man got down from the seat. A moment later Luke heard the tailgate drop and felt himself moving. He knew the old-timer had taken hold of his feet to drag him out of the wagon, even though he couldn't feel the grip.

The rain had tapered off to a drizzle. It was late in the afternoon and darkness was coming on quickly, earlier than usual because of the overcast sky. As they lifted him from the wagon, Luke saw a rectangle of yellow light and recognized it as an open doorway. The glow from a lantern spilled out from the room beyond the door.

Emily and her grandfather wrestled him inside.

The old man said, "We better get him outta these wet duds, or he'll catch the grippe for sure. He don't need that on top of ever'thing else. I ought to take a look at that bullet hole in his back, too."

"You think you can help him, Grampaw?"

"You want me to, don't you?"

"Well . . . yeah, if you can."

"One thing I got to know first." The old man hung on to Luke's arm, but moved enough so he could peer into Luke's face. "Are the Yankees gonna come lookin' for you, mister? Is helpin' you gonna get me and my granddaughter killed?"

"The Yankees . . . don't know I exist," Luke whispered.

That might not be exactly true—there might still be patrols searching for eight or nine men with two wagons—but the Yankees would have no interest in a lone man with what was probably a mortal wound in his back. The bodies of Remy, Dale, and Edgar had surely washed downstream, Luke realized, and when they were found, likely they would be miles from there.

He figured Emily and her grandfather would be safe enough having him. If the Yankees had left them alone so far, they'd have no reason to bother them now.

"All right," the old man said. "I hope you're tellin' the truth. I'll hold him up, gal. Get a knife and cut them clothes off him. That'll be the easiest way to do it."

Luke was in too much pain to worry about the girl

seeing him naked. Anyway, he'd seen her wearing nothing but that soaked woolen shirt, so he supposed turnabout was fair play, as the old saying went.

He heard the faint sound of a sharp blade cutting through fabric. His clothes fell away from him. A chill went through him, and he started to shiver.

"Get somethin' and dry him off," the old man said as he struggled to keep Luke upright. "Then we'll put him in my bunk."

Luke felt her drying his torso. When she moved around behind him, he heard her sharp intake of breath. He figured she had spotted the wound low down on his back.

"It don't look too good, Grampaw."

"I wouldn't expect it to. Come on, we need to get him warmed up some."

Emily finished drying him, and they carried him over to a bunk. As they lowered him face-first onto it, Luke heard a rustling sound that told him the mattress was stuffed with corn husks.

Even with nothing but a rough blanket covering it, it felt wonderful. He let his face sink into the softness.

His head jerked up a second later as something prodded into the wound in his back. His lips drew back from his teeth in a pained grimace.

"Looks like the bullet's still in there," the old man said. "It'll have to come out, but not now. The hole's already festerin' too much. Fetch me that jug o' corn."

"You don't need to get drunk, Grampaw," Emily said.

He snorted. "I ain't plannin' to drink it. It'll clean out that wound better'n anythin' else we got."

After hearing that, Luke knew what to expect. But he

groaned anyway, a moment later, when the liquid fire of the corn liquor burned into his back and seemingly all the way through to the core of his being. Something poked into the wound again, probably the old man's fingers, he guessed.

That was confirmed when the old-timer said, "I can feel the bullet. Should be able to get it. But not yet. I'll dig it out in a day or two . . . if he's still alive."

"He'll be alive," Emily said. "I'm gonna see to that."

"Why in Tophet do you care so much whether this varmint lives or dies? You don't even know him."

"I know his name," Emily said softly. "That's enough for now."

The pain eased a little, and Luke let out the breath he had been holding. As the long sigh escaped him, his eyes closed.

Exhaustion caught up to him, crashing down like a hammer, and once again he knew nothing but darkness.

CHAPTER 14

When he woke up the next time, the only light in the room came from a small candle burned down to almost nothing. The dim glow was enough to reveal Emily sitting in an old rocking chair next to the bunk, dozing. Her eyes were closed.

Now that Luke got a better look at her, he saw that his initial impression had been right: she was beautiful. Her face showed lines that sorrow and hard work had put in it already, even though she was only around twenty years old, but that didn't detract from her beauty as far as he was concerned. Her thick dark hair was plaited into a single braid hanging over her left shoulder as she sat in the rocking chair. She had put on a clean shirt and a clean pair of overalls, maybe the only clothes she owned besides the ones she'd been wearing earlier.

Rough snores came from a long, bulky, blanket-wrapped shape in the bunk on the other side of the room. Luke recalled the bunk in which he lay belonged to Emily's grandfather, which meant the old-timer had claimed Emily's bunk while she slept in the chair.

Or maybe she had insisted on sitting up with him, he thought. That was certainly possible.

The pain in his back had receded to a dull throbbing. He felt it with every beat of his heart, but was able to ignore it by focusing his attention on Emily.

Growing aware of his gaze somehow, her eyes opened, the initial flutter of eyelids as delicate as that of a butterfly's wings. She scooted forward in the rocker and leaned toward him. Quietly, she spoke. "You're awake. How do you feel?"

Before Luke could say anything, Emily shook her head. "You don't have to answer that. I'm sure you hurt like hell."

Incredibly, he felt his lips curving in a smile. In a voice that sounded rusty to his ears, he said, "I do."

"Then why are you smilin'?"

"Because I don't think I've . . . ever run across a young woman who . . . talks like you do."

She looked surprised, and Luke saw a pink tinge spreading slowly through her lightly olive skin. She was blushing, he realized.

"You mean the cussin'? I started doin' it for a reason. After . . . after we got word that my pa and my brothers wouldn't be comin' back from the war, I got worried that Grampaw would miss not havin' any other menfolks around, and since one of the things men seem to do a lot is cuss, I figured it might make Grampaw feel better if I was to do it. They all tried to watch their language around me while I was growin' up, what with me bein' the only gal on the place, but I heard enough. I can cuss up a storm when I want to."

"How did that . . . turn out for you?" Luke asked.

"To be honest, it spooked the hell outa Grampaw at first, but once he got used to it, I think he sorta likes it. And I got used to it, too, I reckon, so I don't hardly know I'm doin' it anymore. Sometimes when you're really mad or frustrated, it sure feels good to let loose with a few ripsnorters."

"Yes, I can . . . imagine."

Emily put a hand to her mouth and looked embarrassed again. "As bad as you must hurt, you must really feel like cussin'. You go right ahead if you want to, Mr. Jensen. It won't bother me none."

"That's all right. What I'd really like . . . is for you to call me Luke."

Emily thought it over and nodded. "I reckon I can do that. I've always been taught to be careful around fellas who were slick talkers, because my pa said there was only one thing they wanted, but I guess the shape you're in, I don't have to worry about that, do I?"

"Not hardly," Luke told her. "And even if I . . . wasn't hurt . . . my pa brought me up to be a gentleman."

"I can see that in your eyes," she said softly, nodding. She reached forward and lightly rested her hand on his forehead. "Oh, my Lord! You're burnin' up with fever."

Luke wasn't surprised. He had already known he felt chilled and light-headed. He supposed the wound in his back had festered and blood poisoning had set in, just like Emily's grandfather had predicted.

"I'll wake Grampaw and see if there's anything he can do for you," she went on.

"There's . . . no need. Just get a wet cloth . . . wipe my face with it . . . That's about all . . . anyone can do for me."

"There's gotta be somethin' else!"

"There's not," Luke told her. "It's pretty much . . . out of our hands now."

He knew that was true. If the fever broke, he might have a chance. If it didn't, he would die. Simple as that.

And it might be better if the fever went ahead and took him, he thought. Emily and her grandfather could bury him and be done with it. They wouldn't have to run even the slight risk of the Yankees finding him and taking action against them.

Better for him, too, because he still couldn't feel his legs or anything below the waist, and he would rather be dead than a cripple. He wouldn't go back to the farm and be a burden to the rest of his family.

Emily got up for a moment and came back with a wet rag. She leaned down and swabbed it over his face. The cool touch felt wonderful.

Sometime while she was doing that, he passed out again. When he woke up, bright sunlight was slanting in through the cabin's open door.

"Huh. You ain't dead after all." That somewhat surprised statement came from Emily's grandfather, who had taken her place in the rocking chair beside the bunk.

Luke licked dry, cracked lips and husked, "I could use . . . something to drink."

"Yeah, you're pretty well wrung out, I expect. I'll fetch you a cup."

The old man came back with a dented tin cup. Luke

took a sip of the clear liquid in it and promptly spit it out in an instinctive reaction.

"That's a waste of good corn, son," the old-timer said. "See if you can keep some of it down this time. You're gonna need it."

"What do you . . . mean by that?"

"I mean your fever may have broken for now, but that wound in your back's in bad shape. That Yankee bullet's got to come out if you're gonna have any chance of makin' it."

Two things were wrong with that, Luke thought. It wasn't a Yankee bullet that had laid him low, but rather one fired by a renegade Confederate. And he wasn't sure he wanted to have a chance of making it, not in the condition he was in.

But the hatred of giving up was bred deeply within him. "All right, give me another sip of that shine."

The old man chuckled. "Emily said you was from up in the Missouri Ozarks. I reckon you prob'ly know good corn liquor when you taste it." He held the cup to Luke's lips.

Carefully, Luke sipped the fiery stuff. His stomach rebelled against it, but he managed to keep it down. He drank enough that it affected him immediately and set his head to spinning. "You're going to . . . cut the bullet of me, aren't you?"

The old man nodded gravely. "That's the only thing to do. As soon as Emily gets back from the tradin' post to hold you down, we'll get started."

"Go ahead and . . . do it now," Luke urged. "I can . . . stay still."

"You don't know what you're sayin'. Even with that liquor in you, it's gonna hurt worse 'n anything you ever felt before."

"Look . . . Emily doesn't weigh enough . . . to hold me down . . . if I start bucking around. I'm going to have to . . . control it . . . whether she's here or not."

The old man rubbed his jaw as he frowned in thought. His fingertips rasped on the white stubble. "More than likely you're right about that," he admitted. "Might not make much difference whether the gal's here or not."

"I don't want her . . . to have to see it," Luke said. "Give me . . . a leather strap or something . . . to bite on."

"My razor strop'll do."

"And maybe . . . some more of that moonshine first."

"We can sure do that," the old man said.

A few minutes later, after several more swallows of the potent liquor, Luke's head was spinning even faster. He set his teeth in the leather strap and watched as the old man heated the long blade of a hunting knife in the fireplace until it glowed cherry red.

He carried the knife quickly back over to the bunk. "The wound's scabbed over, but I'll have to open it again so all the pus can get out. You ready?"

"Just . . . get it done," Luke said around the strap. He took a deep breath and closed his eyes.

The old man was right about one thing: it hurt worse than anything Luke had ever experienced. His teeth bore down on the leather and every muscle in his body turned tight and hard as an iron strap . . . every muscle he could still feel, anyway. The mingled stink of burned flesh and corruption filled the room. Luke groaned.

After what seemed like an eternity of torture, the old-timer exclaimed, "I got it!"

Some of the terrible pressure Luke had felt in his back was released. The pain didn't slack off much, but any relief at all was a blessing.

He felt the old man wiping at his back with a rag. "You're bleedin' like a stuck pig, boy, but I reckon that's a good thing. Maybe it'll wash out all the festerin'. If you don't bleed to death first, that is."

The pain continued to recede. Luke's head slumped back to the bunk, and the leather strap slipped out of his mouth as his teeth released their grip on it. His pulse pounded inside his skull, and he breathed harshly and heavily.

"Grampaw, what in hell are you doin'?" That startled cry came from Emily. "My God, there's blood all over the place! You've killed him!"

"Take it easy, gal. He's alive. And I got that bullet outta his back."

"Is that why you sent me to the tradin' post?" she demanded. "So you could start cuttin' on him without me bein' here to stop you?"

"Shoot, I didn't even know he was gonna wake up. His fever broke, but it would've come right back if I didn't get that bullet out. Look there . . . that's healthy blood comin' out of him now. We can go ahead and stop it, and he can start gettin' his strength back."

Emily went closer to the bunk and bent down to peer

at Luke's face. He saw her only vaguely through his pain and weariness.

"You mean he's gonna be all right?" she asked.

"I mean he's got a chance now," her grandfather told her.

But the biggest question, Luke thought just as he slipped back into unconsciousness, wasn't whether he would live or not.

The question was whether his legs would work . . . or whether he was going to be a cripple for the rest of his life, however long that was.

CHAPTER 15

The fever didn't come back. When Luke woke again, he was ravenously hungry, but able to eat only a few bites of the stew Emily fed him before it started to sicken him. He kept it down, though.

From talking to Emily, he found out it wasn't the day after she'd rescued him from the riverbank. As a matter of fact, three days had passed since that stormy afternoon.

"You were burnin' up with fever and out of your head most of that time," she told him as she sat in the rocker beside the bunk. "You kept ravin', but I couldn't make much sense out of most of it."

"What did I say? Did I talk about anybody in particular?"

"Oh, your ma and pa, of course. I'd expect that. And somebody named Kirby."

"My little brother," Luke said.

"And Janey."

"My sister."

"And Potter."

It was all Luke could do not to snarl in hatred. "He's not part of my family."

"I hope not, the way you were talkin' about him. Remember how I said I could cuss pretty good? Well, you had me beat all hollow while you were talkin' about that fella Potter."

"He's the man who shot me," Luke said. "He and his friends are deserters and renegades."

"Well, then, you've got good reason to be cussin' him. I figured somebody must've waylaid you and robbed you when I didn't find no horse anywhere thereabouts."

Luke waited a moment, then asked, "Did I talk about anything else?" He wanted to know if he had said anything about the gold while he was out of his head.

"Not really. There were some other names . . . Renny, somethin' like that?"

"Remy," Luke said. "A good friend."

"And Dale and Edgar. Who are they?"

"More friends." Luke didn't offer any further explanation. Their bodies must have been taken by the river before Emily found him, otherwise she would have asked him before now who those dead men were.

Just as well, he thought. He didn't want to tell her about the gold, about the way he had lost it and gotten his friends killed. That was a burden he was going to bear alone.

"Grampaw says it looks like that bullet hole in your back is healin' up better now," Emily went on. "I was sure upset with him when I came in and found that he'd been cuttin' on you, but I reckon he did the right thing."

"What's your grandfather's name?" Luke hadn't heard her call him anything except Grampaw.

"Linus Peabody," she told him.

"A fine name. I'm in his debt . . . and yours."

She shook her head. "You don't owe me nothin'."

"You saved my life. I would have died out there if it wasn't for you."

"It's my Christian duty to help folks in need."

"I wish more people felt like you about that," Luke said. "If they did, we might not have had this war."

"Grampaw says we didn't need to have it anyway. We never had no slaves and didn't want any. He tried to talk my pa and my brothers into not goin' off and fightin', but they said it was their duty because the Yankees had no right to invade us."

"They were right about that. I just wish it had never come to that point."

Emily sighed. "Wishin' don't do folks a lot of good, Mr. Jensen . . . I mean, Luke. If it did, there's a whole heap of things in the world that'd be different."

She was certainly right about that, Luke thought.

Because if wishing did any good, his legs would work again, and so far . . . they didn't.

It really hasn't been very long yet since my injury, he reminded himself several times that day . . . and the next and the next and the day after that.

By the time a week had passed, Luke's appetite had returned and so had some of his strength. He was able to sit up in the rocking chair with a pillow to cushion his wounded back, as long as Peabody and Emily helped him get there from the bunk.

But he still had no feeling in his legs, and when he sat there and stared at them and willed them to move, nothing happened. The legs remained limp and lifeless.

"I wish I could help you with the chores," Luke said at supper one evening. "You folks saved my life, you're feeding me, and I can't do a blasted thing to repay you."

"Nobody's asked you to repay nothin'," Peabody said.

"I know that, but I want to, anyway."

"Maybe the time will come that you can. You can't never tell."

Another couple days passed. Luke continued to get stronger. Peabody built him a bunk of his own, so he and Emily could return to their own beds. He checked the wound in Luke's back and changed the dressing on it, then proclaimed, "Looks like that hole's just about healed up, son. I got to admit, I didn't think it'd happen that way, but you must be durned near as strong as a mule . . . and stubborn as one, too."

Emily said, "Grampaw!"

But Luke threw back his head and laughed, which was something he hadn't done much of for a long time. "My pa used to say the same thing about me. The stubborn part, anyway. But the real reason I'm not dead is because you and Emily took such good care of me, Mr. Peabody."

"The gal wouldn't have it no other way," the old-timer said, which brought another blush to Emily's face.

Peabody went out to work in the fields, leaving Emily to finish cleaning up after breakfast before she joined him. With just the two of them to take care of the place, they both worked from dawn to dusk most days. They had gotten behind on the chores during the time they'd had to take turns looking after Luke, and knowing that added to his feeling he owed them more than he could ever repay.

A short time after leaving, Peabody hurried back into the cabin just as Emily was finishing up with the dishes. Luke saw instantly that the old-timer was upset about something.

Peabody didn't keep them in the dark about it. "Yankees comin'."

"Oh, dear Lord," Emily said. "How many?"

"Just a dozen or so . . . but that's plenty if they're lookin' for trouble." Peabody frowned at Luke. "You're sure they ain't huntin' you?"

"I don't see how they could be."

An old single-shot rifle Peabody used for hunting game hung on hooks attached to the wall. He took it down and checked its load.

"You don't want to start trouble," Luke warned him. "Not if there are a dozen of them."

"Don't plan on startin' it. But if they force me to it, I'll fight."

Luke thought swiftly. "How close are they?"

"About a quarter mile, I'd say."

"Put the rocker on the porch and help me into it. I'll hold the rifle in my lap, under a blanket."

"They'd be able to see it anyway," Emily said. "I have a better idea." She opened a cabinet and took out the

Griswold and Gunnison revolver Luke had brought with him from Richmond.

He didn't know what had happened to his rifle, but the sight of the revolver lifted his spirits a little. Only for a moment, though. He recalled how wet the gun had gotten. "The charges in that are bound to be ruined."

"They were," Emily agreed, "until I cleaned it up and reloaded it."

"Where'd you get ammunition for that gun?"

"Bought it at the tradin' post the other day. I thought we might need it sometime."

Luke hoped that time hadn't come. Even with the revolver, he wouldn't be any match for a dozen Yankee cavalrymen, especially stuck in a rocking chair with useless legs.

But being armed was always better than being defenseless, so he held out his hand for the gun and slipped it into the pocket of the overalls he was wearing. It was a good thing Linus Peabody was a fairly big man. His clothes fit Luke without being too tight.

Peabody dragged the rocking chair onto the cabin's front porch, then he and Emily helped Luke get seated in it. She hurried back into the cabin to grab the blanket from the bunk, which she draped over the lower half of Luke's body.

It was the first time he'd been outside since the day of the storm. The air was warm and smelled good. It was a beautiful spring day.

At least, it would have been if it hadn't been marred by the sight of those Yankee troopers riding toward the cabin.

Peabody came out onto the porch holding the rifle. He said to Emily, "Get back inside, gal. And don't come out no matter what happens."

"You know damn good and well I ain't gonna do that, Grampaw."

"Blast it. For once in your life, do what I tell you!"

Emily looked angry and upset, but she said, "I'll be right inside," and moved back through the door.

Luke put his right hand under the blanket, slipping the revolver out of his pocket and gripping it tightly as he watched the Yankees ride closer. He had to fight down the impulse to yank out the gun and start blazing away at the enemy.

Or are they the enemy anymore? he suddenly asked himself. They were laughing and talking among themselves as they approached the cabin. They certainly didn't seem to be looking for trouble.

The officer in charge of the patrol, a lieutenant judging by his insignia, heeled his horse into a trot and rode ahead of the others. He came up to the cabin with the others trailing behind him and reined in. With a friendly nod, he touched a finger to the brim of his hat. "Good morning, gentlemen. Does one of you own this farm?"

"I do." Peabody's voice was flat and hard.

"Then I'd like to ask your permission to water our horses."

Peabody took one hand off the rifle and jerked a thumb toward the north. "River's about half a mile that way. Plenty of water there."

"Oh," the lieutenant said. "I didn't know that. I'm not

that familiar with the area. We're obliged to you for the information. We'll just water our horses at the river."

"That's a good idea." Peabody stood stiffly, both hands tight on the rifle again.

The Yankee officer hesitated, then said, "Sir, you *have* heard the news, haven't you?"

"What news?"

Luke had a hunch he knew what the answer was going to be even before the lieutenant spoke.

"The war's over, sir," the young officer said. "General Lee offered his surrender to General Grant nearly three weeks ago at a place up in Virginia called Appomattox Court House."

Luke closed his eyes. He'd been right.

And Potter and the others had been right, too, about the Confederacy collapsing. They hadn't been traitors, after all.

Just murdering, back-shooting rogues.

"The fighting is all over," the lieutenant went on. "There's no need for you and your son to worry, sir. We're all countrymen again."

Peabody didn't correct the man about Luke being his son. He just said, "The river's up yonder."

The lieutenant nodded. "We'll be going, then. Good day to both of you, and thank you again."

The cavalrymen rode around the cabin and headed north. Luke listened to the sound of their hoofbeats fading as Emily came out of the cabin.

"I'm sorry, Luke," she said.

"About the war being over?" He shook his head. "Don't be. I'm not. I knew that was how it was going to turn out. Better to have it end before more good men were killed for no reason."

"Amen to that," Peabody said.

Luke took the revolver from under the blanket and handed it to Emily. "I guess you can put that away again."

"All right." She hesitated, then said, "Luke . . . what are you gonna do now?"

He looked up at her and realized he had no idea.

CHAPTER 16

Luke balanced himself on the crutches, reached into the bag he held, and slung grain onto the ground for the chickens clustering around him. The fowl went after the stuff with their usual frenzied enthusiasm.

He draped the bag's strap over his shoulder, got a good grip on the crutch handles so he could turn himself around, and stumped back toward the cabin.

Emily came out onto the porch before he got there. "I was gonna feed the chickens," she told him with a grin.

"No need," Luke said. "I took care of it."

"There's just no stoppin' you, is there?"

"Not when it's something I can do." He changed course, angling toward the side of the house where the big stump they used for splitting firewood stood. The ax leaned against the stump, handle up.

"What are you fixin' to do now?" Emily asked.

"You said you needed some wood for the stove," Luke explained.

"I didn't say you had to split it!"

"I don't mind." He reached the stump and propped the

right-hand crutch against it. With only a small amount of awkwardness, he picked up a piece of wood from the pile beside the stump and set it upright in the middle. Then he took hold of the ax and lifted it one-handed.

"You're gonna miss and cut your leg off one of these days," Emily warned.

"No great loss," Luke said.

"Unless you bleed to death!"

Luke swung the ax above his head and brought it down in a precise stroke, splitting the cordwood perfectly down the middle. He used the ax to brush the two pieces off the stump, leaned the ax against it, and picked up another piece of wood to split.

Emily blew out her breath and shook her head in exasperation. "You are the most stubborn man I ever saw, Luke Jensen."

And that was a good thing, Luke thought, otherwise he'd probably be dead. The wound he had suffered a few months earlier would have killed him.

The late summer sun blazed down, and it didn't take Luke long to work up a sweat. His damp linsey-woolsey shirt clung to his back. He lifted his arm and sleeved beads of perspiration off his face.

When he'd first started shaving himself again, rather than relying on Emily to do it, he'd been shocked at the gaunt, haggard face looking out at him from the mirror. That man looked at least ten years older than he really was, Luke thought.

Since then his features had begun to fill out some, and he thought he looked more like himself. Most of the time, the strain of what he had gone through painted a rather grim expression on his face. When he laughed, though, he didn't feel quite as ugly. *Still ugly, mind you,* he told himself, *just not as much.*

Recently he had stopped shaving his upper lip and let his mustache grow. It gave him a certain amount of dignity, in his opinion, and Emily didn't seem to mind. How she thought about things had taken on a lot of importance during the months he had spent on the Peabody farm.

She came down from the porch to gather up the chunks of wood he had split. "Breakfast is ready. Come on inside and eat."

She didn't have to tell him twice, and she didn't have to help him up the steps. He made it just fine with the crutches.

He had carved them himself, putting quite a bit of time and effort into it. He'd wanted the crutches to be as comfortable as possible, since it looked like he'd be using them for quite a while. Some of the feeling had started to come back into his legs, enough that he could get around a little with the help of the crutches, but he was still pretty helpless. He didn't let himself think too much about how long that might go on. He still held out hope that one day his legs would work again, the way they were supposed to.

Because of that, he'd asked Emily to help him exercise the muscles in them. He knew it wasn't fair to place that extra burden on her, but she didn't object. He had seen what happened to Clyde Monroe back home. Doing nothing after his injury had made him worse. Luke wasn't going to give up like that . . . which led right back to that stubbornness Emily had accused him of.

He fed the chickens and gathered eggs and split wood and hoed the vegetable garden and shucked corn. Anything he could do sitting down or balanced on one crutch, he would do. The work put thick slabs of muscle back on his arms and shoulders and back.

He was damned if he was going to be useless. He would die first.

Emily and her grandfather had both asked him if he wanted to send a letter to his family back in Missouri letting them know he was alive. Luke only had to think about it for a second before he shook his head.

After failing the Confederacy and his friends, he didn't want his pa and Kirby finding out about that. One day, if what he planned came about, he would return home, but not until he had done the job he had set out for himself.

Once his legs worked right again, he was going to track down Potter, Stratton, Richards, and Casey and kill each and every one of them. He knew he probably wouldn't be able to recover the gold they had stolen—there was no Confederacy to return it to, anyway—but at least he could even the score for what they had done to Remy, Dale, and Edgar.

And to him.

Then and only then, when he had reclaimed at least a vestige of his honor, would he return to his family. Until then it was better to let them think he was dead, even though they would mourn him.

It had to be that way. On his darkest nights, he admitted to himself there was a very strong possibility he would never walk normally again, no matter how much he tried. In that case, he would live out his life on the Peabody farm, unless Emily and her grandfather kicked him out.

The way he and Emily had started to feel about each other, he didn't think that was likely.

And yet that thought tortured him, too. Emily might be falling in love with him—Lord knew he'd been in love with her pretty much from the moment he first saw her and mistook her for an angel—but was it fair for him to saddle her with a cripple for a husband? He wasn't even sure he could be a real husband to her, although lately he'd begun to feel some stirrings that told him it might be possible.

Feeling *anything* below the level of the wound in his back was a good sign. The bullet wound was completely healed. A pale, ragged scar was the only sign of it that remained. Luke hadn't seen the scar himself, of course, but Emily had described it for him. He could move around now without feeling even a twinge in his back.

He clumped over to the table Emily had set for three people. Setting one of the crutches aside, he gripped his chair and lowered himself into it.

Emily poured coffee for him and set a plate of flapjacks, bacon, and eggs in front of him. They ate fairly well, because the Peabody farm had escaped most of the damage and destruction inflicted by the Yankees when they rampaged through the area a year earlier.

As she sat down opposite Luke, Emily said, "Grampaw told me he's goin' to town today, if you need anything."

The settlement of Dobieville was about five miles down the road. A trading post was closer to the farm, but Linus Peabody refused to do any business there since a Yankee carpetbagger had taken it over a month earlier when the previous owner had been unable to pay his taxes.

Luke shook his head. "I can't think of anything. Unless he can pick me up a new pair of legs."

Emily frowned across the table at him. "I thought you promised to stop sayin' things like that."

"Sorry," he muttered.

"I know you think you got to walk again, Luke, and I don't blame you for feelin' that way, I really don't. But you don't have to. Not . . . not for me, anyway. It ain't gonna change the way I feel about you."

Suddenly the food in front of him didn't seem so appetizing. He didn't want to have this discussion. Of course, it was his own fault for bringing it up.

He looked at the plate. "We don't need to talk about this. It won't change anything, anyway."

His voice sounded harsher than he intended. He didn't look up at Emily, afraid he would see hurt in her eyes.

"All right," she said. "Let's just eat."

Linus Peabody came in a few minutes later. He'd been in the barn, tending to the mules, the milk cow, and the hogs. If he sensed the tension between Luke and Emily, he had the good sense not to say anything about it as he sat down. "Did Emily tell you I'm goin' to town this mornin', Luke?"

"She did, but there's nothing I need right now."

"I was thinkin' you might want to go with me."

Luke frowned in surprise. "To Dobieville?"

"Yep. Actually, I thought we might all go. Been stuck here on this farm all summer."

Luke glanced at Emily and caught a glimpse of excitement on her face.

She hurriedly covered it up. "I don't need nothin' in town, Grampaw."

"Yes, you do. You need to see somebody 'sides a pair of ugly ol' galoots like me and Luke."

"Neither of you is ugly," she protested.

"There's no point in arguing with the facts," Luke said with a smile. "Neither of us is going to win any prizes for being good-looking, are we, Linus?"

The old-timer cackled. "The judges'd have to be plumb blind if we did!" Peabody nodded. "So it's settled. After we eat, we'll all load up in the wagon and head for town."

CHAPTER 17

Luke had to have some help doing it, but he managed to climb into the back of the wagon. From there he was able to use his arms to pull himself to the front, just behind the seat. Peabody settled down on the seat next to Emily to handle the team.

Despite what the old man had said, Luke had a hunch there was more to this trip into Dobieville than Peabody let on. He didn't press the issue, though, as the wagon rolled across fields and along narrow, tree-shaded country lanes toward the settlement.

It was a good test of how well his back actually had healed. The wagon wasn't in the greatest shape, and its ride was pretty rough, even on level ground. But he didn't feel any pain in his back, and that was encouraging.

The mules didn't get in any hurry. The trip to town took more than an hour. Luke was tired by the time they got there, but he still wasn't hurting.

Dobieville had a wide main street running for several blocks between businesses, along with a couple side streets lined with houses. The steeples of the Baptist and

Methodist churches stuck up above the trees on the edge of town. Some of the businesses had been burned when the Yankees came through, but Dobieville had gotten off with less destruction than many Southern settlements.

Several of the businesses that had been burned were being rebuilt, Luke saw as Peabody sent the mules plodding along the street with the wagon rolling slowly behind them. The sounds of hammering and men calling to each other as they worked filled the air.

But Luke sensed something was wrong about what he was hearing, and after a moment he realized what it was. When the workers raised their voices to talk, it wasn't in the slower, softer drawl of Southerners, but rather the hard, brisk tone of folks from up north.

Those were Yankees rebuilding those businesses.

Carpetbaggers.

He had heard Peabody talking about greedy opportunists from up north swarming in all over the South. He saw for himself what was going on. It wasn't just the carpenters. Men in derby hats and gaudy tweed suits and cocky grins strolled along the town's boardwalks, cigars clenched at jaunty angles in their teeth. All Luke had to do was look at them to know they were Yankees.

The true citizens of Dobieville knew it, too. Luke saw the glances filled with resentment, anger, and fear the townsfolk cast toward the newcomers.

Blue-uniformed soldiers lounged here and there. Yankee troopers stood in every block, not necessarily doing anything, but their mere presence was a bitter reminder that the Confederacy had been defeated and the Southern states had been forced back into the Union at gunpoint, after the spilling of rivers of blood.

Peabody brought the wagon to a halt in front of Connally's General Store. He turned on the seat and said to Emily, "Go on inside, gal. I'll join you in a minute."

"What about Luke?" she asked.

"I'm all right sitting back here. It's too much trouble for the two of you to help me down and then back up again."

"No, it's not," she argued. "You came to town so you could see something different from the farm."

"And so I can." Luke smiled. "I can see just fine from right where I am."

"Oh, all right." Emily climbed down from the wagon. "But if you change your mind, we can get you out of there and you can use your crutches."

"I know," Luke assured her.

She still looked a little puzzled, but she went on into the general store. Peabody sighed and turned more on the seat to say quietly, "I wanted a chance to talk to you while Emily ain't around, Luke."

"I thought that might be the case. What's wrong, Linus?"

Peabody let out a disgusted snort. "What's wrong? Just look around you, son!"

"You're talking about all the Yankees?"

"Soldiers and carpetbaggers alike. They've moved in like a swarm of locusts!"

"What did you expect? We lost the war. They can do whatever they want now."

"They could treat us with some respect," Peabody

said as fierce anger edged into his voice. "Instead they've just bulled their way in, run folks off, took over businesses . . . What you're lookin' at, son, is the beginnin' of something that may turn out to be even worse 'n the war itself."

"I don't see how that could be possible."

"You just hide and watch," Peabody said. "Them Yankees got the idea they can waltz in, grab what they want for themselves, and grind the rest of the South into dust under their heels. And they'll laugh at us while they're doin' it."

That was probably right, Luke thought. That was exactly what the carpetbaggers intended to do, and they had the Yankee troops to back them up on it. "Why did you want to show me this?"

"Because there's gonna come a time when we may have to fight for what's ours. So far the Yankees ain't come anywhere near the farm, but one of these days they're liable to. And I don't intend to just let 'em take it away from me."

"You didn't support the war," Luke said. "They should leave you alone."

Peabody waved a gnarled hand. "This ain't about the war anymore. It's about greed, pure and simple, and the chance for a bunch of no-good skunks to grab what ain't theirs."

"And you want to know if I'll stand with you against them?" Luke couldn't keep the dry, acid tone out of his voice.

"I'm just sayin' you may have to make a choice," Peabody snapped. "Legs or no legs."

Luke sighed and nodded. "You're right, Linus. I'm sorry. I appreciate you bringing me to town today and showing me what we may be facing. It's always best to know when trouble's coming."

"That's what I thought."

"And as for whether or not I'll be with you when that trouble comes . . . you ought to know the answer to that. You saved my life, you and Emily . . ."

"I know how you feel about her, too," Peabody said. "I've seen the way she's started lookin' at you lately. I ain't sayin' that I like it—"

"I'm not exactly the man you had in mind for your granddaughter. I know that."

"Maybe not, but you're a good man, Luke." Peabody clapped a hand on Luke's shoulder and squeezed. "I know that, too." He wrapped the team's reins around the brake lever. "Now, I'm gonna go and help Emily pick up a few supplies. Sure you'll be all right out here?"

Luke nodded. "I'll be all right."

"Okay." Peabody jumped down from the wagon and went inside the store.

Luke looked around at the bustling settlement. If it hadn't been for the presence of the Yankees, he would have said Dobieville was well on its way to recovering from the war already.

Unfortunately, under the surface, the truth was that Dobieville was well on its way to being gutted by the carpetbaggers.

Peabody was worried their greedy reach would extend outside the settlement, Luke mused. The old-timer was probably right about that. Even though the prospect worried Luke, too, he didn't see what an old man, a girl, and a cripple could do to stop the arrogant outsiders who now held power in the South.

Peabody wanted to fight if the carpetbaggers came for his property, and he wanted Luke to fight with him. If it came down to that, Luke knew he wouldn't turn his back on the two people who had saved his life. But if that happened, there was a very good chance he and Peabody would wind up dead, leaving Emily alone and defenseless . . .

Or else she would take up arms, and the Yankees would kill her, too.

Maybe the best thing to do, Luke thought suddenly, would be to pack up and leave at the first sign of any Yankees trying to take over the farm. It would mean running from trouble, which stuck in his craw worse than anything. Peabody would probably feel the same, but it might be the only way to save their lives.

The frontier was a big place, with lots of room for folks to settle and start new lives. Luke thought maybe he could even swallow his pride and return home to the Ozarks, taking Emily and her grandfather along with him.

He took a deep breath. No use getting ahead of himself. At the moment, things were all right. Maybe they'd be lucky and it would stay like that.

As he mused, a couple Yankee soldiers came along the boardwalk toward the general store. They stopped and propped their shoulders against one of the posts holding up the awning in front of the store. One of the troopers, a wiry little man with dark hair, glanced at Luke and then looked away, obviously uninterested in him.

The taller, brawnier soldier, with bushy side-whiskers and a thatch of straw-colored hair sticking out from under his forage cap, fastened a cool, appraising stare on Luke.

Keeping an eye on them without drawing attention to himself, Luke tried to ignore them.

A short time later, Emily and her grandfather came out of the store. She was carrying a crate of supplies, while Peabody had a bag of flour slung over his shoulder. As they moved to place the supplies in the back of the wagon, the big trooper straightened from his casual pose.

"Hey, Reb"—he directed the harsh words at Luke—"what kind of man sits by and lets a girl and an old geezer do all the work?"

Peabody turned toward the soldier and snapped, "Who you callin' an old geezer, sonny?"

Emily put a hand on her grandfather's arm and asked the soldier, "Just leave us alone, why don't you?"

"I wasn't talking to either of you." The Yankee soldier pointed at Luke. "I was talking to that big strapping specimen of Southern manhood." A grin stretched across his rough-hewn face. "But I guess he's like the rest of those Johnny Rebs . . . just a lazy coward."

Emily forgot about being reasonable. Even as Luke started to say, "No—", she put herself in the trooper's face. "Shut your mouth, you big, stupid Yankee tyrant."

The man's eyes widened in surprise. He brought his hand up to slap her and growled, "You foul-mouthed little Rebel slut! I'll—"

Luke grabbed the crutch from the wagon bed beside

him and drove the tip of it into the soldier's midsection as hard as he could. He put plenty of the strength in his arms and shoulders behind the punch.

The trooper cried out in pain and stumbled back a step, tripping on a loose board in the porch. He sat down hard, gasping for breath, the blow had been so strong.

His companion acted swiftly, unsnapping the holster at his waist and pulling out a revolver. He eared back the hammer as he raised the gun and pointed it at Luke's face.

CHAPTER 18

Luke knew in that instant how close he was to dying. He had reacted instinctively when Emily was threatened, and it looked like that reaction was going to cost him his life.

But before the little Yankee could pull the trigger, a voice asked sharply, "What's going on here?"

The soldier's gaze darted past the wagon toward a man who had come along the street from the other direction. The short Yankee hesitated, licking his lips. "This Reb just attacked Private Packard, Mr. Wolford."

The newcomer strode past the wagon to confront the soldiers. "It looked to me more like he was defending this young woman. Packard was about to strike her, wasn't he?"

"Beggin' your pardon, sir, but you didn't hear what she called him."

"Nor do I care," Wolford replied. "A man who acts like he's going to hit a lady deserves whatever he gets. And I'm confident Colonel Morrison would agree with me." He used the walking stick he carried to point at the bigger soldier. "Now put that gun away, help Private Packard to his feet, and both of you move along."

The little trooper took a deep breath, obviously reluctant to follow the civilian's orders. But Luke could tell he was afraid not to do what Wolford said. After a couple seconds the soldier holstered his revolver and turned to extend a hand to his companion. "Come on, Packard. We got things to do."

Packard had gotten his breath back, but his face was pale. Anger made twin spots of red glow on his cheeks. He brushed aside the other soldier's hand and climbed to his feet on his own.

"This ain't any of your business, Wolford—"

"Come on," the smaller soldier urged. "Let it go." He got hold of Packard's sleeve and tried to drag him away.

Packard didn't want to, that much was clear. He glared darkly at Luke, who saw a promise in the man's eyes that the skirmish wasn't over. But the soldier turned and stalked off along the boardwalk, his shorter compatriot hurrying to keep up with him.

Wolford turned to Luke, Emily, and Peabody and smiled ingratiatingly. "I'm sorry about that unpleasantness. Unfortunately, too many soldiers haven't gotten it through their heads yet that the war is over." He put out a hand to Peabody. "Vincent Wolford."

The man's accent marked him as being from somewhere in New England. He was about forty, with a lean face, dark hair, and thick, salt-and-pepper side-whiskers. His suit was a subdued blue, and he wore a black beaver hat.

Wolford wasn't just a carpetbagger, Luke thought. He was a *boss* carpetbagger.

Peabody hesitated, clearly not wanting to shake hands with any Yankee, but Wolford had kept the little soldier from shooting Luke. After a moment, he took Wolford's hand and clasped it briefly. "Linus Peabody."

"It's a pleasure to meet you, Mr. Peabody." Wolford smiled at Emily. "And this is your granddaughter, I expect? I can see the resemblance."

"My name's Emily. I ain't much on shakin' hands with Yankees, though."

Wolford smiled. "That's all right, Miss Peabody. A perfectly understandable attitude, considering all the upheavals that have taken place. Believe me, I know what you're going through."

Luke didn't believe that for a second. Wolford had the smooth look of a man who had always been rich and gotten whatever he wanted.

"Or perhaps it's not Miss Peabody," Wolford went on as he turned to Luke. "Are you the lady's husband, sir?"

"That's Luke—"

"Luke Smith. I'm a friend of the family, that's all."

"I see." Wolford glanced at Luke's legs and the crutch still in his hand. "You were wounded in the war?"

"That's right."

"A terrible shame."

Luke was aware that Emily and her grandfather were looking at him curiously, no doubt wondering why he had given Wolford a false name. Without much thought, it had popped out of his mouth. He'd been brooding a lot lately—about the stolen gold and the deaths of his friends—and hated to think the name Jensen would ever be linked to such a shameful failure. That probably had something to do with it.

And the fact he instinctively didn't trust Vincent Wolford.

"Colonel Morrison, the commander of the troops in this area, is a good friend of mine," Wolford went on. "I'll have a word with him and ask if he could order his men to treat the citizens with a bit more respect. After all, we're all partners now in rebuilding the South. If we're going to work together, we should get along, shouldn't we?"

"We don't want trouble with anybody," Peabody said, which didn't really answer Wolford's rhetorical question.

"Of course not." The man smiled and lifted a hand to the brim of his beaver hat. "Well, good day to you folks."

As Wolford strolled away, Peabody climbed quickly to the wagon seat and told Emily, "Get on the wagon, girl. We're gettin' outta here."

The old-timer turned the vehicle around and got the mules headed back toward the farm. Peabody muttered under his breath about how they shouldn't have come to Dobieville today in the first place.

Emily turned around to lean over the back of the seat. "You shouldn't have got mixed up in that, Luke. That big, dumb Yankee never would've been able to hit me. I'm too fast for the likes of him."

Luke shifted on the wagon bed. "Maybe so, but it's bad enough I had to sit by while you and Linus loaded the supplies. You can't expect me to do nothing while that soldier attacked you."

"You almost got yourself killed, that's what you did."

Luke couldn't argue with that.

"If that slick-talkin' Yankee carpetbagger hadn't come along, that mean little varmint would've blowed your head off."

"More than likely," Luke admitted with a sigh.

"And what was that business about callin' yourself *Smith*?" Peabody asked. "Have you been lyin' to us all along, son? Are you some sort of criminal on the run from the law?"

"No," Luke answered without hesitation. "Absolutely not. I may not have told you quite everything, Linus, but I give you my word, nobody's looking for me, lawman or otherwise."

Peabody nodded. "Reckon I can accept that. Just like I can accept it's your business what you call yourself."

"Well, it may take me some gettin' used to, after callin' you Jensen all this time." Emily paused. "Just don't get yourself killed on account of me, Luke Smith or Jensen or whatever the hell name you want to use."

Luke laughed. "I'll certainly try not to."

When they got back to the farm, Emily and her grandfather helped Luke down from the wagon before they unloaded the supplies. He stood at the back of the vehicle on his crutches and said, "If you want to drape that flour sack over my shoulder, Linus, I might be able to carry it in."

"There ain't no need of that," Peabody said. "You don't have to prove anything to us, Luke."

"That's right." Emily turned away from the tailgate with the crate in her hands. "You already do plenty to help out around—

Oh!" she cried out as the heavy crate slipped from her grasp and fell on Luke's right foot.

Luke took a sharp breath.

"Hell and damnation!" Emily exclaimed. "Oh, Luke, I'm so sorry! I didn't mean to drop that on you. It must've—"

He smiled as she stopped short in what she was saying. "Must have hurt? Only a little. That's one thing I don't have to worry about."

Looking flustered, Emily picked up the crate. "Well, when we get inside, I want to take a look at your foot anyway. You could be hurt and not even know it."

"I suppose you're right," Luke said.

A few minutes later, he was sitting in the rocking chair. Emily knelt in front of him and took off his boot and sock. There was a red mark on the top of his foot where the crate had landed, but no blood. Emily poked around on the spot.

Luke blinked.

"Doesn't feel like any bones are broken." Without looking up, she pulled his sock back onto the foot. "You were lucky."

"That's me. Lucky Luke Smith."

Emily snorted.

After they ate a hasty midday meal, Emily and Peabody went out to work in the fields, leaving Luke sitting in the rocker. When he was sure they were gone, he put his hands on his thighs and squeezed as hard as he could, working the muscles. He had succeeded in covering up his reaction so Emily and her grandfather hadn't noticed it, but it had hurt like blazes when that crate fell on his foot, the most sensation he had felt in one of his feet for a long time. And it had been repeated when Emily poked at the site of the injury.

It excited him as no pain ever had.

He stared at his legs, willing them with every fiber of his being to move, but all he could summon up were a few twitches.

He slumped back in the rocking chair, suddenly breathless and exhausted. *That might be the most my legs will ever move,* he told himself. But his heart soared inside him, anyway. For the first time in months he had real hope again.

Hope that someday he might be able to have the things he most wanted . . .

Emily.

And vengeance.

CHAPTER 19

Over the next few days, Luke struggled against the impatience he felt as he looked for another sign that his legs might be improving. Any time he was alone at the cabin, he moved them as much as he could, sometimes unconsciously straining his other muscles until he was breathing hard and sweat popped out on his face. He rubbed his legs and then pounded on them in frustration when they failed to respond as much as he wanted them to.

One day he lifted himself out of the chair with his crutches, then let them fall to the sides in the hope he could force himself to stand.

He fell on his face.

And struggled hard to push himself up with the crutches to get back in the chair.

He didn't give up. He worked at it every day and would continue as long as it took.

He didn't say a word about his efforts to Emily or her grandfather. If he failed—again—he didn't want them to know about it. There would be time enough later to fill them in if he was successful in learning to walk again.

Emily continued to exercise the muscles in his legs, massaging and working them back and forth.

Several days after his fall she noticed a change. "It may be my imagination, Luke, but it seems to me like your legs are getting stronger rather than weaker."

"Really? Well, that's good, isn't it?"

"Yeah, real good. I knew it was just a matter of time before you started healin' up."

He thought she was just trying to be encouraging, but maybe she was more right than she knew. Whenever Emily and her grandfather weren't around and Luke was on his crutches, he let more of the weight of his body rest on his legs.

At first they had buckled, but as the days went on he was able to stiffen them and partially support himself more than he could before. He still didn't say anything to Emily or her grandfather. Hope and resolve filled him, but he was wary.

One evening while Emily was inside cleaning up after supper, Luke sat in the rocker on the porch and the old man sat on the steps. Peabody filled his pipe and lit it, then said quietly enough that Emily wouldn't overhear, "I spotted some fellas on horseback watchin' the place today."

Luke tensed, hearing the worry in the old-timer's voice. "Soldiers?"

"Nope. Civilians. I didn't get a very good look at 'em, but I could tell that much."

"What do you reckon they wanted?"

Peabody shook his head. "Don't know, but Bud Harkness come by today and talked to me. Bud's got the next farm over. He says there's some problem with the taxes and he might lose his place."

"Didn't he pay them?"

"He did . . . but the judge the Yankees put in charge of such things says that Bud didn't pay enough. It's a blamed lie . . . but he's a judge."

"What's this fellow Harkness going to do?" Luke asked.

"What *can* he do? He can stay and fight, or he can leave." Peabody puffed on the pipe for a second or two in silence, then went on. "Bud's got five kids and another on the way. He can't afford to get himself killed."

"So he's going to pack up and leave?"

"I expect so. That's the smart thing to do."

"If they're after his place . . ."

"This one's next in line," Peabody said, his voice heavy. "That's who I think was watchin' us today. Somebody who works for the varmint who's got his eye on this place."

"You happen to know who that is?"

Peabody turned his head to look at Luke in the fading light.

"Wolford."

The answer didn't surprise Luke. Vincent Wolford had stepped in to help them that day in Dobieville when they'd had the trouble with the soldiers, but he had seen through the man's slick façade to the predator underneath. Weighing his words carefully, Luke said, "Maybe Harkness has the right idea. There's Emily to think of—"

"You mean you think we should run, too?" Peabody snapped. "That ain't the way you sounded the last time we talked about this, son."

"I know. I just don't want anything bad to happen to Emily."

"You think I do? But you got to remember this . . . gettin' her to leave wouldn't be easy. This land . . . well, look at it this way. When her pa and her brothers went off to fight, they figured they were doin' it to protect our home. This land. Emily still sees it the same way. She'll feel like she has to defend it, too, just like they did."

Luke understood that. He felt the same way about the Jensen farm in Missouri. So would his pa and Kirby.

There was no good answer. None at all.

Emily appeared in the doorway behind them, drying her hands on a cloth. "What are the two of you talkin' about so serious-like?"

"Who says we're talkin' serious?" her grandfather said. "I was just tellin' Luke a joke."

"I didn't hear anybody laughin'."

"That's because I ain't got to the funny part yet." Peabody turned to Luke. "So then the farmer says, 'You're all mixed up, mister. That there's my prize hog.'" He slapped a hand on his thigh and hooted with laughter.

Luke threw back his head and laughed, too, even though on the inside he had seldom felt grimmer.

Using the crutches, Luke lifted himself from the chair and stood beside the table. He took a deep breath and let go of the crutches, allowing them to fall to the sides like he had done before. As they thumped on the floor, he stood with his hands spread, trying to balance himself.

He didn't fall immediately. He felt the weight on his

legs, felt the muscles struggling to support him. But they began to give out, and he had to slap his palms down on the table to hold himself up. Even that was progress, he thought as his pulse pounded in his head. He hadn't collapsed. Yes, he was leaning on the table, but he was still standing.

A footstep sounded on the porch.

Luke turned his head toward the door, and as he did so, his legs folded up underneath him. He tried to catch himself on the table, but wound up lying on the floor between the chair and the table.

Emily came in and saw him there. "Damn it all to—" She stopped herself. She had been trying to stop cursing so much lately.

He thought maybe she had decided it wasn't ladylike . . . as if acting more like a lady might have become more important to her.

She rushed over to him and bent to take hold of him. "Lord have mercy, Luke, what happened? How did you manage to fall?"

"Don't worry about that," he snapped, furious at himself for letting her distract him. "Just help me up."

He saw the quick flash of hurt in her eyes and wished he could call back the sharp words, but they were already out there. He couldn't do a thing about them except add in a softer tone, "Please, Emily."

As she lifted him, he reached up and grabbed hold of the table. With it to support him, she was able to get him back into the chair.

"I'll pick up your crutches."

He held out a hand to stop her. "I can get them. Thank you."

She looked at him with a slight frown. "Were you trying to walk, Luke? I've told you, I don't care about that, not for me. I want it for you, but it's not going to make any difference how I feel—"

"Of course it makes a difference. It's bound to." Luke frowned at her.

"No," she said as she leaned closer to him. "I swear to you, it doesn't. I'll prove it to you."

Before he could stop her, she lowered herself onto his lap, her arms clasped around his neck, and her mouth pressed hungrily to his.

Luke bit back a groan of mingled despair and desire. His arms went around her. She was such a little bit of a thing, yet the curves of her body were those of a woman. Her lips worked urgently against his, their taste sweet and hot.

As he held her and kissed her, he felt something, no doubt about that.

She did too. Pulling back slightly, her eyes widened. He was about to apologize, but a pleased glow sprang to life in her eyes. "See, Luke," she whispered. "I told you it didn't matter."

She kissed him again, then slid out of his arms and stood up.

"Grampaw might be comin' in any time, so we'll save our sparkin' for later."

Luke nodded. After everything Linus Peabody had done for him, he didn't want to offend the old-timer.

Peabody hurried in a short time later, all right, as

Emily had predicted. He wore a worried expression on his face, and it quickly became obvious the last thing on his mind was who was sparking his granddaughter. "There's a buggy and some riders comin'." He reached for the rifle hanging on the wall near the door.

"Yankee soldiers again?" Emily asked, her body tensing as she stood next to the stove where she had started supper.

Peabody shook his head as he checked to make sure the rifle was loaded.

"Nope. It's that fella Wolford, and unless I miss my guess, the men he's got with him are hired guns."

CHAPTER 20

"Get my revolver," Luke told Emily.

"What're you thinkin' about doin'?" She looked at her grandfather. "What are the both of you thinkin' about doin'?"

"Nothin' we don't have to," Peabody told her. "Could be Wolford just wants to talk. If he does, I'll listen to him. Won't do him any good, but I'll listen."

"Is this about the folks who have been losin' their farms to the carpetbaggers?"

Peabody frowned. "You know about that?"

"How the hell could I *not* know about it?" Emily blurted out. "It's the only thing folks all over this part of the country are talkin' about!"

"I need my revolver," Luke said again. He was trying to stay calm, but the same tense feelings he had experienced before every battle were going through him. He might soon be fighting for his life, and the lives of Emily and her grandfather as well.

But that wasn't exactly likely, he told himself, not just yet, anyway. From what Peabody had said about

Wolford's attempt to take over Bud Harkness's farm, the carpetbagger was using quasi-legal means in his land grabs, relying on corrupt judges and what passed for the law under Yankee occupation.

Wolford would have hired guns in reserve, though, and if he couldn't get what he wanted peacefully, he would use force to take it. Luke had no doubt about that.

He looked intently at Emily until she sighed and went to the cabinet where the Griswold and Gunnison revolver was kept. She took it out and brought it over to Luke. "I can use this gun."

He held out his hand. "You need to stay inside."

A quick flash of anger lit up her eyes. "Luke—"

"Luke's right," Peabody said. "You stay in the house, girl, like you did when the Yankees came."

"Men!" she said in exasperation. "You're the most stubborn critters on God's green earth!"

Luke stuck the revolver in the pocket of his overalls and grasped his crutches. "That's because we're raised by women to be that way." With a smile, he lifted himself to his feet.

She still looked mad, but rested a hand on his arm for a second. "Don't start trouble with them."

"I don't intend to start trouble with anybody," Luke assured her. He didn't say anything about finishing it, if things came down to that. He looked out through the door Peabody had left open. "Here they come."

"Be careful," Emily whispered to Luke. "We just . . ."

She didn't finish, but he knew what she meant. They had just admitted how they felt about each other. She didn't want him going and getting himself killed.

Luke didn't want that, either. He nodded to show her he understood as much.

Peabody went out onto the porch. Luke followed him, moving fairly easily on the crutches. He wished he could have walked out there bold as brass, but that was something for the future if his legs continued to improve.

With a clatter of hoofbeats and wheels, Vincent Wolford drove his buggy up to the cabin and brought the vehicle to a halt, reining in the two fine black horses pulling it. Luke found himself wondering who those horses used to belong to, and how Wolford had gotten his hands on them. He was willing to bet the carpetbagger hadn't bought them fair and square.

Three men on horseback accompanied Wolford. As they reined in, Luke studied them. Back home he had seen Jayhawkers from Kansas on several occasions, and these men reminded him of those ruthless guerrillas.

One wore a derby and a flashy eastern suit. He was big, with broad shoulders and a rough-hewn face dominated by a rusty handlebar mustache. His hands were huge, with knobby knuckles broken more than once in various brawls. He wasn't carrying a gun that was visible, but Luke figured there was probably a revolver in a shoulder holster under that tweed coat.

The other two riders were dressed more like frontiersmen in boots, work clothes, and broad-brimmed hats. They wore their guns out in the open, carrying holstered pistols on their hips. They had rugged, hard-planed faces and cold eyes.

Luke knew all three men were probably killers, paid

by Vincent Wolford to enforce his will and help him take what he wanted. They would be fast on the draw. If Linus Peabody raised his rifle, one or more of the gunmen would drill him before he got a shot off.

Luke was pretty handy with a gun, but knew he wasn't a match for those three. Not with the Griswold and Gunnison stuck in his pocket. If he had a regular gun rig and a pair of revolvers, he might manage to down a couple, maybe all three, but they would get lead in him, too.

It wasn't going to come to that. He couldn't allow the carpetbaggers to kill him and Peabody, leaving Emily at their mercy.

"Take it easy," he said under his breath to Peabody. "Stay calm."

The old man nodded, but the tense way he stood and the urgency with which he gripped the rifle told a different story. He was ready to fight. He *wanted* to fight.

Luke levered himself forward on his crutches, putting himself between Peabody and the buggy. He nodded to Wolford. "Howdy. What brings you out here from town?"

"Mr. Smith, isn't it?" Wolford asked with that phony smile of his, without getting down from the buggy. "I came to speak with Mr. Peabody there. I have a business proposition for him."

Peabody moved up even with Luke. "I ain't interested in doin' business with the likes of you."

"You should hear me out," Wolford said. "That's just a smart rule of thumb. Always listen to the other fellow's proposal. You never know when he might offer something you want."

Peabody glared darkly at the visitors, but after a moment he nodded. "I'll listen. I don't reckon it's very likely you got anything I want, though."

"You might be surprised. What I'm proposing, Mr. Peabody, is that I take this farm off your hands for a very reasonable price."

"Why in blazes would I want to sell?" Peabody snapped.

"Well, the market for cotton, tobacco, and other crops is very depressed right now. You can't hope to make very much for them."

"We'll get by," the old man said.

"Yes, perhaps, but you can do even better somewhere else. I hear people are having phenomenal success migrating to the frontier. There are millions of acres out there just ripe for the taking."

"This is my home. I've lived on this land all my life, and my pa lived here before me. I intend to stay until the Good Lord calls me home."

Wolford's smile didn't budge, but Luke thought he saw impatience growing in the man's eyes.

"You can do that," Wolford said, "but you'd still be wise to sell out to me. If you don't want to leave, you can always stay and work the land on shares."

"Why in the Sam Hill would I want to do that?"

"You wouldn't have all the worries of dealing with the new government. I'd handle all that. You could just work the land the way you always have."

"While you rake in all the profits?" Peabody asked.

"Not all of it. You'd still get by, as you put it." Wolford's voice finally hardened as he went on. "You don't seem to understand, Mr. Peabody, that things have changed around here. It's not the same as it was before the war, and it never will be again. Different people are running things now. I happen to be well acquainted with Colonel Morrison and Judge Blevins, and although I may be speaking out of turn here, I know they're going through all the records and uncovering a number of cases where insufficient taxes were paid on properties in this area."

"You mean you're gonna grab folks' land by claimin' they owe taxes they really don't," Peabody said.

The big eastern tough in the derby glared and edged his horse forward. "Don't you talk to Mr. Wolford like that, you old Rebel," he warned.

Wolford lifted a hand. "Take it easy, Joe. I'm sure Mr. Peabody didn't mean to cast any aspersions."

"What I'll cast is you offa my land," Peabody said. "I paid my taxes, and can't nobody say otherwise!"

"Yes, but you paid them to the Confederates who were in charge here at the time." Wolford shook his head as if he were genuinely regretful. "There's no way of knowing where all that money went, but it isn't in the county's coffers like it's supposed to be. Unfortunately, in order to fund the new government, a new taxation schedule will have to be put in place—"

"Why don't you call it what it is?" Peabody broke in. "Stealin', plain and simple!"

"I'm just trying to help." Wolford leaned over slightly on the buggy seat to look past Luke and Peabody. "Isn't that your granddaughter I see just inside the door?" He raised a hand to his hat. "Good day to you, Miss Peabody. You're looking as lovely as ever."

"You leave Emily outta this—" Peabody began, but she stepped onto the porch and confronted Wolford and his gunmen, too.

"We don't want your so-called help, mister." Her eyes blazed with fury.

She counseled restraint, Luke thought, but her emotions got the better of her and she couldn't practice what she preached.

"You'd better turn that buggy around and get off our land, right now!"

"Or what? An old man and a cripple will run us off?" The gunman leaned over in his saddle and spat. "I don't think so."

"Please, Howell, there's no need for unpleasantness." Wolford smiled at Emily again. "I think if you'd just give me a chance, Miss Peabody, you and I could be good friends. If you were to help persuade your grandfather to be reasonable, why, I can see all sorts of benefits in it for you. A girl as beautiful as you should have some of the finer things in life, the sort of things a man like me could give you—"

"So I could be some sort of backwoods harlot for you?" Emily turned toward her grandfather and reached for the rifle. "Gimme that gun."

Luke saw the three hired killers grow tense in their saddles and knew the situation was teetering perilously close to violence. Under the circumstances, the outcome of that wouldn't be good for him and his friends.

He moved between the Peabodys and the unwelcome visitors and said in a loud, hard voice, "That's enough."

"Do you speak for these people, Mr. Smith?" Wolford asked with a sneer.

"I speak for myself, and this is what I've got to say, Wolford." Luke looked right into the man's eyes. He didn't like taking his attention off the others, but knew they wouldn't act unless Wolford ordered them to. "If there's trouble here today, you'll be sorry. I'll see to that personally."

"That's mighty big talk for a man on crutches." The eastern tough called Joe sneered.

Luke let go of the right-hand crutch, letting it fall behind him, and moved his hand so it wasn't far from the butt of the revolver sticking out of his pocket. "I only need one to balance on," he told Wolford, making it clear as he could. If any gunplay broke out, Luke was going to draw that revolver and kill Wolford, no matter what else happened. He might die, and Emily and her grandfather probably would, too, but Wolford would die first.

Luke was going to see to that.

Reading the deadly message in Luke's steady gaze, fear flared in the carpetbagger's eyes. An instant later, it was replaced by smoldering anger.

But the fear was still there, underneath, and Luke knew it.

"All right," Wolford snapped. "I was just trying to be generous. I thought perhaps we could consider ourselves friends and neighbors, Mr. Peabody. But if you'd rather this . . . this unreconstructed Rebel speak for you—"

"Smith's right," Peabody said. "We've heard enough. You and your boys need to git."

Wolford lifted the reins. "We'll be going, then. Perhaps I was wrong, Mr. Peabody. Perhaps you won't lose your farm"—he paused—"but don't count on it."

With that, he turned the team and sent the buggy rolling away from the cabin. The three gunmen lingered a moment, giving Luke hard, murderous stares before they wheeled their horses and followed Wolford.

"I ain't countin' on nothin'," Peabody said, "except that this trouble ain't over."

Luke knew the old-timer was right about that.

CHAPTER 21

Wolford had been so angry when he drove away Luke wouldn't have been surprised if problems started cropping up right away. But several days passed with no sign of the carpetbagger or his hired guns.

Linus Peabody reported the Harkness family on the neighboring farm had packed up and moved away, abandoning the place because they couldn't pay the exorbitant taxes being demanded by the Reconstruction government. Another worried neighbor had come by the farm and told Peabody about it, adding that the sheriff was going to auction off the Harkness farm in Dobieville on Saturday.

Luke knew Vincent Wolford would win that auction at a rock-bottom price. And he would probably get some of the money back from the sheriff and the judge in the form of a kickback.

The idea of Emily going out to work in the fields with her grandfather worried Luke. If Wolford's gunnies showed up, intent on causing trouble, Peabody wouldn't be able to protect her. In his current condition,

Luke couldn't watch over them, so he made up his mind the best thing for him to do was improve as much and as quickly as he could.

With that determination goading him on, he worked with his legs for long hours each day while Emily and her grandfather were gone. He put more and more weight on his own muscles, forcing them to move and carry him, not just support him.

Back and forth across the cabin's main room he shuffled endlessly, using the crutches. Eventually he was able to take a step, then several steps, without touching the floor with the crutches, although he held them ready to catch himself if he fell.

Those efforts made his legs ache almost intolerably, but he welcomed the pain, even embraced it. To have his legs hurt was so much better than to have them feel nothing at all.

By the time a week had passed since Wolford and his gunmen had shown up at the farm, Luke was able to take actual steps as he walked across the room, no longer sliding his feet in a shuffling manner. He left the crutches behind and walked on his own, something that had seemed utterly impossible a few months ago. His gait was slow and halting, to be sure, and he told himself with a wry smile that he was a long way from being able to dance a jig, but he was getting there.

He was getting there, all right, and it was the best pain he had ever felt, although he sometimes had to bite his lip to keep from crying out when Emily massaged his legs.

It wasn't long before she noticed the change in his

legs. "These muscles are definitely harder and stronger than they were. You're gonna walk again one of these days, Luke. You just wait and see."

"Thanks to you, I am," he told her. Without the way she had kept him going through his darkest days and nights, and without the determination his fear for her safety gave him, he might not have ever walked again. Soon he was going to be ready to reveal his secret to her.

A little later, when Peabody caught a moment alone with him, the old-timer said, "I spotted them fellas who work for Wolford watchin' the place again today."

Luke hated to hear that, but he wasn't surprised. He had known better than to hope Wolford would give up on getting his hands on the farm. Even worse was knowing the man wanted to get his hands on Emily. He had hinted as much when he visited the farm, and Luke had seen the unmistakable lust in the carpetbagger's eyes when Wolford looked at her.

"Why don't I start going out to the fields with you and Emily during the day?" Luke had discarded that idea a week earlier but was beginning to think it might work.

"On your crutches?" Peabody asked with a frown.

"No, you can help me climb into the wagon, and I'll sit up there and keep an eye on things while you're working. We can take along the rifle and my revolver. I can handle a gun just fine."

Peabody scratched his stubbly jaw and shrugged. "That ain't a bad idea."

The next day they put it into practice, even though Emily was insistent on knowing why Luke was coming with them.

"Wolford's men have been watchin' us again," Peabody admitted.

"Oh, them? Shoot, I saw them before. They don't scare me."

"Well, they scare me, and they ought to scare you, too," Peabody insisted. "They're bad men, and the fella they work for is even worse. We got trouble on the horizon."

It was even closer than they suspected.

With help from Peabody and Emily, Luke climbed to the wagon seat and they went out to the fields. He wished he could help them harvest the late summer corn crop. Unfortunately, his legs weren't yet steady enough. Instead, he scanned the surrounding countryside for any sign of Wolford's men without spotting them.

The sound of shots made Emily cry out in alarm and Luke twist around on the seat to peer toward the cabin.

The shots continued from that direction as Emily and Peabody dropped what they were doing and ran to the wagon. Peabody scrambled up to the seat and jerked the reins loose from the brake lever while Emily practically threw herself into the back. Even the normally stubborn mules sensed something was wrong. They broke into a run as Peabody headed them toward the cabin.

Breathing hard, Emily leaned over the back of the seat between the two men. "What are they doin'?" she asked anxiously. "What's all that shootin' about?"

"We'll know in a minute." Luke gripped the rifle tightly. It was only a single-shot weapon, but the revolver in his pocket was fully loaded.

The shooting stopped before they came in sight of the cabin. As they did, Luke caught a glimpse of several riders galloping away from the place. They were already too far off for him to make out any details, but was willing to bet they were the three hired guns who worked for Vincent Wolford.

"No!" Emily cried as her grandfather wheeled the wagon into the open area between the cabin and the barn. Limp, bloody bundles of feathers were scattered around on the ground. The chickens had been blasted to pieces. In the pen over by the barn, the hogs lay motionless in the mud.

Emily leaped out of the wagon and ran into the barn. When she came back a moment later, tears were running down her cheeks. "They killed the milk cow, too. Looks like they just shot everything that moved."

"Why in blazes would they do that?" Peabody asked furiously. "It aggravates the hell out of me, but losin' those animals ain't enough to ruin the farm."

"This is just the opening gambit," Luke said. "Think of it as a warning. Wolford wants to let you know it'll get a lot worse if you don't give him what he wants."

"Never! I'm goin' to town and swearin' out a complaint against the varmints! The sheriff's got to do somethin'. He's supposed to uphold the law around here."

"The sheriff works for Wolford and that judge of his and the rest of the Yankees," Emily said bitterly. "He's not gonna do anything, Grampaw."

"We don't know that. If nobody ever speaks up, nothin' will change around here!"

The old-timer was right about that, Luke supposed.

But like Emily, he didn't think complaining to the law would do any good. They would never know if they didn't try, though. "We'll all go to Dobieville. Maybe round up some of your friends and neighbors who've had trouble with the carpetbaggers and take them with you. If more people are speaking up, the men in charge will have a harder time ignoring them."

Peabody nodded. "That's a good idea."

"Not as good an idea as goin' to town and shootin' that snake Wolford for tellin' his men to do this," Emily said.

It might come to that, Luke thought, *but we have to try reason first . . . then bullets.*

Peabody spent the rest of the day visiting his neighbors and putting together a delegation to complain to the sheriff in Dobieville. The killing of his livestock wasn't the first such outrage in the area. Barns had burned down mysteriously, crops had been trampled on dark nights, wells had been fouled, and cattle had been run off.

Nor would that harassment stop, Luke thought. In fact, he expected it to escalate into outright violence in fairly short order. Wolford and the other carpetbaggers were not patient men.

The farmers rendezvoused outside town and rode in on mules and in wagons and buggies. Some of them walked. A few had brought their wives and children with them, something Luke thought probably wasn't wise. A group about forty strong converged on the sheriff's office.

Their arrival in town stirred up enough of a commotion

the lawman heard them coming. He stepped out onto the porch of his office to wait for them. He was a middle-aged man with thinning brown hair and a mustache. A gun belt was strapped around his waist, and he carried a shotgun in addition to the holstered revolver.

"Fella's name is Royce Wilkes," Peabody explained to Luke as they approached in the wagon. "Used to be a deputy here, but he was too fond of corn liquor. The old sheriff ran him off. When the war was over, the Yankees put him back in office and gave him the sheriff's job. He's local, but he's in the back pocket of them no-good carpetbaggers."

Wilkes had the shotgun cradled in his left arm. He held up his right hand for silence and called, "All right, what the devil's goin' on here?"

Everyone in the group turned to look at Linus Peabody. He had talked them into coming, and they regarded him as their spokesman.

"Sheriff, we're all here to lodge complaints against Vincent Wolford and those fellas who work for him," Peabody said. "I beg pardon of the ladies in earshot of my voice, but Wolford's men have been raisin' hell hereabouts, and it's gotta stop."

"You know for a fact that what you're sayin' is true, Linus?" Wilkes asked.

"I do," Peabody replied with a forceful nod. "They came out to my place yesterday and shot all my chickens and hogs and my milk cow. We seen 'em ridin' off after they done it."

Luke and Emily nodded. In reality the riders had been too far away for a positive identification, but there was no question in Luke's mind that Wolford's men were responsible.

"Well, that's a mighty serious charge," Wilkes said.

Another man in the crowd said, "That ain't all they've done. My barn burned down last week, and I know good and well somebody set that fire. I rode into town and told you all about it, Royce."

"You did," Wilkes said, "but you also told me you didn't see who done it."

"It had to be Wolford's men! You know that!"

"I'm a lawman," Wilkes boasted, his chest puffing out pompously. "I got to have proof. And somebody thinkin' they saw something ain't proof."

"Are you callin' us liars?" Peabody demanded.

"I'm sayin' maybe you were mistaken."

Luke suggested, "Why don't you at least ask Wolford about it? See if he can account for the whereabouts of his men yesterday when Mr. Peabody's livestock was being slaughtered."

Wilkes shook his head stubbornly. "I ain't gonna bother an important man like Mr. Wolford—"

"It's no bother," a new voice said.

Everyone swung around to look. The crowd parted, and Vincent Wolford himself sauntered up to the porch.

"I heard there was a gathering of some sort and decided to come see for myself what it was about," Wolford went on. "I'd be glad to answer any questions you have for me, Sheriff."

"I don't have any questions," Wilkes said.

"I do," Peabody snapped. "Did you send your men to kill my livestock, mister?"

Wolford gave a solemn shake of his head. "Of course not, Mr. Peabody. Why in the world would I do a thing like that?"

"To try to run me off so you can grab my land!"

"I wanted to make you a fair offer for your land, but you wouldn't even consider it," Wolford said. "As far as I'm concerned, our business is over."

"Where were your men yesterday morning?" Luke asked.

"Burnett, Howell, and Prentice?" Wolford shrugged. "I'm not sure. I don't keep track of their whereabouts every hour of the day. As long as they do the jobs I give them, that's all I really care about."

"Did you give them any jobs yesterday?"

"As a matter of fact, I didn't." Wolford smiled. "I didn't even speak to them. So you see, even if there was anything to these ludicrous accusations—and I assure you, there isn't—I can't be held responsible for them."

Wilkes nodded. "Looks like that clears it all up. Sorry to bother you, Mr. Wolford."

"Oh, it's no bother, Sheriff, I assure you. All I want to do is carry on my business and get along with my neighbors."

Wilkes turned back to the farmers. "You've said your piece, now it's time for all of you to go back home and stop botherin' folks."

"Are you runnin' us out of town?" Peabody asked. "Don't we still have a right to go where we please?"

"No, you don't," Wilkes snapped. "Gatherin' up in mobs like this is against the law. So if you don't break it up and leave, it'll be my duty to arrest you . . . and I'll get the soldiers to help me, if I need to."

"You'd better do what he says, Linus," Luke told the old-timer.

"You mean let them get away with it?" Emily asked.

"Getting arrested isn't going to help anything."

Peabody scowled darkly, but he said, "All right, we'll go. But this ain't over, Sheriff. We'll get justice somehow."

"You step out of line and you'll be sorry," Wilkes warned.

With a lot of angry muttering, the crowd turned to leave town. As the wagon rolled past the last buildings, Emily said, "Like I told you, nothin's gonna change."

"At least Wolford knows we're on to him," Peabody said. "He's the one who's really to blame for everything."

"And all he's gonna do is laugh at us," Emily said as her shoulders slumped in despair.

If that's all that happens, Luke thought, *then we might be lucky.* Wolford's smooth façade had never budged, but he had to be angry that the farmers had banded together to complain about his tactics. Luke wouldn't be at all surprised if he decided to teach them a lesson.

And if he did, it would be a painful one. Luke was sure of that.

CHAPTER 22

Emily was cool toward Luke on the ride back to the farm and for the rest of the day. He wasn't sure why she was upset with him, unless it was because he had talked her grandfather out of setting off a showdown in town. Maybe she didn't understand he didn't want anything to happen to her . . . or maybe she did, and that just made her angrier.

Whatever the reason, she didn't have much to say to him around her grandfather, and they didn't get a chance to talk alone. Luke turned in knowing nothing was settled and the situation was likely to get worse before it got better . . . if it ever did.

Sometime during the night he came awake instantly, smelling smoke. It was too strong to be coming from the fireplace or the stove. He sat up. No lights burned inside the cabin, but a flickering red glow came through the cracks around the front door and through the thin curtains hung over the windows.

The barn was on fire. It was the only explanation that made sense.

And he knew it hadn't caught fire by itself.

"Emily!" he shouted. "Linus! Wake up!"

Peabody bolted from his bunk. Emily bolted from hers and cried out in alarm. "Something's on fire!"

"The barn!" With his nightshirt flapping around his legs, Peabody grabbed the rifle from the chair where he had placed it to be handy and headed for the door.

When he flung it open, the garish red light from the blazing barn spilled into the cabin. He rushed outside with Emily right behind him.

Still struggling to get out of his bunk, Luke swung his legs to the floor and stood up, using the back of a nearby chair for support. He picked up his revolver off the chair and grabbed one of his crutches propped against the wall next to the head of his bunk.

Hoofbeats pounded outside. Someone shouted, and Peabody's rifle cracked.

"No, no," Luke panted as he hurried toward the door as fast as he could. He knew without having to think about it what had happened. To get back at Peabody for trying to organize the farmers against him, Wolford had sent his men to the farm to set fire to the barn.

And those killers were still out there, where they threatened Emily and her grandfather. That thought made Luke's blood run cold.

As he reached the porch, he heard Emily scream, "Grampaw!" In the garish light of the fire, Luke saw a man on horseback nearly run down Linus Peabody. The old-timer threw himself out of the way just in time, losing his balance and sprawling on the ground. The rider wheeled his horse around and pointed a gun at Peabody as Emily ran toward her grandfather.

She leaped to shield him as the rider pulled the trigger. Luke fired at the same instant. Flame spat from the barrel of his revolver. The impact of the bullet jarred the man on the horse, knocking him forward.

"Emily!" Peabody cried out. "Oh, my God, Emily!"

Luke suddenly realized he was off the porch and didn't think about what he did next as he cast the single crutch aside and broke into a stumbling run toward Emily and Peabody. The nightmarish glare of the fire revealed Emily's body lying stretched on the ground while her grandfather hovered over her.

Hoofbeats thundered again as two more riders lunged out of the jagged shadows cast by the firelight. The newcomers seemed intent on trampling them. Still stumbling, Luke raised the revolver and thumbed off two more shots. He didn't know if he hit either of the attackers, but they veered sharply away.

The man he'd wounded yelled, "I'm hit! We gotta get out of here!"

Luke recognized the eastern accent of the tough named Joe Burnett. The other two had to be Howell and Prentice. One of them snapped a couple shots at him, coming close enough for him to hear the bullets whine past his head, as the other grabbed the dangling reins of Burnett's horse and all three gunmen fled.

Pain flared through Luke's legs, but they continued to support him. Peabody looked up at him as he reached the old man's side, but he didn't seem to notice Luke was standing and moving around without the aid of the crutches.

"Emily's hurt!" Peabody cried. "When that no-good shot at me, she got in the way of the bullet!"

"How bad is it? Where's she hit?" Luke figured if he knelt down, he wouldn't be able to get back up again, so he made his voice urgent in an attempt to get through the fear and confusion that gripped Peabody.

It seemed to work, because the old-timer looked down, gently grasped Emily's shoulders, and rolled her onto her back. Luke caught a glimpse of blood on her nightclothes, but the stain appeared to be a small one, at least so far.

"I . . . I don't think she's hurt too bad," Peabody said after a moment. "Looks like the bullet just nicked her side."

Emily groaned.

"She's comin' to." Peabody continued to watch his granddaughter.

Luke watched and listened for any sign of the gunmen doubling back. In the firelight, the three of them made good targets, he thought.

Not seeing further danger, he turned his attention back to Emily and Peabody. "You'll need to pick her up and get her back in the cabin. Can you clean that wound and put a dressing on it?"

"Yeah, I reckon I can." Amazement crept into Peabody's voice as he went on. "Luke, you're standin' up on your own! And you ran across there a minute ago! I saw you with my own eyes."

"Don't worry about that. Just take care of Emily."

"I will. What are you gonna do?"

"Something that somebody should have done before now," Luke said.

He didn't know how long his legs would keep working. It had taken the threat to Emily and her grandfather for them to move like they had a few minutes earlier. The mixture of fear, desperation, and rage had burned through him like the fire that was consuming the barn, a cleansing fire that forced muscles and nerves to work again the way they were supposed to. His movements were rusty and a little clumsy, but he could get around again, and didn't want to waste the opportunity.

Peabody was still strong, and Emily was a slip of a girl. He had no trouble picking her up and carrying her back into the cabin.

Luke followed. While Peabody tended to Emily, he got dressed, reloaded the Griswold and Gunnison, and went back outside. His face was impassive in the firelight despite the pain shooting through his legs with every step. The rest of those nerves were waking up again after their long sleep, he thought. If they kept working for a while longer, it would be enough.

He pocketed his revolver and walked over to the spot where he had wounded Joe Burnett. The man's revolver, a Colt Navy, lay on the ground where Burnett had dropped it. Luke picked up the gun, hefting it in his hand, and realized his ammunition would fit it. Both weapons would be fully loaded when he headed for town.

He frowned. How was he going to get there? The luckless mules had been in the barn, and so had the wagon.

His legs were finally working again, but he couldn't walk all the way to Dobieville.

Shouts and hoofbeats made him swing around and raise both guns. The man riding up to the farm reined in sharply and threw his hands in the air. "Whoa!" he exclaimed. "Hold your fire, mister! I'm a friend!"

Luke recognized the newcomer as one of the men who had gone into town with them that morning. He thought for a second and recalled the man's name. "You're Thad Franklin, right?"

"Yeah." The man dismounted. "My place is a couple miles east of here. I saw the light from the fire and knew somethin' had to be wrong. Thought I'd better come see if I could help." He shook his head. "It's too late to save that barn, though."

"Maybe you and the others can help Linus rebuild," Luke suggested.

"Is he hurt? How about Emily?"

Luke jerked his head toward the cabin. "They're in there. Emily was wounded by the varmints who set the barn on fire, but I think she's going to be all right."

"There'll be more folks showin' up soon, I reckon. People always come to help when they see a fire."

"You can help right now," Luke said. "Give me your horse."

"My horse? What? Say, you're the fella who can't walk!" Franklin looked Luke up and down in confusion. "But you're standin' up now."

Luke lifted the Colt Navy and pointed it at Franklin, saying coldly, "I need your horse. I'll get it back to you, if I can. If I can't, you'll find it in Dobieville."

"Careful with that gun, mister! What're you gonna do?" Franklin's eyes widened as he realized the answer to his own question. "You're goin' after the men who did this?"

Luke used his free hand to take the reins out of Franklin's fingers. "Sorry, but it's got to be done." He got his left foot in the stirrup and swung up into the saddle, clenching his jaw at the pain caused by mounting.

"You're crazy," Franklin said. "You can't fight those carpetbaggers. There are too many of 'em, and they got the Yankee army on their side!"

"I don't plan to fight all of them, just one in particular and the men he sent to do this."

"They'll kill you!"

"Probably. But I plan on sending them to hell ahead of me."

CHAPTER 23

Still burning brightly, the fire cast an orange glow into the sky behind Luke as he rode toward Dobieville. Being on a horse again felt good.

Despite his concern for Emily, he felt more alive than he had in a long time.

He hadn't had a chance to reload the Navy after all. Checking the gun's cylinder, he found that Burnett had fired only one round. The other five chambers were loaded. He had eleven shots.

It would have to be enough.

Regret gnawed at him. He hadn't taken the time to say good-bye to Emily and her grandfather. He knew they would have tried to talk him out of forcing a showdown with Wolford. Luke didn't trust himself not to give in to Emily's pleading and stay at the farm with her.

If he had stayed, things would continue to get worse. He didn't know if they would actually improve once Wolford was dead, but at least if the carpetbagger and his gunmen were gone they wouldn't be able to threaten anyone else.

The raiders had come very close to killing Emily, and that knowledge filled Luke with a rage overpowering every other emotion. Somebody had to take a stand against their evil.

He was the man.

Simple as that.

Luke had a good sense of direction and was able to find the settlement without any trouble. When he saw its lights, he reined in for a moment, thinking of the situation and what he should do next.

The three gunmen weren't that far ahead of him. He figured the first thing they would do was report to Wolford, so there was a good chance he could find them together. It would certainly make things easier if all four of his enemies were in one place.

That notion turned his thoughts to Potter, Stratton, Richards, and Casey. He'd had four enemies to deal with that fateful night, too, and it hadn't turned out well. But he'd been taken by surprise, even though he shouldn't have been, and tonight he'd be the one doing the surprising.

He shook his head and turned his thoughts back to the situation at hand. Wolford owned the North Georgia Land Company. Luke had heard talk about it and had seen the sign on a building in town, earlier, when the group of farmers came to talk to the sheriff. He nodded. It was the first place he would look for his quarry.

He used his heels to get the horse moving again. Dobieville was quiet. No reason for it not to be, Luke supposed. The citizens didn't know what had happened out at the Peabody farm. They would hear about it by morning. As he rode down the deserted streets they were blissfully ignorant.

That was about to change.

The saloons were open, and a light still burned in the general store, but most of the businesses along Main Street were dark, including the building that housed Wolford's office. It appeared to be locked up for the night.

A faint glow in the alley behind the place told a different story. Luke looked along the side of the building, saw that glow, and knew one of the windows in the rear was lit up.

He dismounted and his legs sagged for a second, forcing him to grab the saddle horn and hold himself up. He straightened and looped the reins around the hitch rack in front.

Hoping his muscles wouldn't betray him at the worst possible moment, he drew both revolvers from his pockets and started down the narrow passage beside the building. His gait was awkward as he kept his legs rigid, but they got him where he was going.

Reaching the rear corner of the building, he edged around it carefully and saw the lighted window. It was raised a few inches to let in the night air.

As quietly as possible, he moved closer to hear what was being said inside.

". . . doctor," a man said harshly. "This bullet's gotta come out of me."

"If we fetch the doctor, there'll be questions about how you managed to get shot, Joe." That was Wolford's voice. "I'd rather not deal with the potential embarrassment."

"So you're just gonna let me die?" Burnett's voice was drawn thin with pain.

"Of course not. Harve can dig the bullet out, can't you, Harve?"

One of the other gunmen answered, "I reckon I can give it a try." He didn't sound too confident about it.

"And I have a bottle of whiskey right here," Wolford went on. "Take a nice healthy slug, Joe, and then Harve can clean the wound with it, too."

"I don't know about this." Burnett was clearly reluctant to trust his fate to the medical skills of his fellow hired gun.

"You're being well paid to take risks," Wolford snapped, losing his patience. "And you didn't even manage to kill the old man like I told you to."

"That's not my fault," Burnett replied, a whine creeping in his tone. "I told you, boss, the girl jumped right in front of my gun just as I pulled the trigger."

"Yes, well, if she's dead, that's going to be very regrettable . . . for her and for you. I mean to have her, along with her grandfather's farm."

Luke's hands tightened on the guns, wanting to burst in there and start shooting. But it wasn't quite the right moment yet. He needed to wait just a little longer.

"Here's the whiskey," Wolford said.

Luke heard the glugging sound as the wounded man took a healthy swallow of the liquor.

Wolford went on, "You can lie down here on my desk, Joe. Thurman, you hold him down while Harve removes that bullet."

Murmurs of agreement came from the men.

Luke waited as he listened to them moving around.

Burnett let out a yelp. "Damn it, boss, at least give me somethin' to bite down on!"

"All right—"

Now, Luke thought.

While they were all gathered around the desk with their attention focused on the crude surgery he took a couple steps and rammed his shoulder against the building's back door. The flimsy lock gave under the impact and the door flew open.

Luke stumbled over the threshold, catching his balance as he brought up the guns in his hands. "Hold it!" he yelled. "Nobody move!"

They ignored the command and moved, all right. Luke had figured they would. But he had given them a chance to surrender, so his conscience was clear.

One of the gunmen—he still didn't know which one was Prentice and which one was Howell—whirled away from the desk and tried to claw out the gun holstered on his hip. Luke shot him in the face with the Griswold and Gunnison. The .36 caliber slug destroyed the man's nose and plowed into his brain, driving him backward over the desk, where he fell on top of the wounded Burnett.

The second gunman cleared leather, but before he could raise his gun, let alone get off a shot, a slug from the Colt Navy in Luke's left hand ripped into his throat. The man spun around in a half turn, blood from severed arteries spraying across the expensive rug on the floor of Wolford's private office.

Roaring in rage, Burnett shoved the dead man off himself and plucked the man's Colt from its holster. Even wounded, he had the strength to lunge up off the desk.

Luke fired both guns into Burnett's chest. The double impact lifted the big easterner off his feet and dumped him onto the desk again.

A pocket pistol went off with a small popping sound, and Luke felt something lance into his left shoulder. It wasn't much worse than a bee sting, but he knew he'd just been shot. He knew, as well, Wolford had shot him, because the other three men in the room were already dead.

Wolford fired again as he darted for the door leading into the front part of the building. Luke ducked, which gave the carpetbagger time to flee from the private office. As Luke straightened, he fired again and stomped into the bigger, darkened room after Wolford.

Wolford's gun went off again. Luke spotted the little tongue of flame from the muzzle as he heard the slug whine past his ear. He snapped a shot in return. Wolford cried out.

With Luke pursuing him inexorably, Wolford didn't have time to unlock the front door. He took the only way out, throwing himself against the front window. Glass shattered and sprayed as he burst through it and sprawled on the boardwalk outside.

Luke kept moving. His legs hadn't betrayed him so far, and miraculously, he was still alive. His quick reflexes and speed with a gun had saved him, but the job wasn't done yet.

He stepped through the broken window onto the

boardwalk as Wolford tried to scramble away. Wolford screamed for help.

"Should've thought of that before you sent those men out to the Peabody farm tonight," Luke told him.

"You . . . you can't be doing this!" Wolford gasped as he scrambled to his feet. "You can't even walk!"

"Seems that I can." Luke shot the carpetbagger's left leg out from under him, the bullet shattering the kneecap into a million pieces. "But you can't."

Wolford collapsed and clutched his bleeding, ruined knee as he screamed. Luke aimed carefully, since the man was writhing around, and blasted apart Wolford's other knee.

"Drop that gun!" a man yelled over Wolford's shrieks of agony. "Drop it right now!"

Luke glanced over and saw a hatless, nightshirt-wearing Sheriff Royce Wilkes pointing a shotgun at him.

Luke lined the Griswold and Gunnison's barrel on Wolford's forehead and eared back the hammer. His thumb was all that kept it from falling. "You can blast me to hell, Sheriff, but you can't pull those triggers fast enough to keep me from killing Wolford."

The carpetbagger realized how close he was to death, and screamed, "Don't shoot him, Sheriff! Don't shoot him!"

Wilkes held off, but the slight tremor of the shotgun's twin barrels showed how much he wanted to pull the triggers. "Listen here, mister, you'd better put that gun down. Otherwise you'll die here."

"So will this murderer," Luke said, "and I think I'm

just fine with it if that's what it takes to rid the world of him."

"I . . . I never murdered anybody!" Wolford gasped. "Oh, God! Somebody help me!"

"You're beyond help from God or anybody else," Luke growled. "And you paid those gunmen of yours to go out to the Peabody farm, burn down the barn, and murder Linus Peabody. I heard you say that yourself, just a few minutes ago."

"Why . . . why would I . . ." Wolford couldn't go on. He lay whimpering in pain.

"Because with her grandfather dead, you thought Emily would have no choice but to turn to you," Luke continued. "You thought I didn't represent any threat. You were wrong on both counts. Even if you'd killed Linus and me, Emily would have wound up cutting out your heart. Trust me on that, Wolford."

"You . . . you're crazy."

"Am I? Sheriff Wilkes, why don't you ask Mr. Wolford if he sent his men to kill Linus Peabody?"

The shotgun was still trembling in Wilkes' hands, but it seemed to be from fear. "I don't want any part of this. I'm supposed to enforce the law—"

"Then arrest Vincent Wolford. Arrest him for murder and see to it he's tried, convicted, and hanged. And if you do that, then maybe, just maybe, there's still some hope for this country after all."

"Mr. Wolford?" Wilkes said, clearly uncertain what he should do.

"What does it matter?" Wolford suddenly cried. "Of course I sent my men to get rid of that stubborn old geezer! He's just a Rebel! We beat them! We won! We can do anything we want to them!"

"There's still supposed to be some law—"

"Not for Rebels!"

"We're still Americans," Luke pointed out. "Isn't that one of the so-called reasons you Yankees fought the war in the first place?"

Wolford let out a shriek of rage and hatred and pushed himself up from the boardwalk with his left hand. His right flung up the little pistol. "Go to hell!" he screeched.

"You first." Luke lifted his thumb. The revolver roared and bucked in his hand, and the bullet smacked into Wolford's forehead, hammering the back of his skull down on the planks. The gun fell out of Wolford's hand, unfired.

Luke expected to feel a double load of buckshot smash into him, ending his life.

Instead, he realized that other than the echoes of his shot dying away, the street was quiet.

He looked over at Wilkes. The sheriff had lowered the shotgun. Maybe it had something to do with the crowd of townspeople surrounding him. They had been drawn by the shots and the screaming, and probably had heard Wolford's confession. It was possible a lot of them didn't like the way Wilkes had been doing the Yankees' bidding. He had to be worried the crowd would turn on him, if he shot Luke.

"The . . . the soldiers will be coming from their camp," Wilkes stammered out.

"When they get here, you can tell them some criminals have been executed," Luke said.

"There was no trial—"

"More than they deserved. Wolford got to speak his piece." Luke nodded at the crowd. "All these people heard it."

"There's gonna be warrants sworn out on you—"

"Fine." Luke tucked the Colt Navy away, but kept the Griswold and Gunnison in his hand as he stepped down carefully from the boardwalk. The horse he had ridden into town was only a few steps away. It looked like he wasn't going to be able to return the mount to Thad Franklin after all. If he could, later on he would send some money to the man to pay for the horse.

"I thought you couldn't walk," Wilkes remarked.

"It seems that I can," Luke said again.

"Old Peabody and his granddaughter . . ."

"They're all right. Emily was wounded, but I don't think it's bad."

"Then Wolford's men didn't murder anybody after all."

"Not for lack of trying," Luke said. "And there's no telling what other crimes they're guilty of, or how many men they've killed."

"You're the killer," Wilkes said, his voice shaking. "A cold-blooded killer!"

"In that case, Sheriff," Luke said quietly, "I think you'd do well to stay out of my way." He put his foot in the stirrup and swung up onto the borrowed horse. Or stolen horse, if you wanted to look at it that way, he thought.

Part of him couldn't believe he was still alive, or his

legs were still working. But that was the case, and he had learned to deal with things the way they were, not the way he wished they could be.

Wilkes was right. The law would probably come after him. He could never go back to the Peabody farm. It would bring down more trouble on their heads, trouble they didn't need.

One thing had to be left perfectly clear before he rode away. Raising his voice so he addressed the townspeople as much as the sheriff, he said, "Emily Peabody and her grandfather had nothing to do with what happened here tonight! I did it on my own, and the law has no reason to bother them for this or anything else! I'm counting on the good people of this community to make sure that's understood! *I* did this!"

"We don't even know your name, mister," one of the townies called out.

"It's Smith. Luke Smith."

With that, Luke jammed his heels into the horse's flanks. People scrambled to get out of his way as he galloped out of the settlement. The darkness at the edge of town swallowed him.

It swallowed Luke Smith . . . because Luke Jensen was dead. He had died the night the Confederate gold was stolen. His ma and pa, Kirby, and Janey would never know he was a failure and a fugitive.

The swift rataplan of hoofbeats in the night faded and then was gone.

BOOK THREE

CHAPTER 24

1870

An icy wind clawed at Luke through the sheepskin coat he wore as he brought his horse to a stop in front of the squat roadhouse. Settlers' homes and most businesses on the almost treeless Kansas plains were built of sod because it was too expensive to have lumber freighted in. Any grass on the thatched roofs was dead. It was late autumn.

He was glad he'd found the place perched on the bank of a narrow creek with ice forming along its edges. No other human habitation was in sight for miles around on the open plains. At least he'd have somewhere to spend the night out of the frigid weather.

His legs sometimes gave him trouble when it was cold. Usually he got around just fine, as if he'd never been injured, although it had taken months to regain his full strength. The wound in his shoulder was minor and had healed quickly, but his legs had given him trouble for a long time. Every so often the old ache was there, deep in his muscles, and it was worse when the temperature dropped.

Other old aches bothered him more, like the knowledge that he had failed the Confederacy and his friends, and the fact that he had ridden away without saying good-bye to Emily.

At least he knew she and her grandfather were all right.

A few months after leaving Georgia, he'd been tending bar in a little East Texas town when none other than Sheriff Royce Wilkes had walked into the saloon where Luke worked. Former Sheriff Royce Wilkes was more accurate, because as it turned out, Wilkes had been run out of town, just like when he'd been a deputy.

Luke dismounted and tied his horse at the rack with half a dozen others. He glanced at the gray sky. Sleet or snow would probably fall later, but for now there was just the cold wind and the fading light. He shuddered in the cold, remembering that long-ago meeting with Wilkes.

As he came up to the bar, his eyes widened in shock as he recognized Luke. "Smith!" His hand dropped toward the gun on his hip.

Luke reached under the bar and rested his hand on the stock of the sawed-off shotgun the owner kept on a shelf there. "I wouldn't do that, Sheriff. There's a Greener pointing at you under here."

Wilkes moved his hand well away from his gun and

muttered, "Sorry. And I ain't a sheriff no more. Haven't been since not long after you left Dobieville."

"What happened?"

Wilkes' mouth twisted bitterly. "Everybody in the damned county raised hell with Judge Blevins and Colonel Morrison about how Wolford tried to have Linus Peabody killed. That old man's well-liked around those parts. Morrison and the judge tried to brush it off. Blevins swore out a warrant for your arrest on murder charges. But I said I wasn't gonna go after you, so they booted me from the job."

"That's a shame," Luke said. "A man shouldn't lose his job for doing the right thing . . . for once."

"You don't know what it was like back there when the Yankees came in." Wilkes scowled and shrugged. "Or I reckon maybe you do, since you were there. Anyway, the Yankees didn't want me anymore, and the townsfolk didn't have any use for me to start with, so I thought I might as well come on out here to the frontier and see what I was missin'. So far it ain't been a hell of a lot."

Luke asked, "Do you know how Emily is?"

"She was fine when I left. She wasn't hurt bad that night. In fact, she started lettin' Thad Franklin's boy Jess start courtin' her."

Luke drew in a breath. Hearing that hurt, but at the same time he was glad Emily wasn't sitting around and pining away. He wasn't worth her being unhappy.

"What about those murder warrants?"

Wilkes shrugged again. "They're still in effect, I guess, but nobody's gettin' in any hurry to serve them. I reckon there's a good chance that if you stay out of Georgia, nobody's even gonna bother lookin' for you."

Luke hoped that was true. He had spent the first three months looking over his shoulder, even as he worked his way west, taking whatever odd jobs he could find.

"I see you're still up and walkin' around," Wilkes went on.

"Yeah, my legs are a lot better."

"You're a lucky man. How about a beer?"

Luke nodded and reached for a mug. "I can do that."

Wilkes had his drink and left. Luke was relieved, knowing Emily was all right. Maybe she would marry the Franklin boy and settle down to have a long, happy life, Yankees or no Yankees.

It was still on Luke's mind when he left the saloon that night and started back to the shabby little room he rented a block away.

The soft scrape of a footstep behind him was all the warning he had . . . or needed. As he twisted, his hand streaked to the Colt Navy tucked in his waistband. He never went anywhere without being armed. One of his revolvers was always in easy reach, even when he was sleeping.

The gun came out with blinding speed. The muzzle flash from the other man's gun bloomed n the darkness. Luke's revolver crashed. A man cried out and reeled from the mouth of the alley Luke had just passed, collapsing in the muddy street.

He knew, even before he snapped a lucifer to life with his thumbnail, the man he'd just killed was Royce Wilkes. He'd been nursing a grudge against Luke ever since leaving Georgia, and when fate had brought the two of them together again, the moment was inevitable.

And it was a damned shame, Luke thought. Back in Dobieville, Wilkes had acted like a real lawman for a moment, but ultimately, doing the right thing had brought him to a violent end.

The former sheriff was responsible for bushwhacking him, though, so Luke wasn't going to lose any sleep over killing the man. Nor was he going to stay around. He didn't need the attention or the trouble. Before anyone came to see what the shooting was about, he hustled to his room, rounded up what little gear he had, got his horse from the shed behind the boardinghouse, and lit a shuck, heading west again.

In the years since, he had continued to drift, never staying in one place for too long. He had driven a freight wagon, worked as a shotgun guard on a stagecoach run, tended bar, and even worked as a clerk in a store more than once, although he hated that job. Sometimes he sat in on a poker game and usually came out ahead. He had made enough money to send some back to Thad Franklin for the horse, a mount he had traded in on a better one in San Antonio. He owned a decent saddle, a Winchester rifle, and a gun belt and holster in which he carried the Colt Navy. He kept the Griswold and Gunnison either in his saddlebags or tucked in his waistband. He picked up books wherever he could find them and spent most of his nights reading.

It wasn't much of a life, but it was what he had.

The vague idea of going to Denver had struck him, and the way he lived, he didn't spend much time thinking about what he was doing next. He just did it. So he'd set out across Kansas, not figuring on the late autumn storm that was sweeping down across the plains from Canada. He might have to hole up at the roadhouse for a while before continuing his endless journey.

The first thing that struck him as he stepped inside the sod building was the silence. He'd expected some talk and raucous laughter from the patrons, maybe the clatter of coins tossed onto a table as somebody anted up in a poker game, or the clink of a whiskey bottle against a glass.

Instead, once he swung the door closed behind him and cut off the long, hard sigh of the wind, he didn't hear anything.

Then the sound of harsh breathing came to his ears.

The low-ceilinged, windowless room was lit only by a couple dim and flaring lamps, and the air was thick with smoke and shadows. Luke's eyes adjusted quickly to the gloom, and took in the scene before him.

A couple young men who looked like they might be cowboys up from Texas sat at one of the crude, rough-hewn tables scattered around on the hard-packed dirt floor. Another man in an overcoat with a flashy but well-worn suit underneath it sat alone at another table. Luke pegged him as a gambler.

Three men in shaggy buffalo-hide coats had a woman pinned up against the bar, which consisted of planks laid across several whiskey barrels. Long-haired and unshaven, they were about as shaggy as the buffalo that had provided their coats. They turned their heads to glare at Luke.

A few feet away, on the other side of the bar, a skinny, bald-headed man stood, looking nervous. He probably owned the place, Luke thought.

The young cowboys looked a little scared, too. The gambler's face was impassive, but that didn't mean much. Tinhorns made their living by not letting their faces give anything away.

To the room at large, Luke said in a mild voice, "Don't mind me. I'm just looking for a place to get out of that blue norther that's blowing in."

One of the hardcases shrugged and started to turn away, and Luke thought that was the end of it. But the woman said, "I know you."

Luke hadn't gotten a good look at her. He'd seen enough soiled doves in his travels, taking what comfort he could from them when he had to. She tried to step out of the half circle of men around her, and the lamplight hit her face, revealing the curly blond hair, the face that was still pretty despite the hard lines settling in around the eyes and mouth, and the little dark beauty mark near the corner of that mouth.

Luke stiffened. He remembered her, too. It was hard for him to forget somebody who had pointed a shotgun at him. The most vivid memory was of her standing in a shallow creek in wet, skimpy undergarments, but it was followed closely by the mental image of her threatening him and his companions with that scattergun. "Tennessee. Or maybe Georgia."

Before the woman could respond, one of the hardcases put a grimy hand on her chest and shoved her back against the bar. "Mind your own business, mister," he snarled.

"Oh, I intend to," Luke said. "But I'd appreciate it if you wouldn't treat the lady quite so rough, friend."

The blonde said, "They're gonna do a lot worse than that." Her voice rose a little as she tried to control the fear she obviously felt. "They're going to kill us all, once they're through having their fun. These are the Gammon brothers."

The name didn't mean anything to Luke, but he said, "I see."

One of the hardcases said, "Hey, Cooter, you think this fella could be that U.S. marshal who's been on our trail?"

"I don't know, Ben." The man squinted across the room at Luke. "But it don't really matter, does it?"

As soon as the hardcase said that, Luke knew the woman was right. The three of them planned to kill everybody and loot the place before they rode off. They'd probably keep the blonde alive the longest, figuring she could help keep them warm until the storm blew over.

Luke didn't take his eyes off the outlaws, but he asked the cowboys, "You fellas from Texas taking a hand in this?"

"Mister, all we got are rifles, and they're outside on our horses," one of the young punchers said.

"We just came in for a drink," the other added miserably. "Now we'd just like to get out of here alive."

"How about you, Ace?" Luke asked the gambler.

"The deck was stacked against me . . . until now."

The hardcase who had spoken first yelped, "Hellfire, Cooter, they're gonna draw on us!"

Luke told the Texans, "You boys hit the floor *now*!"

CHAPTER 25

Moving fast but not rushing, Luke palmed the Colt smoothly from its holster. At the same time, his left hand twisted at the wrist, grasped the butt of the Griswold and Gunnison sticking up from his waistband, and pulled that gun, too.

He wished the blonde wasn't standing right by the bar where a stray bullet could hit her, but most of the time a man couldn't choose the fights that came to him. All he could do was try to stay alive.

The outlaws swept aside the long buffalo coats and grabbed for their guns. They were fast, but Luke was faster. They had just cleared leather when his guns began to roar.

He shot the one called Ben first, triggering the Colt twice and slamming the slugs into the man's body, hoping two shots would be enough to put the big man down.

The bullets slammed Ben back against the bar and knocked some of the planks loose. Luke fired his left-hand gun at Cooter and saw the man stagger.

To Luke's left, the gambler's pistol cracked, but the

third outlaw had his gun leveled and jerked the trigger twice, sending return shots at the tinhorn.

Luke pivoted and used the Griswold and Gunnison on the third brother while he sent two more slugs from the Colt into Cooter's slumping form. The third man was hit, but he still stood tall and straight and fired at Luke, who felt the hot breath of the bullet as it whipped past his ear.

Something flashed in the lamplight, and the third Gammon brother made a gurgling, gasping sound. Bright red blood flooded from his neck, which the blonde had opened almost from ear to ear with a single backhanded swipe of the straight razor she held in her hand. The man dropped his gun and pawed at his neck, but there was nothing he could do to stop the bleeding. He collapsed onto his knees and then pitched forward on his face to lie motionless as a crimson puddle formed on the dirt floor beneath his head.

Cooter and Ben were both down. So was the gambler, and so were the two cowboys, although they lifted frightened faces to look around as the shooting ended. Luke saw the proprietor peeking out from behind one of the whiskey barrels where he had taken cover.

Luke said to the blonde, "Why don't you step away from those men, ma'am, so I can make sure they're dead?"

"The one I cut is, you can count on that. Looks like just about all the blood he had in him has leaked out."

"It never hurts to make sure." Luke approached the fallen outlaws with both hands still filled with revolvers and toed them over onto their backs. In all three cases, sightless eyes stared up emptily at the low ceiling.

"Told you," the blonde said.

One of the cowboys had gotten up to check on the gambler. "This fella's hurt bad."

Luke tucked away the Griswold and Gunnison but kept the Colt in his other hand as he went over and knelt beside the gambler. The man's white shirt was dark with blood under his once-fancy vest.

"Sorry," Luke said.

"D-don't be," the gambler managed to say. "I knew it was . . . a game of chance . . . when I took cards . . . It's just the way they were . . ." He wasn't able to finish as his eyes went glassy.

"That's right," Luke said, even though the tinhorn couldn't hear him anymore. "It's just the way they were dealt." He looked up at the blonde. "You know his name?"

"I don't have any earthly idea. He just rode in a while ago, like the rest of you. Those cowboys were first, then him, then the Gammons. Then you."

Luke stood up, reloaded the Navy, and introduced himself. "Luke Smith."

"I'm called Marcy."

"Pleased to make your acquaintance . . . again." He noticed the razor she had used to cut the throat of the third Gammon brother was nowhere to be seen. She'd probably slipped it back into a hidden pocket in her dress. "I take it these are some of the local bad men?"

"They're bad, all right. They've robbed, raped, and murdered their way across half of Kansas and Nebraska."

"Then the world's better off with them dead."

"I reckon. The world really would've been better off

if they'd been put in gunnysacks and drowned when they were babies."

Luke couldn't help smiling. "A bit bloodthirsty, aren't you?"

"Men like that deserve it," Marcy said, prodding one of the bodies with the toe of her boot.

Luke turned to the Texas cowhands. "How about giving me a hand dragging them out?"

The proprietor spoke up from behind the bar. "As cold as it is, there's liable to be wolves around tonight. If you put the bodies outside—"

"Then these three will finally serve a purpose in nature, won't they?" Luke looked at the gambler. "We'll put this fellow in the shed where the wolves can't get at him. Maybe the ground won't be frozen too hard in the morning to dig a grave."

The proprietor told Luke his money wasn't any good as long as he was there. Since Luke's funds were running a little low, he didn't argue, and enjoyed the beer, the bowl of stew, and the chunk of hard bread the man brought to his table once the bodies of the dead men had been tended to.

Marcy came over and sat down at the table with him, bringing a glass of whiskey with her. "What happened to those fellas who were with you the last time I saw you?"

"Four of them are dead," Luke said. "I don't know about the other four."

He had kept his eyes and ears open while he was drifting, hoping he might run across something or somebody who could put him on the trail of Potter and the others, but so far he hadn't had any luck. He had no idea where to start searching, so he asked questions about them and waited and hoped. "You haven't seen any of the others since then, have you?"

She shook her head. "You're the first one, Luke."

He swallowed some of the beer from his mug and smiled. "I appreciate you not shooting me that day."

"Don't think I didn't think about it," she said solemnly. Then a faint smile tugged at her lips, too.

"You're about as hardboiled as a lady can be, aren't you?"

"Who the hell said I'm a lady? And do you know any other way for a woman to survive out here? We've got to be tougher than all you men. We just can't let you see it."

Luke grinned and lifted his beer. "To toughness."

She clinked her glass against his and nodded. "To toughness."

After they drank, he said, "What happened to the other women who were with you that day?"

"Turnabout's fair play on that question, eh?" She shrugged. "Damned if I know. Some of them are dead, and the others are scattered. Just like your friends, I reckon."

"The ones who are left alive aren't my friends," Luke said, his smile disappearing.

Marcy regarded him shrewdly for a moment and then nodded. "It's like that, is it?"

"It is."

"Well, then, I don't know whether to hope you find them or not."

"Why's that?" Luke asked.

"Because there's four of them and one of you, and I hate to see any man I let into my bed without payin' get himself killed."

Luke's eyebrows rose a little. "You're going to let me into your bed without paying?"

"Let me finish this drink—" Marcy lifted her glass—"and then we'll see."

Luke and Marcy spent the night in one of the small rooms partitioned off at the back of the roadhouse. Wrapped up in blankets and each other, they stayed warm enough despite the icy wind howling outside.

When Luke woke up in the morning, she was gone, but he smelled coffee brewing and hoped he would find her in the main room. He sat up and dressed quickly. Pushing the curtain aside, he stepped out of the tiny room and saw Marcy standing at the stove fully dressed with a blanket wrapped around her shoulders. Even inside the roadhouse, it was cold.

She looked up at him and smiled. "How do you feel?"

"Not bad." As he walked over to her his gait was a little awkward. His muscles had stiffened up some while he was asleep.

She noticed, and asked, "Something wrong?"

"Just an old injury. Nothing to worry about."

She nodded. "Yeah, I know all about those old injuries. The world's got a way of knockin' folks around, doesn't it?"

"It sure does," Luke agreed.

"Well, sit down somewhere. Coffee will be ready soon, and then I'll whip up some breakfast."

"You're the cook here, too?"

"That's right." Her smile was wry. "I have lots of different jobs."

While Luke was sitting there, the two young cowboys came in from outside. They had spent the night at the roadhouse, too, and Luke figured they'd been out to check on the horses, all of which had been put in the shed behind the building along with the body of the gambler.

"Mornin', Mr. Smith," one of the youngsters greeted him. "Got something here for you." He lifted a gun belt with double holsters. The walnut grip of a revolver stuck up from each holster.

"We took 'em off one of those Gammon brothers when we dragged the carcasses outside last night," the other puncher explained. "Didn't see any point in armin' the wolves that were gonna drag 'em off."

"I see." Luke took the gun belt from the first cowboy. The holsters were reversed for a cross draw. He slid one of the guns from leather and recognized it as a Remington. *Fine weapon*, he thought. "What about the other two brothers?"

The cowboys grinned and pulled back their coats to reveal that they had taken the gun belts from those bodies, too.

"Those looked like the best guns, so we figured you deserved to have them, Mr. Smith. And the horses, too, if you want 'em."

"I'll take one horse as an extra mount," Luke said.

"You fellows can get some good use out of the other two, I expect."

The punchers exchanged grins.

"We sure can," one of them said. "We was just about broke last night, 'cept for our saddles and our hosses. Now we got good guns and extra mounts. Reckon we're plumb rich!"

Luke wasn't sure he had ever been as young and carefree as those two Texas cowboys. If he had been, he couldn't remember it.

Marcy came over with the coffeepot. "You two sit down," she told the punchers. "Breakfast will be ready in a little bit."

They were all eating a short time later when the door opened again. Luke glanced up and saw a bulky figure silhouetted against the gray light of the overcast day. The first things he noticed were the rifle in the man's hand and the tin star pinned to his coat. He recognized it as a United States marshal's badge.

The man wore a thick sheepskin coat and had a broad-brimmed brown hat pulled down tight on his head so the wind wouldn't blow it away. His face was red, either from the cold, a close acquaintance with whiskey, or both, and a close-cropped blond beard stuck out on his cheeks and chin.

Luke took a deep breath. He was still wanted on murder charges back in Georgia.

CHAPTER 26

"Good morning," the man said as he came into the roadhouse and swung the door closed behind him. "Mighty chilly out there to go with the dusting of snow."

"We have coffee if you want it, Marshal," Marcy said. "And grub."

The lawman slapped gloved hands together to warm them and grinned. "That sounds fine, ma'am. Nothing like hot food and drink to warm a man up."

Marcy stood and motioned with her head toward one of the empty tables. "Have a seat. I'll get you a cup and a plate."

"Much obliged."

The marshal went over to the table, set his rifle on it, pulled off his gloves, and dropped his hat next to them. He smiled at Luke and the two cowboys. "Morning, gents."

The punchers muttered greetings, but Luke said, "Good morning, Marshal."

"Deputy Marshal," the lawman corrected him. "Name's Jasper Thornapple."

When a man introduced himself, it was only polite to return the favor, and despite the rough environments in which he spent his life, Luke had come to pride himself on his manners. "I'm Luke Smith."

Thornapple didn't seem to recognize the name, but that didn't mean anything. Maybe he was just good at covering up his reactions.

"Teddy Young," one of the cowboys said.

"Burt Tuttle," the other puncher added.

"Pleased to meet you," Thornapple said.

Marcy set a cup of steaming coffee in front of Thornapple. "What brings you out here in the middle of nowhere, Marshal?"

Thornapple nodded his thanks for the coffee. "Well, I'm trailing some men."

Luke wasn't surprised by the answer.

"Cooter, Ben, and Carl Gammon. Reckon you've probably heard of them," the marshal added.

"I sure have." Marcy went back and sat down next to Luke.

"Or rather, I should say I *was* trailing them," Thornapple went on. "Came across a wolf pack about a mile east of here, having themselves a feast in a dry wash. There wasn't much left of the fellas they'd been after, but I'm pretty sure one of them was Cooter Gammon. He had a streak of white in his hair hard to miss. Since there were two men about the same size with him, I feel confident my boss can close the books on the Gammon brothers."

"Bad luck for them, being caught by a pack of wolves like that," Luke commented.

Thornapple took a sip of his coffee and nodded. "Especially when those wolves were carrying guns," he said with a shrewd smile.

The two cowboys couldn't stop themselves from flinching guiltily. Luke's face was like stone, though. "What do you mean by that?"

"I mean one of those skulls had a bullet hole smack-dab in the middle of its face. Somebody shot that Gammon brother before the wolves got at him. A well-deserved fate, I might add." Thornapple took another sip of coffee. "You folks have anything you want to tell me? Bear in mind I'm a federal lawman who doesn't cotton to being lied to."

"Mr. Smith didn't have any choice!" one of the punchers burst out. "He didn't have any choice at all. Those Gammons were worse 'n hydrophobia skunks. They were gonna kill us all!"

As soon as the words stopped tumbling out of the youngster's mouth, he turned a stricken face to Luke. "I'm sorry, Mr. Smith. I shouldn't've said nothin'—"

Luke lifted a hand to stop the apology. "That's all right. I have a feeling Marshal Thornapple already had a pretty good idea what happened. He strikes me as a man who's been to see the elephant."

"There and back again," Thornapple agreed with a smile. "You killed all three of them, Mr. Smith?"

"Two of them, anyway, and I contributed to the third."

"I cut his throat," Marcy put in. "He probably would have died anyway, but I didn't see any harm in hurrying him along to hell."

"Nor would I, ma'am," Thornapple said. "In that case,

I suppose the two of you will have to come to some sort of equitable arrangement concerning the division of the reward money."

"Reward money!"

"That's right, ma'am. Each of the Gammons had a thousand-dollar bounty on his head."

Marcy leaned back in her chair, her eyes wide with amazement. "Three thousand dollars!"

"That's right. Come with me to Wichita, and I'll authorize payment. You can collect from the bank there."

Marcy looked over at Luke. "My God, we're rich! I never saw three thousand dollars in my life!"

Luke hesitated to say anything. He didn't fully trust Thornapple. Maybe the lawman was trying to trick him into going along to Wichita, where he would promptly place him under arrest.

Giving it more thought, that didn't seem likely. Luke could tell by looking at Thornapple the badge-toter had plenty of bark on him. If Thornapple wanted to make an arrest, he'd just do it instead of trying some fancy trick.

More than likely, Thornapple had never seen any of the wanted posters charging Luke with murder that had circulated back in Georgia.

"There's just one thing," Luke said slowly. "I'm not a bounty hunter."

"You killed three men with a price on their heads," Thornapple offered. "It's not like you have to file papers ahead of time or anything. That money is yours by rights, Mr. Smith."

Marcy looked even more excited. "We've got to do it, Luke. We've got to claim that reward."

He understood then how much it meant to her. She had spent her life struggling just to get by, enduring hardship and degradation. The tough times were starting to take a real toll on her.

Yet there was still a spark of dignity inside her, and a sense of determination that might allow her to make something better of her life if she just got the chance. The bounty money could give her that chance.

"All right," Luke finally agreed. "We'll go to Wichita with the marshal."

She threw her arms around his neck. "Thank you, Luke! You don't know what this means to me."

It meant he had inadvertently done something good for somebody. That wasn't enough to make up for past failures . . . but it was a start.

Thornapple nodded toward the holstered Remingtons and coiled shell belt still laying on the table where Luke and Marcy sat. "Nice-looking guns. Whose are they?"

"They're mine." Luke reached out and pulled a gun out of the holster. *One more bit of bounty for killing the Gammon brothers*, he thought.

They split the reward money down the middle, fifteen hundred apiece. Marcy didn't think that was fair. She wanted to take five hundred for her part and give the rest to Luke, but he refused and insisted she take half.

They set aside an equal amount from each share, and got a room in the finest hotel in Wichita. For a week they ate in the best restaurants the town had to offer, drank champagne they had sent up from one of the saloons, and spent long hours together in bed.

After that week, pleasant though it was, Luke was so restless he couldn't stand it anymore.

He left the room early one morning while Marcy was still sleeping and walked to the livery stable where he was keeping his horses. He had just thrown his saddle on one of the animals when a voice asked, "Going somewhere, Mr. Smith?"

Luke looked around to see Marshal Jasper Thornapple standing in the open double doors of the livery barn with his shoulder propped casually against one of the jambs.

"Thought I might take a ride," Luke answered, assuming as casual an attitude as Thornapple.

"Did you tell the young lady good-bye?"

"Who said I wasn't coming back?"

Thornapple chuckled. "I've seen plenty of fiddlefoots in my time, Smith. Hell, I've been one. I know the look of a man who feels the call of distant trails."

Luke shrugged. "Marcy and I aren't really the sort for sentimental farewells."

"I have a hunch you might be wrong about how she feels . . . but it's none of my business, is it?"

"No, it's not."

"That's right, my business is hunting down lawbreakers. That line of work has given me a healthy curiosity about the people I meet."

Luke turned a little so he could move faster if he needed to reach for the Remingtons. He had started wearing the cross-draw rig, and wished he'd had more time to practice getting those irons out in a hurry. "Out here on the frontier, curiosity's generally considered to be not that healthy," he commented.

"Maybe not, but it's my job. So I sent some wires and did some checking. I wasn't surprised to find out that Luke Smith is a pretty common name."

"Lots of Smiths around," Luke said, his voice tight.

"The only one I came across that might be of some interest to a man like me was from Georgia. He was wanted for killing a land speculator and some hired guns about five years ago. *Was* wanted, Smith. That's important. The charges were dropped last year."

Luke's heart suddenly slugged hard in his chest. He wanted to believe what Thornapple was telling him, but it didn't seem possible it could be true. He managed to ask, "Why would they drop the charges in a case like that?"

"Because once the Reconstruction government was forced to let go of some of its power, the facts of the case came out. Turns out the land speculator was nothing but a carpetbagging thief, and evidence indicated he'd had men killed in order to grab their land. That particular Luke Smith can go back to Georgia without having to worry about the law anymore."

Luke drew in a deep breath. "That's a lucky break . . . for him."

The excitement he'd felt for a second had vanished. There was nothing waiting for him back in Georgia. Emily was probably married to Jess Franklin and raising a couple kids. Even if she wasn't, she wouldn't want to see him again. Not after he'd ridden off that night and never come back.

"I just thought you might be interested in hearing about that before you rode off," Thornapple went on. "Which way do you plan to head? West . . . or east?"

"I set out to go to Denver a while back," Luke said. "I suppose I still will."

Thornapple straightened and nodded. "Have a safe journey, then." He turned to head out of the livery.

Something occurred to Luke. "Marshal."

Thornapple stopped and turned back to Luke. "Yes?"

"Can I ask you if you've heard of some other men? While in your line of work, I mean."

Thornapple's brawny shoulders rose and fell. "Sure, go ahead."

"Wiley Potter. Keith Stratton. Josh Richards. Ted Casey."

For a long moment, Thornapple frowned in thought. Then he shook his head. "None of those names ring a bell, Smith. Should they?"

"I don't know. Thought it was possible."

"Well, I haven't heard of them. Sorry."

"That's all right. I'll catch up to them one of these days."

Thornapple lingered. "What do you plan to do with yourself?"

Luke thought about it for a second, then grunted. "Seems like there's good money in bounty hunting."

"Well . . . there's money in it. Some wouldn't call it good. Some folks call it blood money. And going after it is a good way to get yourself killed." Thornapple shrugged again. "But you saw that for yourself. Not every owlhoot has a price on his head as big as the bounties on the Gammon brothers. But some are even bigger."

"That's what I thought." Luke tightened the cinch on his saddle. "I'll be seeing you, Marshal."

"I wouldn't be a bit surprised," Thornapple said.

Luke didn't wave or even look back as he rode out of Wichita. He hoped Marcy was still asleep, snug and warm in that hotel room bed, dreaming of the new life she could make for herself with her share of the money. He hoped that when she woke up and found him gone, she wouldn't hate him.

But either way, he was going.

CHAPTER 27

Blood money, Thornapple had called it, and that turned out to be true.

As the years passed, Luke Smith saw a veritable lake of blood.

From the Rio Grande to the Canadian border, from New Orleans and the Mississippi River delta to San Francisco, Luke roamed, always on the trail of men with a price on their heads. Whether the bounty was big or small didn't really matter. Kill enough penny-ante owlhoots, as long as somebody was willing to pay for the carcasses, and the money added up.

Sometimes there were big kills, too, high-dollar rewards netting Luke enough cash he wouldn't have to track down any more outlaws for a while if he didn't want to.

But what else was he going to do?

The face looking out at him from the mirror when he shaved became craggier, more weathered. The ordeal he had suffered at the end of the Civil War made him look older than his years, and the life he lived after that certainly didn't make him appear any younger. Those deep-set eyes had seen too much death and suffering to ever be innocent again.

His only consolation was the men he killed had it coming. They were robbers, rapists, arsonists, murderers.

He wasn't arrogant enough to consider himself some sort of avenging angel delivering justice. If he was working for any higher power, it was Lucifer, reaping more souls to be plunged, screaming, into the depths of Hades.

Luckily, there were a few moments of humanity here and there, or he might have gone insane.

Deadwood, 1877

The gold rush that had caused the town to spring into existence a year earlier had dwindled away as mining syndicates and corporations moved in and, for the most part, replaced the individual prospectors who had sunk shafts in the sides of the gulches all around the settlement. It still had its rough edges, though, and enough vice to attract men from all over, including those on the run from the law.

Luke rode in on the trail of a man named Robert Fescoe, who had killed a bank teller during a robbery down in Yankton. Fescoe was reported to be heading west, and Luke hoped the fugitive paused long enough in Deadwood to get drunk and find himself a whore.

Those two things didn't sound that bad to Luke, either, although he wasn't one to indulge his baser appetites indiscriminately. However, a man couldn't just sit and read during all his spare time.

He stopped at a livery stable, and as he turned his horse over to the hostler, he asked, "Have you seen a tall, skinny fellow with a half-moon-shaped scar on his chin?" Luke was grateful for the outlaw's scar because it made him easy to describe.

The hostler frowned in thought and shook his head. "Can't say as I have, mister."

"He would have ridden in within the last day or two," Luke added.

"Nope. Sorry."

"Is this the only livery stable in town?"

The hostler chuckled. "I wish it was. I'd make a lot more money that way. No, there are three or four more. Maybe the hombre you're lookin' for left his hoss at one of them."

"Maybe so." Luke flipped a five-dollar gold piece to the man, who caught it deftly. "That ought to cover my bill for a while . . . and buy your discretion if you happen to see the man I'm looking for."

"If you mean I won't say nothin' to him about you lookin' for him, you're danged right about that. I'll even come see if I can find you."

"I'd be much obliged," Luke told him. "Meanwhile, what's the best place in town to get a drink?"

The hostler scratched his beard-stubbled jaw. "Well, there's the Bella Union. It's pretty nice. Or the Gem, which ain't as nice, but their whiskey is good and they got some fine whores. Folks tend to get shot there from time to time, though."

"An all-too-common occurrence."

"Or there's a new place you could try. It's called the Buffalo Butt."

Luke had to laugh. "What a name for a saloon!"

"Yeah, I don't know why the gal who owns it decided to call it that. *She* don't look like a buffalo's hind end, I can tell you that for dang sure. She's one of the prettiest gals in Deadwood, I'd say."

"Well, that certainly sounds intriguing. I'll give it a try." Luke lifted a hand in farewell and left the livery stable.

It didn't take him long to find the Buffalo Butt Saloon. Despite the crude name, it appeared to be a well-furnished and successful establishment, sitting at an intersection with its bat-winged entrance right at the corner so it was easily visible from both streets.

Luke pushed the batwings aside and stepped in with his usual caution. A man in his line of work never knew when he might run into an old enemy, although most of the men Luke tried to take into custody put up a fight and wound up dead.

A long mahogany bar ran down the left side of the room, with gambling layouts to the right and tables in between. At the far end of the room was an open area where people could dance and a small stage for performers, which was empty at the moment. Men sat at about half the tables, drinking, and the bar was pretty busy, too, although there were plenty of open spots. A couple poker games were going on, and the click and clatter of a roulette wheel mixed with the sounds of talk and laughter. Luke liked the looks of the Buffalo Butt, inelegant moniker and all.

A staircase next to the stage led up to the second floor. If the place was like most saloons, the girls who worked downstairs delivering drinks also worked upstairs delivering something else. Luke glanced at the women moving around the room. Unlike some saloon girls, they were fully dressed in nice gowns cut low enough to reveal the swells of their breasts. Luke might have tried to single out one of them for his attentions later, but a man at a nearby table tilted his head back to look up and said, "Lord have mercy, who's that?"

Luke instinctively followed the direction of the man's gaze. His breath caught in his throat and he stiffened as he saw a woman standing at the railing on the second-floor balcony, looking down at the room. She wore a dark red dress tight enough to reveal her splendid figure, and a thick mass of curly blond hair spilled around her shoulders.

Luke knew her instantly. Marcy hadn't changed much in the seven years since he'd ridden away from Wichita, leaving her in that hotel room.

He saw her suddenly clutch the railing and knew she had recognized him, too. He started toward the stairs, weaving among the tables, as she came along the balcony. He went up the stairs as she came down, and they met halfway, embracing with a desperate urgency as their mouths met.

"Aw, hell!" That disappointed exclamation came from the man who Luke had heard speak when he entered the saloon. "Looks like she's already took."

Luke and Marcy kissed for a long moment, and Luke felt the dull emotional pain that dogged his steps flow out of him. The unexpected reunion was like being plunged into a clean, icy mountain stream.

Then Marcy pulled back a little, lifted her hand, and pressed the barrel of a derringer against the side of his head. "Damn you, Luke Smith. I ought to put a bullet in your brain."

Most of the time, if somebody pointed a gun at him, he reacted violently. He suppressed that urge and smiled instead. "You'd probably be justified. I knew you'd be upset that I left you in Wichita. On the other hand, you appear to be doing well for yourself."

He remembered what the liveryman had said about the owner of the Buffalo Butt being one of the prettiest women in Deadwood. Wherever Marcy was, she would fall into the category. "This is your saloon, isn't it?"

"What if it is?"

"You wouldn't be the owner of a successful business if you hadn't gotten a start from your half of that reward money, would you?"

She let out a snort. "That shows what you know. I used that money to buy an interest in a whorehouse in Wichita. Then it burned down and I lost everything. I had to start over. But by then I'd learned I was pretty good at running things. It took me a while, but I'm doing all right again."

"I'm glad to hear it," Luke said. "Now, if you're not going to pull the trigger on that popgun, I'd appreciate it if you took it away from my head. It might go off by accident."

"I don't do *anything* by accident."

As Marcy lowered the derringer and let its hammer

down carefully, Luke became aware the saloon had gone deathly quiet. He supposed someone had noticed her holding a gun to his head and pointed it out, and as the news spread, everyone stopped what they were doing to watch.

Marcy kissed Luke again, and someone let out a cheer, breaking the silence. Customers returned to their drinking and gambling, filling the saloon with noise once more.

Marcy took Luke by the hand and led him upstairs so they could get reacquainted properly.

That evening, Luke sat with Marcy at her private table in the rear corner of the saloon's main room. One of her bartenders had brought supper over from the dining room of the Grand Central Hotel. It was the best food in the Black Hills, she had explained, and Luke had to admit she was probably right. The roast beef was as good as any he'd had in a long time.

As they ate, washing down the food with sips of fine wine, they talked about everything that had happened since they'd seen each other last.

"I don't have much to tell," Luke told her. "I'm a bounty hunter, have been ever since that run-in with the Gammon brothers."

"I know. I've heard talk about you from time to time. You have quite a reputation." Marcy smiled. "Did you know I named this place after the Gammons?"

"I wondered how come you called it the Buffalo Butt."

"In those buffalo coats, they were as ugly and smelly as buffalo rumps."

"I can't disagree with that," Luke said.

"Even though I didn't want to admit it to you this afternoon, I reckon that was when my life started to change for the better. So I felt like I ought to commemorate the occasion."

Luke thought about it and decided the name was appropriate after all. He lifted his wineglass. "To the good that can come from ugly, inelegant things."

"I'll drink to that." Marcy clinked her glass against his, and he thought her eyes had a meaningful, mischievous twinkle in them as she looked at him.

He *was* ugly and inelegant, he thought. He had so much blood on his hands he could never wash it off, even if he tried.

But he had done some good in his life, too. He had saved Emily and her grandfather from Vincent Wolford. If the carpetbagger had lived, he wouldn't have stopped going after them until he got what he wanted.

And Luke had helped Marcy escape a life that would have eventually killed her if she hadn't gotten out of it. Some people might consider owning a saloon in a frontier town like Deadwood to be pretty disreputable, but those folks just didn't know how low people really could sink. Marcy was better off. He was sure of it.

"What are you going to do now?" she asked.

"I thought I'd have another glass of this surprisingly good wine," he replied with a smile.

"No, I mean with your life. Blast it, Luke, you know that."

He poured the wine and set the bottle aside. "I'll keep doing what I've been doing. I don't see any reason to change now. I'm not sure I *could* change, even if I wanted to."

"I did," Marcy said.

"You wanted to."

"Wouldn't you like to have a normal life? Maybe a business? Like . . . half interest in a saloon?"

He saw the hope in her eyes and knew it would be kinder to dash it right away, rather than letting it linger and grow. He shook his head. "I'm not going to settle down. I can't. Now that I know you're here, I might try to drift this way more often—"

"Don't put yourself out on my account." Her expression turned cold, like a blue norther blowing down across the plains.

"You don't understand. I can't be who you want me to be, Marcy, but knowing that I have a friend somewhere . . . well, it might make those cold nights out on the prairie a little easier to bear."

She wasn't going to give in easily. "I'll think about it." Her voice and body remained stiff with disappointment and anger.

Luke lifted his glass to her. "That's all I can ask."

She came to him that night seemingly as passionate as ever, but he sensed she was holding something back.

His declaration that he would be riding on had changed whatever had been between them.

And how could it fail to do so? he asked himself, regretting it had happened.

Late that night, as Luke was dozing off with Marcy's head pillowed on his shoulder, he heard her whisper, "If you run out on me in the morning without saying goodbye again, I'll hunt you down and kill you."

He laughed softly and promised, "I'll be here."

He was sound asleep when his instincts took over and warned him. Maybe it was the faint creak of a floorboard, but whatever the reason, his eyes snapped open and caught a flicker of movement in the shadows of the room.

Reacting with the speed that had saved his life many times, Luke shoved a startled Marcy out of bed and rolled the other way. With a boom like a crash of thunder, a shotgun went off, twin gouts of flame erupting from its barrels.

Luke snatched up the Remington he had left lying on a chair right beside the bed and thumbed two shots just above the muzzle flash from the scattergun. Momentarily deaf from the shotgun's roar, he couldn't hear if his target cried out or dropped the weapon.

Keeping himself low to the ground, he crept forward. After only a couple steps, Luke tripped on something and stumbled. He put his left hand out to catch himself and it landed on something hot and sticky. He pulled it back and lashed out with the revolver, thudding against something soft.

"Get a light on," Luke told Marcy, hoping none of the buckshot had winged her.

A lucifer flared to life. He squinted against the glare, his eyes adjusting as she lit a lamp on the table beside the bed. Light filled the room and revealed Luke kneeling beside a gaunt man with a scar shaped like a half-moon on his chin. The would-be killer's chest was a bloody mess from the two slugs that had torn through it.

"Who is he?" Marcy asked. "Do you know him?"

Luke heard the question indicating his hearing had come back. He shook his head. "We never met, but I know who he is. His name's Fescoe. I've been on his trail for a while. Somebody must have told him I was in town looking for him, so he asked around until he figured out where he could find me. Thought he'd get me off his trail permanently."

Luke was going to have a talk with that liveryman, who had obviously double-crossed him.

Marcy put her hands on her hips. "My bed's ruined from that shotgun blast, and he's getting blood on the rug, too."

Luke stood up. "I'll send you money for the damages once I've gotten the reward. I'll have to ride back down to Yankton to collect."

"But you won't be coming back?"

"Not for a while. Not after this."

"I've seen men die before, you know. I've even had them try to kill me."

"Death doesn't follow you around, though. Not like it does with me."

Marcy sighed as one of the bartenders pounded on the door and called out to see if she was all right.

"I can't decide if you're the best man I know, Luke Smith, or just a sorry SOB."

Luke walked to the chair by the side of the bed and slipped the Remington back into the holster. "It's a good question. I don't know the answer myself."

CHAPTER 28

Even though his visit to Deadwood had a more bittersweet ending than he would have preferred, Luke took some good memories away from there. He knew Marcy was not only still alive but thriving, and that eased one of the worries he had carried around with him for years. He made himself a promise to drift up to the Black Hills every now and then to visit her and hoped the next time they met, she would still be glad to see him.

The next year, in the summer of 1878, he was in Santa Fe when he saw another familiar face across a crowded cantina. He picked up his mug of beer and made his way across the room until he reached the table where a thick-bodied man with graying fair hair and beard sat nursing a glass of tequila.

"Hello, Marshal," Luke said to Jasper Thornapple.

The two of them had crossed trails several times over the years. Luke had turned over to Thornapple a few fugitives he'd captured and sometimes it was sheer coincidence how they met. The frontier, for all its vastness, could sometimes seem like a small place.

The lawman looked up with a pleased smile. "Luke! I was hoping I'd run into you again one of these days. I've got some news for you." Thornapple gestured for Luke to have a seat at the table. "Heard about it from another deputy marshal."

Luke settled down into the chair. "What kind of news?"

"Remember a long time ago, the first time we met up in Kansas, you asked me about four men?"

Luke stiffened. "You mean Potter, Stratton, Richards, and Casey?"

"Those are the ones. You never found them, did you?"

Luke frowned but didn't say anything. His mind was too full of bitter memories. He had looked for the four men who had betrayed him, betrayed their country, murdered his friends, nearly killed him, and stolen the gold. As much as he roamed, as many people as he met during his travels, he had thought it was inevitable that he would pick up their trail.

But instead he had run into stone wall after stone wall. Nobody knew the men he was looking for. Maybe they were all dead already, he often told himself, but never really believed that. It was as if fate had conspired with those four no-good deserters to keep them safe from his vengeance.

Finally, in a quiet voice, he told Thornapple, "No, I never found them. To tell you the truth, after a while I quit looking so hard." He looked at the marshal, his pulse quickening. "Do you know where they are?"

"I do," Thornapple said, then dashed Luke's hopes. "They're in the ground. They're all dead, Luke."

A strange feeling washed through Luke. It wasn't disappointment, really, or even relief, but rather an odd, hollow mixture of the two. He wanted them dead, but he took no real satisfaction from knowing that they were.

"What happened to them?" he asked Thornapple, although he didn't really care.

"They were killed up in Idaho Territory a while back, at a settlement called Bury. The name turned out to be fitting. They started the town and ran everything in the area. Ran roughshod over everybody in those parts, too. A gunfighter calling himself Buck West rode in and raised hell. Wound up killing all of them. Turns out that wasn't really West's name at all. He was really a fella named Smoke Jensen."

The surprise Luke had felt at hearing his enemies were dead was nothing compared to the shock that went through him upon hearing his family name. It had been so long since he'd used the name Jensen it seemed like he had always been Luke Smith.

Despite that, he had never forgotten his family. Sometimes it was hard to remember what his ma and pa had looked like. They might both be dead. Probably were. And Janey and Kirby would be grown. He might pass them on the street and never know them.

But who in blazes was Smoke Jensen?

Luke shook his head. "I haven't heard of him."

"No reason you would have," Thornapple said. "There were wanted posters out on him for a while, especially while he was calling himself Buck West, but from what I hear there are no charges against him now."

"Did you ever see him?"

Thornapple shook his head. "Nope. Supposed to be a big, sandy-haired fella who's really fast with his guns. He'd have to be, because from what I've heard, not only did he kill those men you were looking for, but he and some old mountain man friends of his wiped out a small army of hired killers who worked for Potter and the others, too. It was a full-fledged war up there."

Kirby had ash-blond hair, Luke recalled. If he'd grown big enough, he might fit the description of Smoke Jensen. But why in the world would he have taken that name?

Why not? That wry thought crossed Luke's mind. *I took a different name, and for a good reason, didn't I? Maybe Kirby did, too.*

"You know where he is now?"

"Jensen?" Thornapple shook his head. "No idea. The way I heard it, he rode away from Bury with some good-looking gal he met up there, and they never came back. Do you want to find him?"

"I thought I might look him up. Thank him for doing my job for me."

"I had a feeling you had a score to settle with those hombres you asked about," Thornapple said. "Well, it's done, so you can forget about it now."

"I suppose so." Luke drank down the rest of his beer and set the empty mug on the table. Inside he felt as empty as that mug.

* * *

He continued to ride, drifting from one place to another. Over time that feeling faded. Glad Potter and the others were dead, Luke would have liked to have been the one to pull the trigger and send them to hell, but nobody ever said life was fair. Justice had caught up to them, and he had to be satisfied with that. He had other killers to hunt down and bring in. But as he went about it, he kept his ears open and learned everything he could about the man called Smoke Jensen.

Smoke was said to be fast with a gun, mighty fast. Maybe the slickest on the draw in the entire West. Luke heard stories about some of the battles Smoke had had with a wide assortment of outlaws and cold-blooded killers, and Smoke always emerged triumphant.

But those who had met him, without fail, said Smoke Jensen was no arrogant, vicious gunman, but rather a stalwart friend, a decent man, and a loving husband to his wife Sally. They had a successful ranch somewhere in Colorado called Sugarloaf, and judging by all the stories Luke heard about the man, Smoke wanted to live a peaceful life and never went out looking for trouble.

He sure didn't back down from it, though, and just about the worst mistake anybody could ever make was to threaten one of Smoke's friends or relatives. That was a mighty quick way to wind up dead.

Yes, Smoke Jensen sounded like the sort of man Luke would be proud to know, but despite what he had told Thornapple, he never made any attempt to find

Jensen. Maybe the famous gunfighter really was his little brother Kirby, or maybe he wasn't, but either way, he figured Smoke wouldn't want a bloody-handed bounty hunter showing up on his doorstep claiming to be kinfolk. Luke felt sure if any of his family had even thought about him during the long years since the end of the Civil War, they must have assumed he was dead.

Because of that, whenever Luke was in Colorado, he was always careful to steer well clear of the Sugarloaf Ranch and the nearby town of Big Rock, the same way that he had never returned to the Ozarks of southwestern Missouri. It was entirely possible there weren't any Jensens left back there, but he didn't want to take that chance.

It was better for Luke Jensen to just stay dead.

He was in northern New Mexico Territory, in the town of Raton, with the Sangre de Cristo Mountains and Raton Pass looming to the north, when he heard a rumor that Solomon Burke and his gang had been spotted in the area.

Luke had been trailing Burke for a couple weeks, so he took a keen interest in what he heard and finally located the old-timer who was the source of the rumor. He bought the man a drink in the High Hat Saloon and asked him about Burke.

The garrulous old man was glad to talk. "I seen 'em while I was out huntin' one day. I got me some diggin's up there, so I keep a pretty close eye on all the comin's and goin's thereabouts."

Luke didn't figure the old-timer's mining claim

amounted to much, but that wouldn't stop him from being fiercely protective of it.

"I heard riders comin' and took cover in some trees," the wizened, bearded oldster continued. "Seen 'em ride right past me, no more 'n fifty yards away. I seen ree-ward dodgers on Burke with his picture on 'em before, so I recognized him right away. Had a couple o' big Mexicans with him, so I figured they had to be Hernandez and Cardona. I've heard mighty bad stories about them two. Don't know who all the other hombres were, but they was prob'ly Burke's regular bunch of owlhoots."

Luke didn't doubt that. "Could you tell where they were going?"

The old prospector hesitated, licking his lips, and Luke signaled for the bartender to bring another round. That got the old-timer talking again.

"I don't know for sure, no, but they rode on outta the valley where my diggin's are and over the pass into the next valley. They's an old abandoned cabin over there they could be usin' as a hideout, right on the banks of Bluejay Creek. I can tell you how to get there"—a shrewd look appeared on the man's whiskery face—"And I will, if you swear to give me a cut of the bounty you collect on 'em."

"How do you know I'm a bounty hunter?" Luke wanted to know.

"Well, you don't really look like a star packer, and I can't think of nobody else who'd be trailin' a bunch of hydrophobia skunks like Solomon Burke and his gang. Gimme your word you'll cut me in?"

Luke nodded his agreement and then added, "If I come back alive, that is."

"Yeah, it's kind of a sucker bet on my part, ain't it? But here's how to get to that cabin . . ."

Luke had followed the old-timer's directions. The valley was a two-day ride from Raton. He thought he was still in New Mexico Territory, but up in the high country it was difficult to be sure. He might have crossed over into Colorado without realizing it.

Colorado . . . the place where Smoke Jensen lived. It wouldn't take but a few days to reach Big Rock, Luke mused as he trailed the Burke gang. He might be able to get a look at Smoke without having to introduce himself. Would he recognize his own brother, if that's who Smoke turned out to be?

That question still lurked in the back of Luke's mind as he dismounted and crept forward through some trees to spy on the old cabin where he thought the outlaws might be hiding.

Then bad luck cropped up again, as José Cardona, out hunting or taking a leak or just looking around, stumbled on him, tackled him, and tried to kill him. Nothing could ever just be easy. Not for Luke Smith.

He'd wiped out the gang, but he'd taken three bullets in return. His efforts to patch himself up hadn't done much good. He wound up passing out and crashing to the floor in the cabin.

Just like fifteen years earlier, when he'd been left for dead on the banks of a shallow river in Georgia, as blackness claimed Luke he was sure he would never wake up again, that it was the end.

BOOK FOUR

CHAPTER 29

Luke winced a little as light struck his eyelids. He turned his head away and felt something soft and smooth against his cheek. *A pillow? Light?*

He was alive. Like the other times over the years when he had come awake after being convinced he was going to die, he struggled to grasp the concept that he wasn't dead after all. Once again, his stubbornness had somehow kept him breathing . . . although he was sure he'd had help, too. Someone had found him in that cabin after he'd passed out from losing so much blood.

Wondering where he was and how much time had passed, he tried to open his eyes, but the light was too bright. *Sunlight,* he thought, but it didn't seem like he was outside. He didn't feel any wind. Moving his hands, he felt crisp fabric. He was lying on a mattress covered with clean sheets. So . . . he was in a bed, inside a house somewhere, and the sun was shining on him through a window.

Keeping his eyes closed, he turned his head back and

heard a sweet sound that puzzled him. It reminded him of the music of a mountain stream.

It was music, all right, he realized. What he heard was a woman humming softly to herself.

His tongue felt twice as big as it should have as he licked his dry, rough lips. He had to swallow a couple times before his throat loosened enough for him to speak. All he could manage was to rasp, “H-hello . . . ?”

“Oh, my!” the woman exclaimed.

Luke heard the rapid patter of her footsteps as she crossed the room. The mattress shifted a little, and he figured she had rested a hand there as she leaned over him. Even through his closed eyes he felt the light change as she came between him and the light, so he tried opening them again.

For the second time in his life, he found himself looking up at what seemed to be an angel. This woman was older than Emily Peabody had been, but she had the same sweet, dark-haired beauty.

She smiled. “You’re all right. You’ve been wounded, but you’re going to be just fine. You’re among friends.”

“F-friends?” Luke repeated, his voice weak. “I don’t . . . have any friends.”

That wasn’t strictly true. He considered Jasper Thornapple to be a friend, and Marcy, too, of course. But Thornapple was nowhere around, as far as Luke knew, and he was a long way from Deadwood.

“You’re wrong,” the woman told him, still smiling. “Anybody who’s in trouble has friends here.” She straightened. “You just lie there and rest. I’ll go tell Smoke you’re awake.”

Once again Luke felt a shock go through him. As the woman turned away she moved out of the sunlight, causing him to flinch as the brilliant rays fell on him again. But he was able to say, "Wait . . . Did you say . . . Smoke?"

She paused, still smiling down at him, although it was hard for him to see her with the light filling his eyes.

"That's right. Smoke Jensen. He's my husband. I'm Sally Jensen. You're on the Sugarloaf Ranch, near Big Rock, Colorado."

That was loco, Luke thought. Smoke Jensen's place was days away from where he'd fought that battle with Solomon Burke and the rest of those outlaws. How in the world had he gotten to the Sugarloaf?

Someone had brought him, of course, he realized as he forced his brain to work and struggled to put his thoughts in order. But why had they brought him to the ranch of a man who might well be one of his relatives? How had they known?

"I'll be right back." Sally hurried out of the room, leaving a very confused Luke lying there.

He continued wrestling with his thoughts. He must have been unconscious for days since he was far north of where he'd been the last time he knew where he was.

Slowly, he became aware of something tight around his torso, and moved his hand to his chest. Someone had wrapped bandages around him. He moved his hand upward and discovered his shoulder was bandaged, too, and so was his arm. The wounds he'd received during the shootout had been tended to.

With a sigh, he tuned into his wounds. They ached,

but not too bad. With the instincts of a man who lived somewhat like a wild animal, Luke knew he wasn't going to die from his injuries after all. For that, he could thank whoever had come along and found him in that old cabin.

Footsteps sounded in the hallway outside the room. Sally came back in, followed by a tall man with very broad shoulders. She stepped over and pulled the curtains over the window, shielding Luke's eyes from the bright light. "I'm sorry, I should have thought to close these before I left. The sun must be blinding you."

Luke was looking at the man who stood next to the bed, but cleared his throat and managed to squeak out a few words. "That's all right. The sun was warm. Felt good."

The man's face was too rugged to call handsome, although it was the sort of face women usually found attractive. The strong features were topped by close-cropped, ash-blond hair. In him, Luke saw both his mother and his father, the resemblance vivid enough to almost take his breath away.

He knew he was looking at his brother. He almost said Kirby's name, but stopped himself in time.

The man gave him a friendly smile. "Welcome to the Sugarloaf. Sally was afraid we were going to lose you, but I took one look at her and told her not to worry. I know a stubborn varmint when I see one."

"He ought to," Sally put in. "He sees one looking back at him from the mirror every morning."

The man chuckled. "I'm Smoke Jensen. This is my ranch."

"L-Luke. Luke Smith."

"Pleased to meet you. We'll shake and howdy later, when you're feeling better. Right now you need some rest, Mr. Smith. You lost a lot of blood. Stubborn or not, it's a miracle you survived the trip up here from the Sangre de Cristos."

"How . . . how did I . . ."

"How'd you get here?" Smoke asked. "An old prospector heard a bunch of shooting and decided to go investigate."

The old-timer had been trying to protect his potential payoff, Luke thought.

"He had a couple friends visiting him at the time," Smoke went on, "a pair of old mountain men. They all went looking and found you still alive in a cabin with a bunch of dead men outside. It must have been quite a battle."

Luke managed to nod slightly. "It was," he whispered.

"Anyway, you'd been shot up and were running a fever. You were out of your head and did a lot of ranting and raving while they were taking care of you. You mentioned my name several times, and those mountain men knew who I was. I have a lot of friends among those old-timers. They figured I might know you, and when they thought you were strong enough, they decided to bring you up here." Smoke paused and gave Luke an intent look. "*Do* we know each other, Mr. Smith?"

Luke forced himself to shake his head. "S-sorry. Never saw you before." Those words practically broke his heart. He knew he was looking at his own flesh and blood.

Nearly twenty years had passed since he'd seen his little brother, and he couldn't even acknowledge that. Kirby—Smoke—had built a fine life for himself. Why ruin that by admitting the shot-up stranger was really his disreputable, bounty-hunting failure of a brother?

Smoke frowned. "Then why were you talking about me while you were feverish?"

"Hell . . . I don't know. Like you said . . . I was out of my head. Maybe I heard somebody else talking about you . . . before I got shot. I know the name . . . You're some sort of . . . gunfighter."

"That's a reputation I never set out to get." Smoke's face settled into grim lines.

The moment passed quickly, and he smiled again. "Well, I suppose it doesn't really matter. What's important is that you're safe here, and your wounds are starting to heal. Now that you're awake again, you can concentrate on resting and getting better."

"Why would you . . . go to so much trouble for me?" Luke asked. "For a . . . stranger?"

Sally answered his question. "Nobody who needs help is a stranger on the Sugarloaf, Mr. Smith. That's just the way we are around here."

"I can't . . . pay you."

Smoke's face hardened again. "You don't know Sally and me, so we'll let that pass. Are you hungry?"

Luke suddenly realized he was ravenous. It had

probably been quite a while since he'd had any solid food. "Yeah. I could . . . sure eat."

"I have a pot of stew on the stove downstairs," Sally said. "I'll bring some up to you, although it'll be mostly broth starting out."

"That sounds . . . mighty good, ma'am. I'm . . . obliged to you." Luke looked at Smoke. "And to you."

"*De nada,*" Smoke said, then before he could go on, somebody knocked on the open door.

Luke cut his eyes in that direction and saw a tall, gangling cowboy standing in the doorway, holding a battered black hat in one hand.

Smoke looked toward the doorway and asked, "What is it, Pearlie?"

"Hate to bother you, Smoke, but Cal just rode in and told me somebody caved in a bunch of boulders on the Fortuna Ridge waterhole. Covered it up completely. We'll have to move the cows on that range, since they won't have any water."

"Could it have been a natural rockslide?" Smoke asked with a troubled frown.

"Didn't sound like it from what Cal said. He told me he rode up to the top of the ridge and found a place where a bunch of horses stopped this mornin'. He figured some of Baxter's men dabbed their loops on one of them boulders and used their horses to start it rollin'. That's all it would've took. But you can ride up there and take a look for yourself, if you want."

Smoke shook his head. "I trust Cal's opinion. He's a good hand, even if he is pretty young. But there's no way of knowing it was Baxter's men who ruined the waterhole."

"We don't know they were the hombres who took them potshots at us the other day, or ran off that jag of cattle, but who else could it be? You got any other enemies around here right now?"

"Simeon Baxter claims he just wants to be neighbors with us."

Pearlie let out a disgusted snort, then glanced at Sally. "Sorry for almost sayin' what I almost just said," he apologized.

"Don't worry about it," Sally told him with a smile. "I was probably thinking the same thing about Simeon Baxter. All I had to do was look at the man to know he can't be trusted . . . and I think you know that, too, Smoke. You just want to give him the benefit of the doubt."

"Yeah, well, that's starting to wear a little thin," Smoke admitted. "Pearlie, tell the boys to saddle up. We're going to take a ride over to the Baxter spread."

"Now you're talkin'," Pearlie said with undisguised enthusiasm. "I'll tell 'em to oil up their smoke poles, too."

"We're not going to ride in shooting."

"No, but we may have to ride out that way."

Smoke didn't dispute that speculation.

Luke saw the worried glance Sally directed in her husband's direction as Pearlie hurried away down the corridor.

"Is this going to turn into another range war, Smoke?" she asked.

"I hope not. I've had my fill of those, and I know you

have, too. But I'm not going to let Simeon Baxter bull his way in and take over. You know me better than that."

"Yes. I do."

"And you wouldn't want me to be like that, anyway." Smoke went to her and kissed the thick dark hair on top of her head.

"No, I don't suppose I would," she agreed. "But I wish you'd be careful, anyway."

"Always," Smoke said with a grin. He hugged her and then hurried out after Pearlie.

"Sounds like . . . you folks have some trouble around here," Luke acknowledged.

"It's nothing for you to worry about, Mr. Smith," she assured him. "Just some range hog who moved in recently. He's got the loco idea in his head that he can bully Smoke Jensen."

"Sounds like . . . a pretty foolish thing to do."

"It is." Sally sighed. "I just hope this isn't the time Smoke's luck finally changes."

"It's not . . . luck." Luke knew it was the Jensen blood. The sheer determination to do the right thing and stand up for yourself. He had failed in that respect so long ago, and he'd been trying to make up for it ever since. He could take another step on the long road back . . . if he could strap on his guns and stand beside his brother as Smoke faced down this trouble.

But that wasn't possible, at least not at the moment. Luke had lost too much blood, been unconscious for too long, grown too weak. All he could do was lie there and regain his strength.

When he was stronger, he could offer to help Smoke

with his troubles. He wouldn't have to reveal who he really was. He'd just be a grateful stranger returning a favor.

Time enough for that later. He could barely keep his eyes open.

Sally recognized his weariness. "I'll bring you some of that stew later, Mr. Smith. I think you need to rest a bit more before you eat."

"Maybe . . ." Luke murmured, trying to fight off the exhaustion threatening to wash over him. Realizing he couldn't, he gave in and let it claim him.

His last thought was that he wasn't passing out. It wasn't unconsciousness, it was good honest sleep. Healing sleep—just what he needed.

And when he woke up next time, he would be that much closer to being able to help his brother.

CHAPTER 30

The stew Sally Jensen brought up to him tasted as good as it smelled, Luke discovered after the delicious aroma roused him from his slumber. It seemed to possess some magical power, as well, he decided, because after one bowl of it, he felt strength coursing back into his body.

She sat in a chair beside his bed and fed him, and when the bowl was empty, Luke asked, "Did your husband get back from talking to that fellow Baxter?"

Sally had been smiling and cheerful when she came into the room, but a shadow passed over her face at his question. Luke didn't like that he had caused her distress, but he needed to know what was going on.

"They talked," Sally said. "Baxter denied having anything to do with the trouble we've been having. From the way Smoke sounded, it was pretty tense between them for a few minutes, but there was no shooting."

"That's good. Range wars usually don't work out well for either side."

"I know that. Sometimes you have to stand up and fight for what's yours, though. I know that, too."

Luke couldn't argue with her. Earlier, the exact same thought had crossed his mind. He said carefully, "I've heard stories about your husband, Mrs. Jensen. I would think a man would have to be pretty foolish to come in and try to hog Smoke Jensen's range."

"Some men are so arrogant they think they can have whatever they want," she replied with a shrug. "Baxter has plenty on his payroll who are fast with their guns. Smoke just has our ranch hands, although Pearlie had a reputation as a gunman, too, before he gave that up to be Sugarloaf's foreman."

"How did Smoke leave it with Baxter?"

"With a warning that nothing else had better happen."

Luke thought that was unlikely. He knew what Sally meant about the arrogance of some men driving them on, even when the smart thing to do would be to back off. He counted on the outlaws he hunted having the same attitude. They could usually be goaded into doing something stupid that would give him a chance to bring them down.

Sally changed the subject, saying she wanted to check the dressings on Luke's wounds. He let her do so, feeling a little bit embarrassed about having his sister-in-law poking around his body. She didn't know they were related, and he didn't tell her.

"Everything looks fine," she announced when she was finished. "Those old mountain men who found you probably had plenty of experience patching up bullet wounds. They took good care of you and put you on the road to recovery."

"How long do you think it'll be before I'm up and around?"

"Not long," she assured him. "It's mostly just a matter of getting your strength back." Sally hesitated. "I noticed a terrible scar on your back . . ."

"An old war wound," Luke said, trying not to sound too curt but making it clear he didn't want to talk about it.

"Smoke was too young for the war, but just barely. His father and brother fought in it, though."

Luke's interest quickened. "Did they make it through?"

"His father did . . . but he was killed not long afterward by some men responsible for the death of Smoke's brother Luke during the war." She cocked her head to the side as she looked down at him. "You have the same name as him."

Luke suddenly worried that he had probed too much. "There are plenty of men around named Luke."

"Of course there are."

Even though he knew he probably shouldn't, he risked another question. "What happened to those men? The ones responsible for the deaths of Smoke's pa and brother?"

"Smoke found them."

The flat sound of Sally's answer told Luke all he needed to know. Jasper Thornapple's information had been correct. Smoke had settled that long-standing score.

Only it was worse than Luke had ever known. From what Sally had just said, Potter and the others were responsible for the death of his father as well. The confirmation that Emmett Jensen was dead, and had died violently at the hands of trash like that, was like a knife inside Luke for a second.

"Good riddance, I'd say," he forced out.

"Yes, indeed," Sally agreed. She brightened. "You get some more rest now. Let that stew do its work."

"I'll do that," Luke promised. He leaned his head back against the pillows and closed his eyes. He owed a debt to Smoke Jensen for killing those four no-good thieves. He would find a way to pay that debt, he promised himself.

Even if it had to be as Luke Smith.

A couple nights later, Smoke brought him a cup of coffee and a plate of bear sign. Luke was glad to see him. After being unconscious for so long, once he began to get his strength back he wasn't nearly as sleepy.

"Need me to break pieces off this and feed 'em to you?" Smoke asked as he settled down in the chair beside the bed.

"I think I can handle a pastry." Luke sat up, moved the pillows behind him, and then proved it by taking one of the doughnuts off the plate.

"You sound like a cultured man, Smith."

Luke managed not to laugh. "Far from it. I just have a taste for reading. I suppose I've picked up a few things from that. Most of my life has been spent about as far from what people would consider culture as you can imagine."

"I have some books downstairs. Would you like me to bring a few of them up here for you?"

"That would be very much appreciated," Luke said.

"In the meantime, you can tell me about all those dead men scattered around the place where my friends found you."

Luke smiled. "You've been wanting to ask me about that ever since I woke up, haven't you?"

"That old prospector said they were outlaws. Somebody named Solomon Burke and his gang. Supposed to be pretty bad hombres. Did you kill all of them by yourself?"

"Seemed like the thing to do, especially since they were trying to kill me at the time."

"If they were using that place for a hideout, that means they didn't ambush you. It was the other way around, wasn't it?"

"I was hunting them, yes," Luke admitted with a nod. "I was after the bounty on them." He had to laugh. "I'll bet that old pelican claimed it for himself, though."

"I wouldn't be surprised," Smoke said. "So you're a bounty hunter."

"That's right."

"There was a time I had a price on my head." Smoke shrugged. "But I suppose a fella's got to do whatever is necessary for him to get by."

"I don't blame you for not being fond of the idea of

having a bounty hunter under your roof. For what it's worth, all the men I've gone after were bad sorts, the kind of men who really need to be behind bars or six feet under."

"As far as you know," Smoke said.

Luke inclined his head in acknowledgment of that point. "I believe I'm right, but no one knows everything about the other people in this world."

"That's true. For example, you strike me as the sort of man who has secrets of his own, Smith."

Luke didn't like the turn in the conversation. "You already know all that's worth knowing about me, Jensen."

It sounded odd to him, saying his own name like that.

"I'm not sure," Smoke said. "There's something about you . . . something I can't put my finger on. I feel like I ought to know you. Are you sure we've never met?"

"Positive." Luke hoped he kept the tension out of his voice. "I know who you are, but I never heard the name Smoke Jensen until a couple years ago." That was true, as far as it went.

Smoke made a face. "I never asked for a reputation as a gunfighter. I just wanted to be left alone. But then I found out some men had done my family wrong—skunks who had be dealt with—and I set out to do it. I'd already met an old mountain man named Preacher. He taught me how to handle a gun. Taught me everything worth knowing that my pa hadn't already taught me. Along the way I got married to a fine woman, even had a son, but some other evil lowlifes took that family away from me. I met a young fella named Matt Cavanaugh and took him under my wing the way Preacher did with me. Matt's the same as my brother now, even goes by the name Matt Jensen. Then Sally came along—" Smoke stopped and shook his head.

"I don't know why I started going on about all of that. You're not interested in my checkered past, as they say in the dime novels. But it might be boring enough to help you sleep."

"I wasn't bored," Luke said honestly. In fact, he had a hard time keeping the emotion out of his voice. Hearing about his brother's life stirred up a lot of feelings inside him. He wished he had gone home after the war, that he had been at Kirby's side when trouble came to call. Things might have turned out completely different.

But he hadn't been able to return. He'd been a wanted fugitive, and didn't know Kirby—Smoke—had gone through the same sort of ordeal for a while.

All that was behind them. Luke couldn't think of a single reason why he couldn't tell Smoke who he really was.

And suddenly that was exactly what he wanted to do.

I've been a damned fool all these years, he told himself.

As soon as Thornapple told him the gunfighter named Smoke Jensen had killed Potter, Stratton, Richards, and Casey, Luke should have gone looking for him and found out the truth. That blasted prideful stubbornness of his had stolen two more years out of his life, two years he could have spent with his brother . . . or at least knowing he had a brother.

The coffee and the bear sign were forgotten. Luke wasn't sure exactly how he would go about it, but it was long past time for the truth to come out.

And it might have, if fate hadn't chosen that moment for the sudden, harsh sound of gunfire to fill the night.

CHAPTER 31

Smoke was on his feet instantly, blowing out the lamp on the bedside table and stepping to the window to flick back the curtain so he could look out without being silhouetted. "Masked raiders shooting up the place," he snapped, dropping the curtain.

Luke opened his mouth to say he wanted to help, but it was too late. Smoke was through the doorway and gone, leaving Luke sitting in the bed listening to the sounds of battle as gunmen attacked his brother's ranch.

Not while I can do anything about it, by God, Luke thought as resolve stiffened his muscles. Especially since his revolvers were within reach.

Earlier, he had asked Sally where his guns were. She'd tried to tell him not to worry about that, but he had persisted, learning his gun belt and the twin Remingtons were in a wardrobe at the side of the room, along with his clothes. His Winchester was downstairs.

He didn't think he could handle stairs, but he could get to his revolvers. He pushed the covers aside, swung his legs out of bed, and stood up.

A wave of dizziness swept through him. He fought it off as his eyes adjusted to the moonlight filtering through the curtains. Tightly bandaged as he was, he found he could move around without his wounds hurting too much. Wearing only those bandages and the bottom half of a pair of long underwear, he made his way to the wardrobe and opened it.

It had been too long, he thought as his hands closed around the smooth walnut grips of the guns. For a decade and a half, the weapons he carried had been the closest friends he had. That might not be true anymore—he had a brother again—but it still felt mighty good to heft the Remingtons as he turned around and walked back to the open window.

The night breezes were tainted with the acrid bite of powder smoke as Luke thrust the curtains aside and looked out. Riders with bandannas tied over their faces galloped through the open area between the ranch house and the bunkhouse. The guns in their hands spat flame and lead as they sent shots in both directions.

Return fire came from the Sugarloaf's defenders, but they were heavily outnumbered. Luke figured there were at least thirty raiders in the yard.

He could improve the odds a little, he thought as he thrust the right-hand Remington out the window, drew a bead on one of the riders, and fired. The masked man rocked back in his saddle and had to drop his gun and grab the saddle horn to keep from toppling off his mount.

One low-down sacker out of the fight, Luke told himself. He eared back the Remington's hammer and shifted his aim to another of the masked men.

He got off several rounds, dropping a couple more men, before the raiders noticed the shots coming from the second-floor window of the ranch house. A few twisted in their saddles and flung their guns up to fire in that direction. Luke was forced to reel back from the window as glass shattered and bullets whipped through the opening.

He waited until the barrage stopped and then moved forward again, kneeling at the window so the wall gave him some cover. It looked thick enough to stop most bullets.

Still galloping back and forth, the raiders continued their barrage, but the deadly accurate fire of the defenders was starting to take a toll. Luke added to it by triggering both revolvers and spraying bullets among the marauders. Gun thunder rolled from the Remingtons.

The masked killers finally had enough. The one who seemed to be in command wheeled his horse and yelled, "Let's get out of here!"

Those still mounted—some badly wounded—followed him as he galloped off into the darkness, leaving seven or eight bodies scattered on the ground.

Luke didn't stand up immediately. He didn't want to catch a final wild slug thrown through the shattered window.

Also, he was tired. When he was sure they were all gone, he placed his left-hand gun on the floor and used that hand to brace himself as he leaned forward and drew in several deep breaths. The bandages around his midsection prevented him from breathing too deeply, but he did the best he could.

The door opened behind him. Sally Jensen stood in the doorway, wearing a nightdress and a coat slung around her shoulders. "Mr. Smith! Are you all right?"

Luke looked back over his shoulder at her, noticing immediately the rifle in her hands. He figured she had been right in the middle of the fight downstairs. "I'm fine."

Feeling a little stronger, he picked up the gun and pushed himself to his feet.

"Smoke said he thought he heard shots coming from up here. You really shouldn't have gotten out of bed."

"After all you folks have done for me, I wasn't going to just lie there while you were under attack," Luke argued. "That's not the way I'm built."

Sally smiled. "I know. We haven't been acquainted for long, Mr. Smith, but you remind me a little of my husband. He can't turn his back on a fight, either."

It was the Jensen blood, Luke thought, but he couldn't say that. Instead he asked, "Was anybody hurt?"

Sally's smile was replaced by a look of grim anger. "We're fine in here, but Smoke's gone out to the bunkhouse to see about the men. I'm worried some of them were wounded."

Luke became uncomfortably aware that he was standing in his underwear with a pair of empty guns in his hands. He wasn't sure which of those things bothered him more. He didn't think the masked raiders would double back and launch another attack, but the possibility couldn't be ruled out entirely. First things first, he decided. "I'd better reload. Just in case."

"No, what you'd better do is get back in that bed and let me check your dressings. I want to make sure none of your wounds have broken open again."

Luke thought about it for a second, then chuckled. "I always try not to argue with a woman, especially one holding a loaded rifle."

"That's a good policy," Sally told him, smiling again.

He was back in bed and she had taken a look at his bandages, determining that none of the wounds were bleeding again by the time Smoke came into the room with a Colt in his hand. Sally turned toward him with a worried frown on her face.

"Two men were killed," Smoke reported. "Steve Rankin and Charlie Moss."

Sally cringed. "Oh, no. What about the wounded?"

"A bullet busted Phil Weston's arm. Other than that just some nicks and scratches." Smoke's face was set in hard, bleak lines. "But they killed two men who rode for me, and I'm not going to let Baxter get away with that."

"You don't know they were Baxter's men," Sally maintained.

"Yes, I do. I took a look at the bodies of the men they left behind. I remember seeing all of them at Baxter's place when I was over there a couple days ago."

"Then you can go tell Monte about it and let the law handle this," Sally suggested.

Smoke shook his head. "I'll send a rider to Big Rock tomorrow to tell Monte what happened, but Pearlie, the rest of the men, and I will be heading for Baxter's ranch."

Sally opened her mouth, and for a second Luke thought she was going to argue with her husband. But then she nodded. "You're right, Smoke. We need to stomp our own snakes."

Smoke grunted. "Damn right we do." His expression eased a little as he looked at Luke. "Are you all right, Smith?"

Luke nodded. "I'm fine."

"You were burning some powder up here, weren't you? I heard the shots."

Luke grinned. "Like I told your wife, I owe you folks too much to sit by and do nothing. If you'll let me borrow a horse, I'll ride over to Baxter's with you in the morning for the showdown."

"Oh, now, I don't think that would be a good idea at all," Sally protested. "You're not in good enough shape to ride yet, Mr. Smith."

"I agree with Sally," Smoke added. "But I appreciate the offer. I'm obliged to you for taking a hand tonight, too. You're probably responsible for some of those men we downed."

Luke knew he was, but didn't say anything. He'd never been one to boast.

Smoke went on. "You just keep recuperating. I'll handle Baxter."

Luke nodded. "All right." He looked at Sally. "I'd be obliged, though, if you'd bring my gun belt over here. I sure don't like having empty guns." He smiled. "Gives a man the fantods."

* * *

Pearlie, Calvin Woods, and the rest of the Sugarloaf hands were so upset about the deaths of their friends they had wanted to charge over to Simeon Baxter's ranch right away and settle the score. But Smoke had decided to wait for daylight, thinking Baxter might have an ambush set up for them.

He mentioned that reasoning to Luke early the next morning, before dawn actually, when he stopped by Luke's room.

"That's good thinking," Luke agreed. "I've ridden into more ambushes than I should have, just because I was too eager or too careless. Gunfighting is almost as much about thinking as it is about shooting."

"You sound like a man speaking from bitter experience," Smoke commented.

"Is there any other kind?"

Smoke hefted the rifle he had carried into the room. "I brought your Winchester up. I don't expect you to need it, but I thought you might feel better having it close at hand."

Luke smiled. "Thanks. You'd better not put it on the bed, though. Mrs. Jensen wouldn't like it if you got gun oil on her sheets."

"Wouldn't be the first time," Smoke said with a grin as he placed the rifle on the floor next to the bed. He didn't look like a man who was about to ride off and fight a battle to the death with a ruthless enemy. But like Luke, life on the frontier had taught Smoke how to live in the moment.

"Still wish I was going with you," Luke said.

"I know that." Smoke stuck out a hand. "And I appreciate it."

They shook. Again, Luke wished he could tell Smoke who he really was, but he had decided that could wait. Smoke already had enough on his mind without the shock of finding out the brother he had thought to be dead for the past fifteen years was really alive.

"Sally will be up with some breakfast in a little bit." Smoke lifted a hand in farewell and left the room.

Luke looked at the holstered revolvers and coiled shell belt on the table beside the bed, then pushed the covers back and swung his feet to the floor. He stood up, feeling a lot steadier than he had the night before. Getting back into action seemed to have had a bracing effect on him.

With the approach of dawn, the sky outside was lighter. He went over to the wardrobe, opened it, and could see his clothes hanging on hooks inside the wardrobe. As he pulled on the black shirt and buttoned it up he realized it was clean. Sally had cleaned and patched his clothes. He took the black trousers off the hook, braced himself with one hand on the wardrobe and hung the pants as low as possible with his other hand. Gingerly, he put one leg, then the other into the pants and pulled them up around his hips.

He picked up his boots and clean socks from the floor of the wardrobe and carried them to the chair. Carefully, he lowered himself down. Taking a big breath, he crossed one leg over the other and pulled on a sock. He grimaced. One sock, and he needed to rest before crossing the other leg and pulling on the other sock. It had taken more effort than he had anticipated. After another moment or two, he stood and stuck his feet into his boots. It wasn't easy, but he managed without doing any damage to his wounds.

Being dressed made him feel even better, but he wasn't *fully* dressed yet, he thought with a wry smile as he turned toward the bedside table. He picked up the cross-draw rig and buckled it on.

A footstep sounded at the doorway. "What in the world are you doing, Mr. Smith?" Sally stood with her hands on her hips.

Luke turned toward her. "I was thinking I might come downstairs for breakfast for a change."

"I'm not sure that's wise."

"I've got to get up and start moving around again sometime. The sooner I do, the sooner I'll get better."

She gave him a stern look for a moment, then shook her head and laughed. "I've seen Smoke act exactly the same way, and arguing with him never did any good, either. I swear, if I didn't know better—" She stopped short, and a puzzled frown came over her face.

To keep her from thinking too much, Luke said hurriedly, "If you'd just pick up that rifle and hand it to me . . . I'm not sure I'm ready to do a lot of bending yet."

"All right." She went over to the bed, picked up the Winchester, and gave it to him. "You want your hat, too? It's in the wardrobe."

"A gentleman doesn't wear his hat indoors. I know I may not look like one, but I strive for a certain standard of civilized behavior."

"No offense, Mr. Smith, but you're an odd man."

"So I've been told."

Keeping the rifle in one hand and the other on the wall for support, Luke followed Sally down the stairs. As they reached the kitchen, he heard the sound of numerous horses leaving the ranch.

Her face tightened at the sound. Smoke and the other men were riding off for the showdown with Simeon Baxter and his hired gunmen. She knew her husband was going into danger, but what woman ever truly got used to it?

Sally brought Luke a cup of coffee and a plate of flapjacks, bacon, and eggs, and he dug in with gusto. His appetite had come back as strong as ever, and Sally's good cooking had already put some meat back on his bones.

As he ate, he asked, "Did Smoke get any sleep last night?"

"Not much," Sally admitted. "He was upset about the men who were killed. He was up early this morning, well before dawn, digging graves for them in the little graveyard we have here on the ranch. Pearlie went out to help him, but Smoke would have done it by himself."

"He's a good man," Luke said.

"The best I've ever met, by far," Sally agreed. "And I thank God every day that the two of us found each other."

Luke would have liked to think he had something to do with the way Smoke had turned out, but that wasn't likely. Kirby had been only twelve years old when Luke went off to war, so he hadn't had much chance to mold the boy into the man he had grown up to be. Their father had more to do with that, along with the old mountain man called Preacher. Luke hoped to hear a lot more about him before his visit to the Sugarloaf was over.

And it was only a visit, no doubt about that. Even if he told Smoke the truth and Smoke invited him to stay at the ranch, Luke knew that wasn't going to happen. Smoke sure as hell didn't owe him a home, and after all the years of drifting, Luke didn't think he was even capable of settling down.

After breakfast, he said, "I think I'll go sit out on the front porch for a while, and take the rifle with me. I believe the sun might be good for me."

"You're probably right. I'll clean up in here, and then I might come out and join you." Sally paused, then added, "I'm really curious about something, Luke . . . but we can talk about that later."

He frowned as he made his way to the porch. He had an idea what Sally wanted to talk about, and it wasn't a conversation he wanted to have just yet. Not until he'd discussed it with Smoke, anyway.

She might not give him any choice, though, he thought as he carefully sat down in one of the rocking chairs on the porch and slowly cocked his right ankle on his left knee. After the way she had taken care of him, he didn't think he could bring himself to lie to her.

His head was so full of those thoughts he almost didn't notice the wink of sunlight on something metal in the trees about two hundred yards away from the ranch house. But his instincts still worked and shouted a warning to him. He hadn't stayed alive by ignoring what his gut told him.

He threw himself forward, landing on the porch on his knees, just as a rifle cracked in the distance. He felt the wind-rip of a bullet passing close beside his ear.

CHAPTER 32

Two hundred yards was too far for a handgun, so Luke drew his rifle and fired a shot in the direction of the hidden rifleman, aiming high so the bullet would carry a little farther. Ignoring the pain lancing through his side, he rolled toward the doorway as another shot blasted. He didn't want the wound on his side to break open and start bleeding again, but that pain was better than being a sitting duck.

The slug struck the rocking chair he'd been sitting in, and a chunk of wood flew off the back of it.

"Mr. Smith!" Sally cried as she jerked the door open. "Luke!"

He dived at her, tackling her around the knees and taking her down as a bullet plowed into the door. They scrambled farther into the house, and Luke kicked the door closed behind them.

"Luke!" Sally gasped. "I heard shots! What—"

A rumble of hoofbeats sounded outside, and Luke knew Smoke had miscalculated . . . and so had he. Neither had realized Baxter's attack on the ranch the night before was just a feint. Baxter had counted on some of his men being killed, and on Smoke recognizing them. He'd been trying to goad Smoke into rushing over to the neighboring spread and taking most, if not all, of the Sugarloaf crew with him.

"It's Baxter," Luke told Sally in a taut, grim voice. "He's come for you. He figures with you as his prisoner, Smoke won't have any choice but to do what Baxter tells him."

"Men have tried that before," Sally informed him. "Smoke killed them. He'll kill Baxter."

"More than likely," Luke agreed as the rush of hoofbeats came to a stop outside the house. "If I don't kill him first." He jerked his head toward the stairs. "Get up there. I'll stop them."

"You're one man against two dozen, and you're wounded!" Sally protested. "You can't—"

"Go!" Luke told her as he climbed to his feet. He didn't have anything to lose, making him more dangerous than any number of men Baxter could muster.

Sally didn't understand that. She stood up beside him, and suddenly threw her arms around him and came up on her toes to brush a kiss across his gaunt cheek. "Luke," she whispered, "I don't know how it's possible, but I think I know—"

"Just go," he cut in, "while you still can."

A man shouted orders outside. The gunnies knew Baxter wanted Sally alive, but they also knew at least one man with a gun was inside. Luke figured they wouldn't come in shooting for fear of hurting her, but they would rush the place, counting on the force of numbers to overwhelm any opposition.

Sally squeezed his arm and turned to run to the stairs. As she started up, Luke faced the door, squaring himself to the opening and bracing his feet. He had both guns drawn and pointed at the doorway, waiting grimly to start their thunderous song.

He didn't have long to wait. Something crashed against the door and it flew open. Hard-faced men with guns in their hands rushed into the room, and at the sight of the tall, lean man dressed in black waiting for them, they raised the weapons to open fire.

They were too late. The revolvers in Luke's hands were already spouting flaming death.

As it always did at such moments, everything else faded away for Luke. The world receded until there was nothing left in the universe except him and the men he was trying to kill . . . the men who were trying to kill him. The roar of guns was like the bellow of great primordial beasts, the clouds of powder smoke rolling through the room like the eruption of ancient volcanoes, and the blood flowing the bright crimson of man like going all the way back to the dawn of time.

Luke didn't feel the smash of bullets like he expected. He was still on his feet and fighting, and that was all that mattered to him. Men fell before his guns like wheat before a scythe.

Vaguely, he became aware of shots pealing out from other places. There seemed to be a battle going on *outside* the ranch house, as well as a rifle blasting somewhere close by.

Suddenly, as the hammers of both Remingtons clicked on empty chambers, only one enemy faced him, a tall, burly man with a rough-hewn face and silver hair under a black Stetson. The man's clothes were better and more expensive than those of the others, and Luke had a hunch he was facing Simeon Baxter.

That was confirmed a second later when the man pointed a fancy, nickel-plated revolver at Luke and yelled, "I don't know who you are, you lousy interloper, but you've ruined all my plans! Now you're gonna die, you and that skirt both!"

Luke glanced over and realized Sally was standing beside him, holding the Winchester. "I'm empty. You?"

"Me, too." But she was smiling, unafraid.

Luke realized why when a powerful voice bellowed from outside, "Baxter!"

The would-be cattle baron whirled around. A shot blasted from his gun, soaring harmlessly into the air, and was answered by a pair of crashing reports from a Colt. The bullets drove Baxter through the doorway and spilled him onto his back, almost at the feet of Luke and Sally. He writhed in pain, pawing at his chest with blood welling through his fingers, and ended up on his side looking up at Luke. "Who . . . who are you?" he gasped.

Smoke appeared in the doorway. "His name's Luke Jensen. He's my brother."

Baxter's head sagged back, an ugly rattle came from his throat, and he died.

Normally the first thing Luke did when he held empty guns was reload them, but he was just too tired. He slid both guns back into their holsters and looked himself over, expecting to see more blood on his clothes. It was a shock to realize he didn't seem to be hit. With all the lead that had been flying around the room, he didn't see how it was possible, but he didn't feel any new pains, just a dull ache in his side from that old wound.

Smoke pouched his iron and rushed across the room to draw Sally into his arms. He cupped a hand behind her head and kissed her. "Are you all right?" he asked when he lifted his mouth from hers a moment later.

"I'm fine . . . thanks to Luke. Smoke, he's—"

"My brother. I know. I can't figure out how it's possible, but there's no doubt in my mind." With his arms still around Sally, Smoke turned his head to look at Luke. "All I had to do was see him standing there with the dead men he'd killed defending you heaped at his feet, and I knew." He shifted so that he could hold out a hand to Luke. "Welcome home . . . brother."

Luke didn't hesitate. Reaching out, he clasped his brother's hand.

Pearlie and the other hands had dragged the corpses out of the living room and dumped sand on the floor to soak up the blood. Cleaning it all up was going to take a while.

In the kitchen, Smoke filled Sally and Luke in on what had happened after he left the ranch. "I figured out what Baxter was up to when we were about halfway to his ranch. We turned around and got back here as fast as we could, with me kicking myself for being a damned fool the whole way."

"You were upset about your men being killed last night," Luke said. "It's understandable you wanted to have a showdown with Baxter."

"And that's what he was counting on." Smoke shook his head. "I'm just glad we got back in time."

"So am I," Luke said with a wry smile. "I didn't have enough bullets to kill all of Baxter's men."

"Maybe not, but from the sound of it I expected to find a small army trying to fight them off inside the house, not just the two of you."

"Luke did most of it." Sally gave credit where credit was due. "I never saw anybody handle guns like that, Smoke . . . well, nobody but you, that is."

"It's a skill that seems to run in the family." Smoke took a sip of his coffee and fixed Luke with an intent look across the table. "I heard you were killed fighting Yankees in the wilderness, and then told later you were murdered by those varmints who stole that shipment of Confederate gold. What's the real story, Luke?"

"I suppose if anyone has a right to hear it, it's you." Luke looked away. "Some of it's not too pretty, though."

"I want to know anyway."

"Of course."

For the next half hour, Luke told them everything that had happened since that fateful night in Richmond with the Yankee artillery pounding away at the city. He didn't leave out anything. When he was finished, he glanced at Sally and saw tears shining in her eyes.

"You considered yourself a failure because those terrible men ambushed you?" She wiped at a tear.

"They stole the gold I was supposed to protect. They killed my friends."

"And they nearly killed you! My God, Luke, that wasn't your fault. You could have gone back home to your family."

He shrugged. "I saw it differently." He knew from the look in Smoke's eyes that his brother understood.

"That wasn't all. I was wanted for murder in Georgia."

"Well, that just wasn't right," Sally declared. "You were only trying to protect that girl and her grandfather."

"Yes, but I figured I'd caused enough trouble for them."

"*You* didn't cause the trouble." Sally was starting to sound a little exasperated with him. "You saved them from it!" She blew out her breath and shook her head. "You stiff-necked Jensen boys! Matt's the same way, and he's not even a blood relative. You all think you have to be perfect and that you can never let anybody down."

"Well, that's something to aspire to, isn't it?" Smoke asked with a faint smile.

"Maybe . . . but it's not human." Sally took Smoke's hand, then reached across the table and clasped Luke's hand, too. "At least the two of you are back together, after all these years. Now I understand why you seemed so familiar to me, Luke. Even though you and Smoke don't look that much alike, I was seeing him in you. I knew there was something special about you all along."

"That's nice to hear," he told her as he squeezed her hand.

"And you have a home again at last," Sally added.

Luke didn't say anything. Glancing at Smoke, he saw the knowledge in his brother's eyes and realized Smoke knew he wasn't going to stay on permanently. Luke could never adjust to that sort of life. The wanderlust was just too strong in him.

Anyway, he still had outlaws to hunt down.

But not right away.

At that moment, he was content to sit in a quiet kitchen with his family and know that, while the place would never be his home, it was as close to one as he would ever come.

EPILOGUE

Three weeks later, on a cool morning with streamers of fog hanging around the mountain peaks in the distance, Luke saddled the fine horse Smoke had insisted was his and led the animal out of the barn, leading a packhorse behind him. He had thought he might be able to slip away from the ranch without anybody noticing until he was gone, but he supposed that was too much to hope for.

Smoke stood waiting for him. "You don't have to go, you know."

"Yeah, I do." Luke checked the cinches one more time. "I've been talking to Monte Carson, and he tells me that Badger McCoy was spotted up in Laramie a few days ago."

Monte Carson was the local sheriff in Big Rock, and he had a whole desk drawer full of wanted posters he had let Luke look through.

"Badger McCoy," Smoke repeated.

"Train robber. The reward's only eight hundred dollars, but I have a hunch I can get more out of the railroad if I'm able to recover some of the loot McCoy's stolen, too."

"So you're bound and determined to go on risking your life hunting down fugitives?"

"It's what I do," Luke said. If anybody could understand that, it was Smoke.

After a moment, Smoke nodded. "Sally won't be happy you didn't tell her good-bye."

Luke shook his head. "Not good at that."

"I know. I'll try to explain it to her. And I'll tell her you promised to come back. You will, won't you? I want you to meet Preacher and Matt."

"I'd like that." Luke put out his hand. "Next time."

"Next time," Smoke agreed as he shook hands.

Luke swung up into the saddle, but before he could ride away, Smoke went on, "There's one more thing."

"What's that?"

"Forget about calling yourself Luke Smith. You've got a name. You should use it."

Luke frowned. "You really want people to know me as Luke Jensen? A bounty hunter?"

"You're a good man and you're my brother." Smoke looked up at Luke. "That's all I care about. Jensen's a proud name, and I think you should wear it."

Luke thought about it for a moment and then nodded. "All right. If that's what you want, I can do that."

"Good. So long, Luke."

Lifting a hand in farewell, Luke turned his horses and rode out of the ranch yard.

"Don't forget!" Smoke called after him. "You always have a home here if you want it!"

Luke waved, but didn't look back as he rode north. *Home*, he thought. He hadn't had one of those for a long, long time. The idea would take some getting used to.

But it was a pretty thing to think about. It surely was.

Turn the page for an exciting preview of

**SAVAGE TEXAS:
A GOOD DAY TO DIE**

In Hangtree, Texas, any day could be your last.

On the heels of the Civil War,
the town is drawing gamblers, fast women,
and faster gunmen. Amid the brawls and
shooting, the land grabbing and card sharking,
two men barely hold the boomtown together:
Yankee Sam Heller and Texan Johnny Cross.
Heller and Cross can't stand the sight of each other . . .
and Hangtree needs them more than ever.

Comanche War Chief Red Hand leads a
horde of warriors on a horrific path of bloodshed
and destruction, with Hangtree sitting right in his path.
For a town bitterly divided, and for Heller and Cross,
the time has come to unite and stand shoulder to
shoulder—and fight, live, or die for their
little slice of hell called Hangtree.

CHAPTER 1

On a night in late May 1866, Comanche Chief Red Hand took up the Fire Lance to proclaim the opening of the warm weather raiding season—a time of torture, plunder, and murder. For warlike Comanche braves, the best time of the year.

Six hundred and more Comanche men, women, and children were camped near a stream in a valley north of the Texas panhandle, on land between the Canadian and Arkansas rivers. The site, Arrowhead Rock, lay deep in the heart of the vast, untamed territory of Comancheria, home grounds of the tribal nation.

The gathering was made up mostly of two main subgroups, the Bison Eyes and the Dawn Hawks, along with a number of lesser clans, relations, and allies.

Red Hand, a Bison Eye, was a rising star who had led a number of successful raids in recent seasons past. Many braves, especially those of the younger generation, were eager to attach themselves to him.

Others had come to hear him out and make up their own minds about whether or not to follow his lead. Not a few had come to keep a wary eye on him and see what he was up to.

All brought their families with them, from the oldest squaws to the youngest babes in arms. They brought their tipis and personal belongings, horse herds, and even dogs.

The Comanche were a mobile folk, nomads who followed the buffalo herds across the Great Plains. They spent much of their lives on horseback and were superb riders. They were fierce fighters, arguably the most dangerous Indian tribe in the West. They gloried in the title of Lords of the Southern Plains.

Farther southwest—much farther—lay the lands of the Apache, relentless desert warriors of fearsome repute. During their seasonal wanderings Comanches raided Apaches as the opportunity presented itself, but the Apache did not strike north to raid Comancheria. This stark fact spoke volumes about the relative deadliness of the two.

The camp on the valley stream was unusual in its size, the tribesmen generally preferring to travel in much smaller groups. The temporary settlement had come into being in response to Red Hand's invitation, taken by his emissaries to the various interested parties. Invitation, not summons.

A high-spirited individual, the Comanche brave was jealous of his freedom and rights. His allegiance was freely given and just as freely withdrawn. Warriors of great deeds were respected, but not slavishly submitted to. A leader gained followers by ability and success; incompetence and failure inevitably incited mass desertions.

It was a mark of Red Hand's prowess that so many had come to hear his words.

The campsite at Arrowhead Rock lay on a well-watered patch of grassy ground. Cone-shaped tipis massed along the stream banks. Smoke from many cooking fires hazed the area. The tipis had been given over to women and children; the men were elsewhere. Packs of half-wild, half-starved dogs chased each other around the campgrounds, snarling and yapping.

The horse herds were picketed nearby. Comanches reckoned their wealth in horses, as white men did in gold. The greater the thief, the more he was respected and envied by his fellows.

For such a conclave, an informal truce reigned, whereby the braves of various clans held in check their craving to steal each other's horses . . . mostly.

North of the camp, a long bowshot away, the land dipped into a shallow basin, a hollow serving as a kind of natural amphitheater. It was spacious enough to comfortably hold the two hundred and more warriors assembled there under a horned moon. No females were present at the basin.

To a man, they were in prime physical condition. There was no place in the Comanche nation for weaklings. Men were warriors, doing the hunting, raiding, fighting, and killing—sometimes dying. Women did all the other work, the drudgery of the tribe.

The braves were high-spirited, raucous. Much horseplay and boasting of big brags occurred. It had been a long winter; they looked forward to the wild free life of raiding south with eager anticipation. An air of keen interest hung over them as they waited impatiently for Red Hand to take the fore.

At the northern center rim of the basin stood a triangular rock about twenty feet high. Shaped like an arrowhead planted point-up in the ground, it gave the site its name. Among Comanche warrior society, the arrowhead was an emblem of power and danger, giving the stone an aura of magical potency.

A fire blazed near its base. Yellow-red tongues of flame leaped upward, wreathed with spirals of blue-gray smoke. Between the fire and the rock, a stout wooden stake eight feet tall had been driven into the ground.

The braves faced the rock, Bison Eyes grouped on the left, Dawn Hawks on the right. Both clans were strong, numerous, and well respected. Nearly evenly matched in numbers and fighting prowess, they were great rivals.

A stir went through the crowd. Something was happening.

A handful of shadowy figures stepped out from behind the rock, coming into view of those assembled in the hollow. They ranked themselves in a line behind the fire, forming up like a guard of honor in advance of their leader. Underlit by the flames' red glare, they could be seen and recognized.

Mighty warriors all, men of renown, they made up Red Hand's inner circle of trusted advisors and henchmen, his lieutenants.

Ten Scalps was a giant of a man, one of the strongest warriors in the Comanche nation. He'd taken ten scalps as a youth during his first raid. After that he stopped counting.

Sun Dog, his face wider than it was long, had dark eyes glinting like chips of black glass.

Little Bells, with twin strings of tiny silver bells plaited into his lion's mane of shoulder-length hair, stood tall.

Badger was short and squat, with tremendous upper body strength and oversized, pawlike hands.

Black Robe, clad in a garment he'd stripped from a Mexican priest he'd slain and scalped, was next. Part long coat, part cape, the tattered garment gave him a weird, batlike outline.

The cadre's appearance was greeted by the crowd with appreciative whoops, shrieks, and howls. The five stood motionless, faces impassive, arms folded across their chests. They held the pose for a long time, their stillness contrasting with the crowd's mounting excitement.

After a moment, a lone man emerged from behind the rock into the firelight. He wore a war bonnet and carried a lance.

The Bison Eyes clansmen vented loud, full-throated cries of welcome, for the newcomer was none other than their own great man, Red Hand. But Red Hand's entrance was almost as well received by the rival Dawn Hawks.

He was a man of power, a doer of great deeds. He had stature. He had stolen many horses, enslaved many captives, killed many foes. With skill and daring he had won much fame throughout the plains and deep into Mexico.

Circling around to the front of Arrowhead Rock, Red Hand scrambled up onto a ledge four feet above the ground. Facing the assembled, he showed himself to them.

Roughly thirty years of age, he was in full, vigorous prime, broad-shouldered, deep-chested, and long-limbed. Thick coal-black hair, full and unbound, framed a long, sharp-featured face. His eyes were deep-set, burning.

He was crowned with a splendid eagle-feather war bonnet whose train reached down his back. He wore a simple breechcloth and knee-length antelope skin boots. A hunting knife hung on his hip.

From fingertips to wrists, the backs of his hands were painted with greasy red coloring, markings that were stripes, wavy lines, crescent moons, and arrows. His right hand clenched the lance, holding it upright with its base resting atop the rocky ledge. Ten feet long, it was tipped with a wickedly sharp, barbed spear blade.

This was no Comanche war spear. He had taken it in Mexico the summer before from a mounted lancer, one of the legions of crack cavalry troops sent by France's Emperor Napoleon III to protect his ally Maximilian of Austria-Hungary.

Red Hand knew nothing of the crowned heads of Europe nor of Napoleon III's mad dream of a New World Empire that had prompted him to install a Hapsburg royal on the throne of Mexico. Red Hand knew killing, though, dodging the lancer's lunging spear thrust, dragging him down off his fine horse, and cutting his throat.

Word of this enviable weapon spread far and wide among the Comanches. More than a prize, the lance became a talisman of Red Hand's prestige. It evoked no small interest, with many braves pressing forward, craning for a better look.

Red Hand lifted the weapon, shaking it triumphantly in the air. It was met by a fresh round of appreciative whoops.

Notably lacking in enthusiasm was Wahtonka, a Dawn Hawks chief standing in the front rank of his clan. He, too, was a great man, with many daring deeds of blood to his credit. But he was fifty years old, a generation older than Red Hand.

Of medium height, Wahtonka was lean and wiry, all bone, sinews, and tendons. His hair, parted in the middle of his scalp, was worn in two long, gray-flecked braids. His face was deeply lined, his mouth downturned, dour.

Red Hand's enthusiastic audience did nothing to lighten his mood. Others were not so constrained in their appreciation of the upstart, Wahtonka noticed, including many of his own Dawn Hawks. Too many.

The young men were loud in their whooping and hollering, and a number of older, more established warriors also stamped and shouted for Red Hand.

Wahtonka cut a side glance at Laughing Bear standing beside him. Laughing Bear was of his generation, himself a mighty warrior, though with few deeds in recent years to his credit. He was Wahtonka's kinsman and most trusted ally.

Laughing Bear was heavyset, with sloping shoulders and a blocky torso, thick in the middle. His features were broad and lumpish. The gaze of his small round eyes was bleak. He looked as if he had not laughed in years. Red Hand's appearance this night had not struck forth in him any spirit of mirth. He shared Wahtonka's grave concerns about the growing Red Hand problem.

The hero of the hour basked for a moment in the gusty reception given him, before motioning for silence. The Comanches quieted down, though scattered shrieks and screams continued to rise from some of the more excitable types. The clamor subsided, though the crowd kept up a continual buzzing.

"Brothers! I went in search of a vision," Red Hand began, his voice big and booming. "I went in search of a vision—and I have found it!"

The warriors' cheers echoed across the nighted prairie.

Red Hand's face split in a wicked grin, showing strong white teeth. "In the old times life was good. The game was thick. Birds filled the skies. The buffalo were many, covering the ground as far as the eye could see." He had a far-off look in his eyes, as if gazing through the distance of space and time in search of such onetime abundance.

He frowned, his gaze hardening, dark passions clouding his features. "Then came the white men," he said, voice thick, almost choking on the words.

The mood of the braves turned. Whoops and screeches faded, replaced by sullen, ominous mutterings accompanied by much solemn nodding of heads in agreement. Red Hand was voicing their universal complaint against the hated invaders who were destroying a cherished way of life.

"First were the Mexicans, with their high-handed ways," he said, thrusting his lance toward the south, the direction from which the initial trespassers hailed.

"They came in suits of iron, calling themselves 'conquerers.'" Red Hand sneered at the conquistadors who had emerged from Mexico some three hundred and fifty years earlier. It might have been yesterday, so fresh and strong was his hate.

"They rode—horses!" Red Hand's eyes bulged as he assumed an expression of pop-eyed amazement, his clowning provoking shouts and laughter. "We had never seen horses before. The horses were good!"

He paused, then punched the rest of it across. "We killed the men and took their horses! We burned the settlements and killed and killed until only cowards were left alive, and we sent them running back to Mexico!"

The braves spasmed with screaming delight, some shouting themselves hoarse.

Red Hand waited for a lull in the tumult, then continued. "From that day till now, they have never dared return to our hunting grounds. We could have wiped them off the face of the earth, chasing them into the Great Water, had we so desired. Aye, for we Comanche are a mighty folk, and a warlike one. But we were merciful. We took pity on the poor weak creatures and let them live, so they could keep on breeding fine horses for us to steal.

"One black day, out from where the sun rises, came the Texans."

Texans—the Comanches' generic term for Anglos, English-speaking whites.

"Texans! They, too, wanted to steal our land and enslave us. They had guns! The guns were good. So we killed the Texans and took their guns and killed more, whipping and burning until they wept like frightened children!

"Not all did we kill, for we Comanches are a merciful people. We let some live so we could take more guns and powder and bullets from them. Their horses are good to steal, too! And their women!

"But the Comanche is too tenderhearted for his own good," he said, shaking his head as if in sorrow. "For a time, all was well. But no more. The Texans forget the lesson we taught them in blood and fire. They come creeping back, pressing at our lands in ever-greater numbers. They will eat up the earth if they are not stopped.

"What to do, brothers, what to do? I prayed to the Great Spirit to send me an answer. And I dreamed a dream. The sky cracked open! The clouds parted, and an arm reached down between them—a mighty red arm, holding a burning spear. The Fire Lance!

"The hand darted the spear. It flew down to earth, striking the ground with a thunderclap. When the smoke cleared, I alone was left standing, for all around me the Texans lay fallen on the ground. Man, woman and child—dead! Dead all, from oldest to youngest, from greatest to most small. All dead. And this was not the least of wonders.

"Everywhere a white person had fallen, a buffalo rose up. Here, there, everywhere a buffalo! They filled the plains with a thundering herd, filling my heart with joy. So it was shown to me in a dream, as I tell it to you. But I tell you this. It was no dream, but a vision!"

Wild stirrings shot through the crowd, a storm of potential energy yearning to be released.

"A true vision!" Red Hand bellowed.

The braves chafed at the bit, straining to break loose, but Red Hand shouted down the rising tumult. "The Great Spirit has shown us the Way—kill the Texans!

Take up the Fire Lance! Kill and burn until the last white has fled from these lands, never to be seen again! The buffalo will once more grow thick and fat! All will be well, as in the days of our fathers!"

Brandishing his lance, Red Hand shook it at the heavens. Pandemonium erupted, a near riot. The hollow basin became a howling bedlam as the wild crowd went wilder.

So great was the uproar that, in the tipis, the women and children marveled to hear it. Any outsider, red or white, hearing it crashing across the plains would have taken fright.

Red Hand hopped down off the ledge that had served him as a platform and stepped back into the shadows, partly withdrawing from the scene while the disturbance played itself out. His henchmen followed.

Presently, order was restored, if not peace and quiet. The braves settled down, in their restless way.

Red Hand put his head together with his five-man cadre, giving orders.

Carrying out his command, Sun Dog and Little Bells moved around to the east side of Arrowhead Rock, where a lone tipi stood off by itself in the gloom beyond the firelight. Sun Dog lifted the front flap and went inside.

A moment later, a figure emerged headfirst through the opening as if violently flung outward, falling face-down in the dirt at Little Bells's feet.

Sun Dog reappeared. He and Little Bells bracketed a sorry figure, grabbing him by the arms and hauling him to his feet. The newcomer was a white man in cavalry blue. A Long Knife, one of the hated pony soldiers!

There was a collective intake of breath from the mob in the hollow, followed by ominous mutterings and growlings. As one, they pressed forward.

The captive wore a torn blue tunic and pants with a yellow strip down the sides. He was barefoot. His hands were tied in front of him by rawhide strips cutting deep into the flesh of his wrists. He sagged, legs folding at the knees. He would have fallen if Sun Dog and Little Bells hadn't been holding him up.

He was Butch Hardesty, a robber, rapist, and back-shooting murderer. He had a system. When the law got too hot on his trail, he would enlist in the army and disappear in the ranks, losing himself among blue-clad troopers and distant frontier posts. When the pursuit cooled off, he would steal a horse and rifle and go "over the hill," deserting to resume his outlaw career. He'd go about his business until the law started dogging him again, once more repeating the cycle.

In the last years of the War Between the States, he worked his way west across the country, finally winding up at lonesome Fort Pardee in north central Texas. He deserted again, and had the extreme bad luck to cross paths with some of Red Hand's scouts. He'd been doubly unfortunate in being taken alive.

He'd been beaten, starved, abused, and tortured near the extreme. But not all the way to destruction. Red Hand needed him alive. He had a use for him. Hardesty was taken north, to the conclave at Arrowhead Rock. Kept alive and on hand—for what?

Out of the tipi stepped a weird hybrid creature, man-shaped, with a monstrous shaggy horned head.

Coming into the light, the apparition was revealed to be an aged Comanche, potbellied and thin-shanked. He wore a brown woolly buffalo hide headdress complete with horns. He was Medicine Hat, Red Hand's own shaman, herbalist, devil doctor, and sorcerer.

Half carrying and half dragging Hardesty, Sun Dog and Little Bells hustled him to the front of the rock. Medicine Hat shambled after them, mumbling to himself.

The cavalryman produced no small effect on the crowd. Like a magnifying lens focusing the sun's rays into a single burning beam, the trooper provided a focus for the braves' bloodlust and demonic energies.

Hardesty was brought to the stake and bound to it. Ropes made of braided buffalo hide strips lashed him to the pole with hands tied above his head. He was too weak to stand on his own two feet, and the ropes held him up.

When Comanches took an enemy alive, they tortured him, expecting no less should they be taken. Torture was an important element of the warrior society. How a man stood up to it showed what he was made of. It was entertaining, too—to those not on the receiving end.

Hardesty bore the marks of starvation and abuse. His face was mottled with purple-black bruises, features swollen, one blackened eye narrowed to a glinting slit. His mouth hung open. His shirt was ripped open down the middle, his bare torso having been sliced and gouged. Cactus thorns had been driven under his fingernails and toenails. Twigs had been tied between fingers and toes and set aflame. The soles of his feet had been skinned, then roasted.

Firelight caused shadows to crawl and slide across

Hardesty's bound form. He seemed as much dead as alive.

Black Robe now went to work on him with a knife whose blade was heated red-hot. It brought Hardesty around, his bellows of pain booming in the basin.

Badger shot some arrows into Hardesty's arms and legs, careful to ensure that no wound was mortal.

Each new infliction was greeted with shouts by the braves. It was great sport.

Hardesty was scum and he knew it, but he played his string out to the end. His mouth worked, cursing his captors. "The joke's on you, ya ignorant savages. I ain't cavalry a'tall. I'm a deserter. I quit the army, you dumb sons of bitches, haw haw! How d'you like that? Ya heathen devils."

A few Comanches had a smattering of English, but were unable to make out his words. All liked his show of spirit, however.

"The gods are happiest when the sacrifice is strong," Red Hand said. "Make ready for the Fire Lance."

Medicine Hat muttered agreement with a toothless mouth, spittle wetting his pointed chin. Reaching into his bag of tricks, he pulled out a gourd. It was dried and hollowed out, with a long neck serving as a kind of spout. The end of the spout was sealed by a stopper. Pulling the plug, he closed on the captive.

Hardesty slumped against the ropes, head down, and chin resting on top of his chest. He looked up out of the tops of his eyes, his pain-wracked gaze registering little more than a mute flicker of animal awareness.

Red Hand moved forward, out of the shadows into

the light. It could be seen that his face was freshly striped with black paint.

War paint! The sight of which sent an electric thrill surging through the throng.

Red Hand motioned Medicine Hat to proceed. The shaman's moccasined feet shuffled in the dust, doing a little ceremonial dance. Mouthing spells, prayers, and incantations, Medicine Hat neared Hardesty, then backed away, repeating the action several times.

He held the gourd over the captive's head and. began pouring the vessel's contents on Hardesty's head, shoulders, chest, and belly, dousing him with a dark, foul-smelling liquid. Compounded of rendered animal fats, grease, and mineral oils, the stuff was used as a fire starter to quicken the lighting of campfires. It gurgled as it spewed from the spout.

Groans escaped Hardesty as his upper body was coated with the stuff. Medicine Hat poured until the gourd was empty. He stepped away from Hardesty, who looked as if he'd been drenched with glistening brown oil.

Red Hand moved forward, the center of all eyes.

The shaman was a great one for brewing up various potions, powders, and salves. Earlier, he had applied a special ointment to the spear blade of Red Hat's lance. The main ingredient of the mixture was a thick, sticky pine tar resin blended with vegetable and herbal oils. It coated the blade, showing as a gummy residue that dulled the brilliance of the steel's metallic shine.

Red Hand's movements took on a deliberate, ritualistic quality. Holding the lance in both hands, he raised it horizontally over his head and shook it at the heavens.

Lowering it, he dipped the blade into the heart of the fire. A few beats passed before the slow-burning ointment flared up, wrapping the blade in blue flames.

Red Hand lifted the lance, tilting it skyward for all to see. The blade was a wedge of blue fire, burning with an eerie, mystic glow—a ghost light, a weird effect both impressive and unnerving.

Quivering with emotion, Red Hand's clear, strong voice rang out. "Lo! The Fire Lance!"

He touched the burning spear to Hardesty's well-oiled chest. Blue fire sparked from the blade tip, leaping to the oily substance coating the captive's flesh. The fire-starting compound burst into bright hot flames, wrapping Hardesty in a skin of fire, turning him into a human torch.

He blazed with a hot yellow-red-orange light. The burning had a crackling sound, like flags being whipped by a high wind.

Hardesty writhed, screaming as he was burned alive. Fire cut through the ropes binding him to the stake. Before he could break free, he was speared by Red Hand, who skewered him in the middle.

Red Hand opened up Hardesty's belly, spilling his guts. He gave a final twist to the blade before withdrawing it. He faced the man of fire, lance leveled for another thrust if needed.

Hardesty collapsed, falling in a blazing heap. The fire spread to some nearby grass and brush, setting them alight.

At a sign from Red Hand, members of his five-man cadre rushed up with blankets, using them to beat out the fires. Streamers of blue-gray smoke rose up. The night was thick with the smell of burning flesh.

Red Hand thrust the blue-burning spear blade into a dirt mound. When it surfaced, the mystic glow was extinguished, the blade glowing a dull red.

Chaos, near anarchy, reigned among the Comanches. The horde erupted in a frenzy, many breaking into spontaneous war dances.

Above all others was heard the voice of Red Hand. "Take up the Fire Lance! Kill the Texans!"

Much later, when all was quiet, Wahtonka and Laughing Bear stood off by themselves in a secluded place, putting their heads together. The horned moon was low in the west, the stars were paling, the eastern sky was lightening.

"What should we do?" Laughing Bear asked.

"What can we do? Go with Red Hand to make war on the whites." Wahtonka shrugged. "Any raid is better than none," he added, philosophically.

Laughing Bear grunted agreement. "Waugh! That is true."

"We shall see if the Great Spirit truly spoke to Red Hand, if his vision comes to pass," Wahtonka said. "If not—may his bones bleach in the sand!"